SEMPER FLY

A SIERRA HOTEL NOVEL

PRAISE FOR KENT MCINNIS & *SIERRA HOTEL*

"Balancing pathos and comedy is a challenging task for a writer, and McInnis does this beautifully. Lead protagonist Rob Amity's internal conflict is carried throughout the book in both tragedy and hilarity."

—Alan B. Hollingsworth
Author of *Flatbellies*

"An exciting story of American history and patriotism, a gifted author and historian, and a former USAF pilot. What better formula for your next page-turning thriller than Sierra Hotel*?"*

—John J. Dwyer
Will Rogers Medallion-winning
Author of *Shortgrass* and *Mustang*

"Kent McInnis is a man who has served his country. We are fortunate that God made men like Kent who was willing to do the tough job, and still continues to have a smile on his face."

—Harvey Pratt
Designer, National Native American Veterans Memorial, Washington, D.C.
Cheyenne Peace Chief, U. S. Marine

"McInnis spins a vivid tale of... an American culture in conflict. With an authentic depiction of events peppered with humor, McInnis has another page turner."

—Col. Larry Hoppe, USAF (ret.)
F-105 Pilot during the Vietnam War, Recipient of the Silver Star

"Author Kent McInnis's depiction of young Air Force airmen in wartime is raw and honest—a man's book that will also appeal to women."

—Major General Donald F. Ferrell, USAFR (Retired)
Former Oklahoma Adjutant General

"The genius in Kent McInnis's writing is his ability to submerge you into the good, the bad, and the ugly of military life."

—Bob Giel
U.S. Army Veteran and Author of *A Crow to Pluck* and *Shawnee*

also by

Kent McInnis

Sierra Hotel

Clear and a Million

SEMPER FLY

A NOVEL OF LIFE AFTER WAR

Kent McInnis

HAT CREEK

HAT CREEK

An Imprint of Roan & Weatherford Publishing Associates, LLC
Bentonville, Arkansas
www.roanweatherford.com

Library of Congress Cataloging-in-Publication Data
Names: McInnis, Kent, author
Title: Semper Fly/Kent McInnis | Sierra Hotel #3
Description: First Edition. | Bentonville: Hat Creek, 2023.
Identifiers: LCCN: 2023951103 | ISBN: 978-1-63373-887-4 (hardcover)
ISBN: 978-1-63373-888-1 (trade paperback) | ISBN: 978-1-63373-889-8 (eBook)
Subjects: | BISAC: FICTION/War & Military | FICTION/Historical |
FICTION/General
LC record available at: https://lccn.loc.gov/2023951103

Hat Creek trade paperback edition June, 2024

Jacket & Interior Design by Casey W. Cowan
Editing by Amy Cowan

To the Rio River Rats
Pilot Training Class 71-06
Laredo AFB, Texas

PREFACE

MY DRAFT BOARD IN 1968 was a powerful motivator. I chose pilot training in the Air Force because the pay would be better—and it might cure my fear of flying. I did learn to enjoy flying, even if tall buildings still make me nervous. The experience quickly changed my tolerance for challenges. Commanding a squadron may have been the most challenging aspect of my short military career. With my eternal gratitude I learned the value of a good first sergeant. The military was worthy of my admiration. So, when twice I heard acquaintances of mine express gladness over the death in combat of one of my own, I plotted my revenge. Since actual physical assault is not my strong suit, I chose instead to write about it and let my characters do the dirty work. It feels good when I read it. I hope you, too, will enjoy the vicarious thrill of vengeance.

ACKNOWLEDGEMENTS

THE MORE I WRITE, THE greater grows the list of those I must thank. My publisher, Casey Cowan of Roan & Weatherford Publishing, took a chance on 72- year-old author. My editors Anthony Wood, Amy Cowan, and Dennis Doty always give me a wide latitude. So many members of the R&W family, including Bob Giel, have shared hours of their encouragement and sage advice. My parents, Marvin and Betty McInnis, gave me two great gifts. They introduced me to the world of travel along Route 66 for seven years as a child. They also made each day of my childhood a 24/7 grammar classroom. Because of them, I learned to love composing in the English language. I'm grateful also for my fellow Teamster Union truck driver, Harold Owen, who for three years introduced me to the real people in America as we delivered furniture, appliances, and assorted merchandise for Sears to urban and rural Oklahoma homes. His knowledge of history and his gift of keen observation taught me much about how to treat people and how to speak the language of the least among us and the refined above us. Cheryl, my wife and best friend, has always encouraged me to do what gives me joy. If I can write and be by her side, I am content. I send a big thanks to otolaryngologist, Jerry Renfroe, M.D., who advised me on the proper description of the surgical procedure depicted in this work. The late Brad Baldwin, my high school classmate and civil aviation sidekick, brought me back to aviation after a 23-year hiatus from my Air Force days. I miss him every day and hope someday we will meet again so I can say, "Let's go fly!"

1

"PARTNER, WHAT ARE YOU DOING up so early?" I asked Sean, as he sat at our kitchen breakfast bar, a bowl of dry Cheerios in front of him.

"I just woke up," he said, shrugging his shoulders.

"But it's still dark. Nobody should get up this early. Why did you get up?"

"'Cause I wanted to be with you." He gave me a Cheerio-incrusted smile.

How could I argue with that? He sat there kicking his two bare feet repetitively against the side of the breakfast bar. If the moment weren't so endearing to watch, it would be difficult to enjoy nonstop.

"Coffee?" I poured my first cup, then added milk before returning it to our refrigerator.

He started to snicker at the mere idea of having something only Mom and Dad drank. "No-o-o-o! It's too hot for me."

"And how did you find out it's too hot?"

"Mom told me it was hot, but once I stuck my tongue in her coffee to find out. Mom wasn't looking."

"Did you burn your tongue and cry?"

"A lot! But I was little then. That's when Mom found out I stuck my tongue in."

"That is how we learn."

"I need some milk for my cereal." It was more of a childish demand than a request.

"Go get it."

"I'll have to eat this cereal dry then." His voice was whiny.

We looked at each other in a father son standoff. You can't blame a kid for trying. I sipped my coffee, savoring the smell of the brew and taste of the milk I had added one minute earlier. He continued to stare hopefully. He hated dry cereal. Dads are heartless.

"As I said, son. That's how we learn."

I peered out our east kitchen window, watching the first orange hints of sunrise. On his way to get milk, Sean joined me in looking at the brightening dawn. Like my son, Oklahoma was learning valuable lessons. Flat farmland of the Oklahoma plains afforded an unobstructed sky, except for the silhouettes of the two giants of industry and wealth in the state.

The round bales of hay were like golden money rolls laid out scattered fat in the fields. So, too, were oil drilling rigs sprouting like money trees for those brave enough to grow them. Oklahoma was flush with cash, and the boom would never end. Except, in autumn of 1980, Iran shelled Iraq. Iraq invaded Iran. World oil prices plunged to less than half. Within two years, the small Penn Square Bank in Oklahoma City collapsed, the first of 139 Oklahoma banks to follow. The oil boom went all to hell, leaving agriculture once again king.

Tricked out pickup trucks, neoclassic Excalibur and Clénet roadsters, and red Ferraris suddenly sported *FOR SALE* signs. The car companies that made them fared no better. The price of housing dropped over a year's time. Mortgages went unpaid. Early Oilies, the ones who had never read their history and lived only for the moment, abandoned their homes and cars, and left everything else they owned at the pawn shop.

By contrast, the many Oilies who saved half their money and drove modest Chevys, Fords, and Chryslers proved why being sensible always pays off. Money can't buy you happiness, but it can pay off a lot of misery.

It became my goal to help people in misery. Houses were easier to buy than airplanes. Oil executives with aircraft hung onto the hope that oil prices would rise again and save them from their profligacy. They often chose bankruptcy over selling assets while they could. Often, the worth of assets lost value faster than the oilmen lost hope. Some savvy executives and oil field workers clearly saw the handwriting on the wall. They were selling out at the ideal time. As citizens grew desperate to sell everything to avoid the shame of going bust, buyers fell into short supply—a buyer's market. The supply of opportunities grew larger with every failed bank. Thus, with both the seller and buyer ecstatic over our transaction, I bought our new family home for a steal. And I paid with cash.

I was an early adopter of that approach—buy low, sell high. I sold my part-ownership of the formerly named A to Z Oilfield Services back to the corporation that bought us seven years before when the oil industry was rapidly expanding. Stanton BigHeart, my original partner now retired, taught me to value the advice of the elderly. In 1982, he was the elder whose advice I sought. The Iran-Iraq War was gaining intensity. Both countries began selling oil as fast as they could extract it from the ground to pay for their conflict. Then the oil glut came. OPEC, the international cartel of oil producing nations, lost its grip on prices. Prices dropped to disastrous levels of negative profitability. It cost more to pump oil out of the ground than it did to sell it. Stanton said it was time to bail out. The corporation, which owned all the remaining shares, assumed prosperity would return soon. My instincts matched Stanton's. I sold months before disaster hit Oklahoma. In life's rearview mirror, the oil dollar was already getting smaller.

The irony of my good timing was exemplified nicely in the Oklahoma race for governor in 1982. Running for a second term, Democrat Governor George Nigh had ridden the wave of oil prosperity through his whole first term. To voters he appeared to be a genius of politics. He not only reduced taxes, but he eliminated many sources of taxation. The remaining taxes still produced revenues that were unheard of by most Oklahomans. Few were around to remember the boom-bust cycles that alternated between good and bad oilfield days in the century's first thirty years. Governor Nigh triumphed in his reelection, being the first Oklahoma governor to win a second term. He won all seventy-seven counties in the state, another first. Wildly popular, Governor Nigh ran on a simple unspoken but obvious slogan—The state of the State is Great. In his second inaugural address, the governor quoted the most famous iconic line from the comic strip, Pogo.

"We have found the enemy, and he is us."

Soon after, Governor Nigh addressed the Oklahoma media and said something to this effect.

"Friends, we are in deep trouble."

When the governor said those words, I already had millions in the bank and in other safe havens. I had sold my company shares the year before in good faith and had no remorse over the results. No one forecast the debacle in the oil industry that would eventually take down corporations and banks together. Stanton BigHeart and Robert Amity had made A to Z into a hugely successful oilfield service provider with a sterling reputation for integrity. Our sold company pride and joy collapsed a year later into the blackhole of Oklahoma's worst ever oil bust. That was the catalyst that convinced me it was a perfect time to buy a house.

2

SUZY AND I TOOK OUR son Sean with us to see what houses we could find for a bargain. For Sale signs began to proliferate in nearly all the upscale neighborhoods of Oklahoma City, Edmond, and Nichols Hills. The signs were up, but no one was buying. The prices offered were way too high for the collapsing economy. No one could afford to sell at those low prices. Asking prices were now lower than the mortgages on the houses for sale. Homeowners contemplated paying someone to buy their house before the value dropped even further. It was in that mindset that we drove every day through neighborhoods, patiently scouting out homes that we hoped to buy in a way that made both the buyer and the seller satisfied. It was not that easy, as banks holding those mortgages began to fail.

High mortgage rates did not help banks. In March 1983, the 30-year fixed rate for a Freddie Mac mortgage loan peaked at 12.8%. Banks would not lend money at that rate. Home buyers could not afford to buy a home at rates of nearly 13%. Houses went abandoned because it was the perfect trifecta—banks could not lend, buyers could not borrow, and homeowners could not pay. The only way to buy a house was with cash, which gave our family a bargaining chip highly sought by sellers. For the right seller, we became their ticket to avoid foreclosure or bankruptcy.

The Department of Housing and Urban Development (HUD) muscled into the state, buying up mortgaged properties of failing banks. It was prudent to avoid these properties. HUD often stripped the homes of valuable components, which they then auctioned off at pennies on the dollar. It was unforgivable seeing valuable homes gutted for the expedience of the federal government. But the housing slaughter continued at an increasing pace, in line with the growing number of banks collapsing.

Realtors were desperate for business. To their horror, more homeowners tried For Sale by Owner. The cost to the home seller by a realtor charging six to seven percent of a sale was the difference between salvation and repossession.

Within this environment we spotted a property with a For Sale by Owner sign in far north Oklahoma City on a six-acre lot in the Cross Timbers near the edge of the flatland plains. The Cross Timbers, a mix of prairie and woodland, was the hardwood forest that divided the eastern woodland prairies of the United States from the western Great Plains. Stretching from Texas, through Oklahoma, and into Kansas, it split Oklahoma in half. Although not directly following the terrain line of the Cross Timbers, it made sense why the original Indian Territory comprised the east half of Oklahoma and Oklahoma Territory encompassed the west.

We parked our car at the midway point of the long ascending brick-paved driveway. This impressive house was set far back and up from the road. From below it looked massive to the eye.

"Wow!" Sean was out of the car on a run to the front door.

"Oh, Rob, this is beautiful." Suzy's voice was soft and full of awe.

"Let's get closer before we go gaga over this."

"You don't like it?"

"Oh, I like it all right."

"We agreed that we both had to be wowed before we would consider a house. Please tell me you are wowed."

I moved my eyes from the house to her. "I am wowed." Her grin, I feared, was leaving permanent smile lines in her cheeks.

The three-story house was done in blond brick with ornate limestone corner and window accents. An oversized double doorway served as a center focal point to its symmetrical layout. Double limestone Corinthian columns framed each side of the adequate porch and entry. Balustrades on each side of the four-step entryway, converged with each step to the front door. At the columns, the balustrades diverged left and right to frame a porch walkway that permitted access to either side of this ample house. Reminiscent of the architecture of House and Senate wings of the U.S. Capitol, the columns supported a third-floor balcony atop the entablature overlooking the grand driveway entrance. I envisioned Suzy the Queen on that balcony regally waving to all her adoring fans.

The long brick driveway led to a circle drive. A life-sized marble sculpture of a heavily maned lion roared warning to visitors who dared enter. To the left near the porch walkway stood, in all her resplendent and naked glory, a life-sized marble of Venus. She was proportioned more to the tastes of modern man than to the Greeks of ancient times. Our son, having run all the way to the house, stopped when he caught his first glimpse of the nude. Sean's gaze fixated on Venus with a fascination fostered by my own love of beautiful women.

"Can we keep it, Mom?" I asked, attempting to sound like Sean.

Suzy turned to me. "We better move that to the backyard. I'm sure there is a place way at the back that would be perfect."

"Yes," I said, gazing at Venus. "We'll always know where to find Sean."

Suzy jumped out of the car and ran faster than I was able to follow. I called to her as discreetly as possible. "Suzy, we should call the phone on their For Sale sign. Maybe they will show it to us then… and don't let Sean ring their doorbell."

I hiked back to the end of the driveway to read the phone number on the sign. Suzy, with Sean in tow, was returning as I jotted down the numbers.

"I don't think we'll find a pay phone nearby out here," she said. "Hop in the car, Sean, and let's find somewhere to call."

I glanced at the house in disappointment for having to leave. A man and woman stepped out on the front porch.

"I don't think we'll be making that call," I said. "We have visitors."

The couple waved their hands in welcoming gestures. We turned around to acknowledge their presence and began the long hike to their front door.

They were middle aged, well dressed, looked prosperous but looked eager to sell. As we approached, I feared they were going to hug and kiss us with joy.

"I see you read our sign," the lady said. "We are the Archers."

"I'm pleased to meet you, I'm Rob Amity." I shook her outstretched hand and introduced Sean and Suzy. "Have you had any lookers?"

"Hundreds," Mr. Archer replied.

"Oh, I bet so," I said.

"You're the first," Mrs. Archer said.

We all chuckled. It was hard to keep Suzy from looking eager, but she still wasn't as eager as were the Archers. It would be impolite to ask for a tour at this moment, but we hoped for a better look around in the future. Surprise visits were never the proper approach.

"Tell us about your house," I said.

"I like that." Sean was pointing at Venus.

"Well, you should, young man," said Mr. Archer. "That's the only girlfriend my wife lets me have. What's your name, son?"

"Sean."

"Well, Sean, I think you should buy this house. Come in, and I'll show you around."

With a wave of his hand, he led Sean toward the front door, where we all joined him to enter the most beautiful home we had yet seen in our search.

3

IT TOOK LITTLE TIME FOR Suzy and me to conclude that this was the home we wanted. When we stepped inside, a similar sense of good and warm feelings hit both of us. The home was five years old. While the popular décor of earth tones prevailed in most new homes we visited, this home defied the trend of the time. It had a Thomas Jefferson at Monticello feel to it—elegant and refined appointments with a smattering of the great unexplored West woven into the interior. White craftsman classic square recessed columns inside blended with a rustic beamed ceiling of the large entryway. The beams paralleled our line of sight, serving to draw us inside. Two grand staircases gave the home a grandeur I had never experienced outside of movie-inspired fantasies. Beyond the entryway a fifteen-foot ceiling of the great room lured us further into a surprising view at the back where large windowpanes revealed an extensive well-manicured lawn. Beyond that grew a wonderland of prairie and woodlands. Sean put his nose against the heavy glass.

"Dad! We could play catch out here."

As a dad who loved to throw a ball, that was icing on the cake. Suzy kept smiling. Sean's eyes were as wide as the backyard. I tried hard to keep my expression neutral.

I looked at the homeowners curiously. "Why would you sell such a beautiful home."

"Oil, or the lack of same," he said.

"I don't wish to intrude, but may we see the other rooms?"

"Of course," she replied. "We've kept it nice for so long, it's a treat to show it off."

The couple led us up a grand banister staircase to the four bedrooms on the second floor. The four full bathrooms looked unused. I suspect most of their house was unused. It was large for an empty nest couple up in years, especially with all the stairs to climb. Not for Sean, though.

"Could I slide down the stairs, please?"

There were four simultaneous nos. We carefully held Sean's hand as we stepped down. When he got to the last five steps, I arrested his leap to the bottom. Holding him back by grabbing under his arms, he nearly launched me off the steps with him. After a short lesson about conduct in someone else's home, we sat Sean down with us to talk more with the owners.

They sat us down in an adjoining room between the kitchen and the exceedingly large master bedroom and master bathroom. This well-crafted library caused Suzy and me to turn toward each other to show our amazement. The richly upholstered sofas and chairs made for an inviting space of calming colors, enormous built-in bookshelves, adequate wet bar, and inviting fireplace. It was a room designed for genuine comfort after a grueling day at the office. It spoke to Suzy, to Sean, and especially to me. I claimed one wall as a final resting place for my Air Force mementoes—my hero wall.

The Archers had no objections to a house inspector running through the property. When I was younger, my parents built their house. Their experience would also be helpful to us. Still, I remembered a great deal from that experience as a young observer. We asked about city services. The house was hooked up to the Oklahoma City water and sewer system. Trash pickup was twice a week. Neighbors were widely separated and nice to each other. Rush hour traffic was a challenge, both morning and evening.

Mr. Archer pulled out the architectural blueprints of the house to show me how it was put together. The first thing I noticed was how big the downstairs master bedroom and master bath were and nearly the same size. There was an overabundance of plugs and light switches on the walls. The supporting piers and walls were clearly marked. A separated and oversized three-car garage connected to the house by a concourse. Above the garage was a mother-in-law apartment of sufficient size to have a separate kitchen, bedroom, and bathroom away from the cozy living room. The blueprints displayed how the dining room lay on the other side of the kitchen from the library. It was convenient, having dinners in such close proximity to the kitchen. A passthrough to the dining area made kitchen service so much easier.

Suzy came over to see what the men were gazing at.

"So, what do you think? You want to buy my house?"

"I dearly love it," Suzy said. "I may do some work on the kitchen. I don't like the layout of the appliances, and I will want all new ones anyway."

The man flinched when she hinted at gutting the kitchen, his wife's place of tranquility and source of pride. Mr. Archer expressed frustration.

"If you do that, keep it from the Missus. She would be upset to know you did anything to her precious kitchen."

"Mum's the word," she said, looking around the large family room and its array of bookshelves. "This room is marvelous. I wouldn't change a thing."

"You can tell that to her." He began to laugh. "You want to know why? Because she hates this room."

We agreed to call on them tomorrow or as soon as an inspector came out and issued his report.

4

SUZY AND I KNEW THAT hasty decisions were always bad ideas. We called an inspector with good credentials, assuming it might take days of waiting because he would be busy. We should have known when he jumped on the job the next day, that all facets of life in Oklahoma were in a slump. He had little work to do most days and was overjoyed by our call.

Being a large house, it took parts of two days to thoroughly cover all aspects of our dream home. I followed along with him for both days, remaining out of the way, but assured to my satisfaction that the job was done well. Aside from a dripping faucet, a blocked central air vent, and a rotted soffit on one corner of the house, the inspection uncovered nothing structurally deficient. There was no settling. Mr. Archer had laid the foundation over steel piers. To my delight he had architecturally overdone all aspects of the house from foundation to walls to roof.

I also researched Mr. Archer. I wanted to learn all I could about the man—his company, his friends, his customers. What described his personality? I did the same inquiry on the house itself. Did it have a lien? Were real estate taxes up to date? Did he own the house outright?

I learned he was well respected but no pushover. His home was constructed like he viewed himself—first class. My report to Suzy was an enthusiastic call to action.

"Are you with me?" I asked.

"It's time you go bargain for a decent price. Don't buy it unless we pay what it's really worth." She didn't mean that it was underpriced.

I went to see Mr. and Mrs. Archer the next morning to gauge how eager they were to sell. My initial impression was promising. I was sorry that they were desperate to stay afloat, but I had no intention of being a pushover. I knew from stopping by the county assessor's office what the original cost of their home was. I offered them fifty cents on the dollar—cash.

Mr. Archer squirmed in his easy chair. He began tapping a finger on the arm of his chair. Mrs. Archer lowered her head either out of shock, pain, or shame. Finally, he broke the silence with an effort to bully a younger man.

"Son, that's an insult to me and my wife. It's worth much more than that. You're too young to realize you can't talk to us like that. Give me a reasonable offer, or you can leave."

"Mister Archer. Ma'am. You may think I am taking advantage of you, but you know by now that you can't sell it. No one can take out a mortgage anymore. You think I'm trying to exploit you, but from my perspective, my family counts on me not to put them in peril. If I had to sell this house today, at the price I am offering you, you know in your heart that I couldn't sell it."

"It's not fair to us," Mrs. Archer said.

"Let me ask the two of you a question. Why are you selling the house? Why would you? Is it because you are about to lose it?"

"No, not at all," he said.

"I looked up your company and did a little investigation. You didn't incorporate. It's all on you. I know your situation. You're heavily in debt, but you have no lien on your house. You built it and paid for it without a loan. Now you can't even afford to pay the utilities and taxes on it. That's why you are selling. You need to sell your house to keep the collectors at a safe distance."

Mrs. Archer was the first to hint with a subtle nod that I had nailed the issue for them. I waited for a response which was not forthcoming. I turned to face the gentleman, who now sat slumped in defeat.

"Sir, I'm offering you cash in six figures. It can be in your hand before the week is over. This deal can be good for you. It can be good for my family. Please say yes."

I waited. I was definitely not going to speak again. If I did, the deal would be lost. He turned to me, his left hand extended in a plea.

"I'll make the deal if you throw in another hundred grand."

"No."

Another pause as he looked at his wife, whose tears were flowing freely. Now I could see desperation in their faces.

"Could you throw in and extra fifty thousand?"

"No."

"You expect us to…." His voice trailed off. He was out of words.

"You know it's a good deal for both of us." I looked at his wife who nodded her head again.

"Honey, we don't have a choice."

The man looked utterly defeated. I could have sympathized, but part of my research revealed that in the business world, he developed a reputation for treating his customers like I was treating him. If I had learned anything about dealing with big shots, it was that if you want their respect, treat them like they would treat you. I had his respect now if I simply waited in silence. He continued to tap the arm of his chair. His other hand gave him away by its tremble. To my relief, he looked up and spoke.

"Okay. Where can we sign?"

And that is how Suzy and I bought our first house.

5

WHILE OIL COUNTRY WENT BUST, the rest of the nation went boom, the result of policies of a new president in Washington. The fresh awakening of American pride and patriotism was to change my life in ways I never expected.

For others, who lived like the grasshopper in the ancient fable of Aesop, unemployment and bitterness fed a return to old grievances and destructive lifestyles. And nothing brought out more bitterness in the underdog than the lasting effects of the Vietnam War.

I left the Air Force as the war in Vietnam wound down. With my opinions about the war still in flux, I viewed my role with mixed feelings. I found it best to keep my veteran status as a former jet pilot under wraps. Not that I was any hero warrior. Rather than flying in Vietnam, I spent my time in south Texas as an instructor pilot, introducing students to their first jet aircraft. The T-37 was a primary jet trainer, the smallest jet in the Air Force with the loudest and most ear damaging jet engines in the inventory. Many military pilots suffered hearing loss, and I was no exception. The T-37, unlike all other military aircraft, had no official nickname. The unofficial name was descriptive but not often meant as a compliment. My T-37 didn't get a rugged name like Mustang, Thunderbolt, or Talon. Other airplanes got raptor names like Falcon or Eagle. The T-37 acquired the name "Tweet." With ironic humor, we named it the "6500-pound Dog Whistle." The Continental J-69 engine turned at the ear-piercing rate of 25,000 rpm when at full military power. At idle it turned at the perfect speed to sound like a whistle. Adding to its hazards, the Tweet was the only unpressurized jet in the Air Force. That fact contributed to my short career in flying. I didn't know what a sinus cavity in my head was until mine imploded one day as I descended through 10,000 feet. My hospital stays and ultimate grounding from flying gave me my out from military service. Now, ten years later, and to my shock, I missed military life.

That was why I was happy after I checked my mailbox and found a letter from my friend and fellow pilot, Hal Freed. A combat veteran of the Vietnam War, he recently landed a part time job as a college professor of political science. What could go wrong mixing a combat veteran with a bunch of antiwar students? Evidently, a lot went wrong. With exposure to Agent Orange when in Vietnam, Hal developed a treatable form of leukemia but was still cleared to fly. He worried before each medical visit, but so far, he was keeping his currency in the air. His college students were harder to manage.

Dear Rob,

I had to write and share my frustration with somebody, so you're it. Lisa gets enough of my gripes already. To save the integrity of my marriage, I write to you.

You would be shocked at the poor quality of freshmen students that are coming into our universities now. This is my first semester teaching at the university level. These students need to be top notch to get here. After the first week of class, introducing them to political Science 101, I was shell-shocked. Not by their behavior but by their ignorance. It's bad! God forbid they ever find out I was in Vietnam. They don't know come here from sic 'em. I asked them the simplest questions to gear them up for the course itself. This is college. They are supposed to learn the fundamentals in high school. I thought at first that it couldn't possibly be as bad as I heard. So, I decided it was fair to test their knowledge before we began discussions of the curriculum I'm supposed to teach.

I gave my freshmen a 100-question multiple choice test over what I thought should be common knowledge. Here are examples.

1. If Oklahoma has two U.S. Senators, how many does the larger state of Texas have?

2. What nation in 1941 attacked the United States at Pearl Harbor?

3. Where is Pearl Harbor?

4. What U.S. President was elected four times?

5. How many branches of government are there in the U.S. Constitution?

6. Abraham Lincoln was U.S. President during what war?

7. What are the two primary political parties in the U.S.?

8. The Korean War and the Vietnam War were fought to prevent the spread of what system of economic and political theory?

9. The United States is composed of how many states?

10. What are the two entities that make up what we call Congress?

These are just ten of 100 questions I asked them to answer. They should have had classes every year in secondary school that kept them knowledgeable of government, the constitution, and history. Instead, their grammar and spelling are terrible, they can't find Europe on a map, and Texas fared no better. Add to that—they are all pissed off about something. I have a few veterans in my class who have a much better attitude. They're older, but they are just as ignorant as the younger freshmen. I'm worried about what's happening in our country.

Okay. I feel better. Thank you for reading this diatribe. It's really worrisome what's happening in education.

My best to Suzy,
Hal

P.S. I forgot to give my test results. The average score in my first college freshman class was 35%. I tell you, we as a nation are going to hell fast.

THROUGH WORKING IN THE OIL patch for all these years, I encountered a mix of ignorant and well-informed citizens in small towns, where refinement and articulation were not always admired as desirable traits. If you were a politician, it was best not to act too uppity. But they were down to earth, hardworking, and God-fearing patriots. The difference now was that the urban citizens—city slickers—were passing their country folk on their way down to the depths of ignorance. Schools were dropping concentration in civics, history, patriotism, and, most important, discipline. The big difference between them now was a smug embrace of socialism, communism, and anarchy in the college educated. It started with the free speech movement at Berkley, California. Slowly, protests became all about being anti-establishment and tearing up things. Then the Vietnam war began and all three—socialism, communism, anarchy—became the fad of the enlightened masses. Protests were what you did if you were cool. If you preferred pride in country, the oil patch was a great place to start—where men worked with their hands.

The change in attitudes of the enlightened before and after the Vietnam War was like cussing in front of your parents. The child would say "hell." The parent would say, "don't say that word." So, the child says the word hell from then on because it's forbidden. Then one day the child says "damn." The parents have given up on stopping the use of hell, so they forbid the child to say "damn." Then the child, now a new teenager, discovers that scatological term. That's forbidden, thus it is added to the teen's routine vocabulary. Then the teen discovers the mother of all bad words, but the parents have given up trying to forbid cussing because it doesn't work. Now the teen has developed a complete cussing lexicon, and the parents are resigned to a life of shame, failure, and embarrassment.

The same thing had happened to the enlightened masses. The road to being part of the college in-crowd had digressed to violent protests, rejection of convention, free love, and political activism. Soon the daily protests involved routine heckling and spitting at returning Vietnam veterans. The next step to come was the Weather Underground that set off bombs at the U.S. Capitol, Pentagon, and State Department. Anarchy was the fad of the day. Sadly, many citizens clapped their hands in joy every time something bad happened. It began to affect me personally in early spring.

It started with a conversation I had with a stranger named Phil Snart at a McDonald's in the northwest quadrant of Oklahoma City. He was treating his son to a Happy Meal when he noticed I was wearing an Air Force ball cap. Tall and slightly overweight with long greying hair in a ponytail, his stylish nonconformity stood out from the crowd. It caught my attention. Dressed more like an ageing hippie than a caring father, he kept staring at me between bouts of attention to his son. Finally, he came over to introduce himself and to ask me about my ballcap. It was a dark blue cap adorned with silver Air Force pilot wings. I wore it often because few knew what the wings meant unless they were former military. It was my subtle way to hint at my veteran status without arousing comments from detractors. The Reagan wave of overt displays of pride in America's military strength had not yet fully taken place.

"Excuse me," he said as I chewed on my Big Mac. "My name is Phil Snart. Are you Air Force?"

"Yes, sir," I replied. "I served five years during Nixon's time in office. How about you?"

"Army field hospital in South Vietnam. I served under Johnson and Nixon both. Army Medic. *OO–RAH!* I saw a lot of terrible wounds in my year." His face lowered. His expression revealed the angst of his memories. He might cry any moment. That's odd for a complete stranger.

"I'm sorry you had to go through that. It was a terrible time. You must have worked with the Marines, too."

"No, just army types. Where did you get that idea?"

"Oh, nothing," I replied. "Just asking." There was something there that puzzled me.

"Did you work on any of the airplanes?"

"Yes, but...." Snart rudely interrupted me.

"Then maybe you went through enough yourself. I had plenty of amputations, stomach wounds, and blood to keep me awake most nights. I performed surgery and anesthesia in the field hospital. So, where in Vietnam did you serve?"

"I was going to say, I never was in Vietnam. All my nightmares were stateside. I was in an accident that killed my commander. We were pilots together, had to bailout, and I pulled him out of the wreckage."

"You were an Air Force pilot?" He sounded surprised.

"I was an instructor pilot. We flew in south...."

He again interrupted me with a wave of his hand. Now he looked furious. What a piece of work. "That's interesting. You were an instructor pilot. You didn't go to Vietnam like I did. You're saying you trained the pilots who went over there. Is that right?"

What a strange question.

"That's right." This was an odd line of questions and statements from a veteran. Often people told me the war was bad for the country, but never had I listened to a complete stranger ask for such detail from me. I suspected he was setting me up.

"So, let's see. You train the pilots to go over and bomb the countryside while you stay home in your air-conditioned luxury. How sad for you?"

This moron was acting like someone who walks into a bar and insults the first person he meets. Snart acted like a smug individual, college educated, a professional student, and in love with his odd sense of reasoning. A prissy know-it-all walks into a bar and assumes everyone agrees with the first insult he hurls. That's what this guy is doing.

"I take it you're not a fan of us pilots."

"If you're an Air Force pilot, I have no respect for you."

"I don't understand that short-sighted opinion. We all sacrificed and gave up something."

"You never saw the blood and guts that I did... while you... way up there at thirty thousand feet, never had to look at your handiwork."

"Like I said...."

"Baby killer! I think that is what you mean to say."

My adrenaline kicked into high gear as my flight-or-fight mechanism took over. I looked over at his son, a boy about the same age of nine as mine. I was too grown up to consider the merits of teaching this smug dope what a fist in the kisser feels like. Those days, I hoped, were over. He needed to know that I didn't give a damn what he believed.

"You may not be aware...."

"You have no right to say anything. You prima donnas strutting around in your flight suits with your air-conditioned hooches, never seeing what I saw. You can all go to hell!"

Confused as I was by this sudden vile turn from a fellow veteran turning my relaxing McDonald's experience into an insult, I tried to press on in defense.

"How could you say that? My friend was killed... burned alive. I think I've seen quite a bit myself."

"I have no sympathy for you or your friend." He was shouting. "I'm glad he was killed. He deserved to die. All of you did... for what you did."

And there our conversation ended. I stood up, glaring at him. I hearkened to another time that someone told me, "he deserved to die." Back then, I responded with a right hook. My initial shock was that there could be more than one person in the world who would dare say that. But Phil Snart's son was present. I couldn't do what I wanted to do to the man. Not this time. So, I let it go. From my own experience I remembered how much my fist hurt after it landed powerfully on a man's face. Vietnam had screwed up the whole world. This man was the sickest screwed up protester I had yet seen in person since I returned to civilian life. For a veteran to say such vile things about another loyal American veteran was unimaginable. But I had seen it before—one veteran shaming another for not being in Vietnam or not serving in combat in Vietnam or not having a Purple Heart in Vietnam. The degrees of supposed patriotism among veterans were endless. All caused by a war so frustrating that no one was happy and nearly everyone knew in their hearts that it was a losing effort. Now, it appeared that rubbing our nose in it was the new direction of the peace-at-any-cost crowd. Knowing that there were many people who did not serve their country, I understood their reluctance to fight a war that was never meant to be won. But I had only seen this anti-military sickness on television news. The heartland was home to few of these people. In my last year of college in 1968, there was only one man on campus with hippie-length hair. That was the only protest he did—growing long hair. There were strong sentiments about the Vietnam War, of course, but no one was a vitriolic radical. Protests, if there were any, were more like college pranks than destructive protests. Being glad that someone died while in the service of our country was not something that would come from the heartland of America. It was from the lunatic fringe, which was hellbent on beating a dead horse. The war was over. I wanted them to get over it.

As I pondered his revolting comment, I had a taste of stark reality. There were people who hated the guts of any veteran they met. They were ignorant, self-absorbed, and certain of their own virtue. Just as there is a difference between ignorance and stupidity, there is a difference between education and indoctrination. From Phil Snart's comment, 'he deserved to die,' this man and his ilk were now my sworn enemies.

6

THAT AFTERNOON I SHARED WITH my wife the pain of my recent conversation. It reflected on my somber face.

"Suzy, I can't believe anyone could say that to another veteran. That war screwed up everybody."

"Rob, don't be so hard on yourself. We've done okay. There's no need to dwell in the past."

"It took courage for me to hold back. Nobody should wish John dead and say he deserved to die. My goodness, that moron just hated pilots for some reason."

"Ignore him. You want to get him back? Make the guy disappear from your thoughts. There is nothing worse than being forgotten."

Suzy looked at me, her face sad but loving. In her adult life she would have had a right to be gloomy. It was her husband who had burned up in an airplane crash. I was the one who failed to save his life. I was the one who later married his widow. It was personal to me because of the sadness in losing a friend and the guilt I carried for taking his wife in marriage. John Alexander didn't deserve either event to happen. Even though it was a good marriage for Suzy and me, it made the sadness of someone ripping open those old wounds all the more acute.

Suzy Amity was a beautiful woman of thirty-five and not nearly past her prime—one of those lucky souls with ageless porcelain skin and boundless energy. She had the figure of a model who was finally able to eat—still slender but with the roundness in her figure that spoke of more maturity. The way she carried herself showed a carefree comfort in her soul. There was no doubt that she turned heads. I saw it many times. Her reaction was always a smile, a direct connection with a man's eyes, and a happy look away as she walked on. She was genuine in everything she did, whether in public or at home. Only around me did she respond in kind when I admired her beauty. Our passion for each other always started with her happy eyes gazing upon my grateful smile. Oh, how she could arouse me more with each passing year. Suzy was not a truck driver's dream. Instead, she was a fighter pilot's dream—sleek, low drag, highly maneuverable, and with powerful thrust.

She dressed well and had impeccable manners from years of being a Southern Belle's daughter. This afternoon she wore clothes appropriate for after-Easter, which coincided with the 95th anniversary of the first Oklahoma Land Run, Eighty-niner Day, April 22nd. She sported head to toe pastels of crisp pink slacks to midcalf and a white cotton collared blouse with small abstract shapes of pastel yellows, pinks, greens, and blues. She kept three buttons open at the collar, without fear of revealing too much. She liked to wear an ornamental flower in her now lighter honey blonde shoulder length hair. Today it was a pink rose clipped in her hair on the left side. She complemented all of this with a pair of comfortable white sandals. Toenails and fingernails of pale pink added to the total beauty of this luscious, springtime feminine package. I was lucky enough to afford to pamper her. At first, she resisted being treated so lavishly, but, at my insistence, she went back to try again. Now she enjoyed the experience of manicures, pedicures, and beauticians. I enjoyed it more than she.

A lover of reading, Suzy earned her degree in Library Science at Oklahoma State University, which turned into a pathway to technology. She was one of those girls both brilliant in grades and brilliant in common sense. From my own experiences, it was rare for someone her age. We had met in school, dated for a year, then went our separate ways with other people. Back then I viewed dating as a means of evaluating a mate for life. Sadly, I convinced Suzy by my own senseless actions that I was not marriage material. She was right, and I had been stupid. It was only through the tragedy of her husband's death that we ended up back together again, finally as one.

In the years since her tragedy, we spent many hours together recovering from the loss of her husband, who was also my best friend and college roommate. Added to the mix was a son, Sean, that John and Suzy brought into the world at Laredo Air Force Base in Texas. He was now a healthy boy, full of energy, curiosity, and independence. Since Sean never knew his father, I became the only father figure he knew. It was an easy decision to adopt Sean as my son when Suzy and I married. As close as John and I had been, Sean was an easy boy to love as my own. To see Suzy each day, I was blessed to have such a loving wife, mother, and friend. She accepted me, warts and all, and gently coached me to my potential as a focused, mature, and confident man. She reminded me daily that it worked both ways. I did the same for her. We were truly two souls in one.

"Do we need to talk about it more?" Suzy asked, interrupting my thoughts. We was her favorite word to describe us.

"No, I guess not." I sounded more discouraged than comforted. "We've moved on, haven't we?"

"I would say we have. A lot of good things have happened to us since we came home to Oklahoma. It has all been good."

I looked at Suzy pensively. "I hate it when you're right."

She laughed, even if I had uttered the same cliché a thousand times before. She had her own library jokes that I knew by heart. Her favorite crack was also very true. Suzy was keenly aware that I always admired a beautiful woman.

"Being a loyal husband means treating other women like books in a library. You're only checking them out. You're not buying them."

Out of my view a boy of almost ten years old crept up. I quickly turned around and together, as if choreographed, we both said "BOO!"

Sean laughed when I grabbed him under his arms and pulled him face to face. It was getting harder to do. He must have grown heavier overnight.

"Bueno," I said. I tapped the top of his head with my knuckles, like I was knocking on a door. It was a humorous blast from the past. That was

how people in south Texas answered their telephones during my Air Force flying days.

"Dad, don't say *bueno.* I don't like it," he said, laughing more.

"But you were born in Texas. How about, howdy? How's my partner?"

"I'm fine, Dad. Where have you been today?"

I moved close to his ear and whispered, "Don't tell Mom. I've been to the doctor again."

His eyes grew large. His mouth opened in mock surprise. "Are you going to fly again? Mom wants me to learn to fly."

"Our doctor says that I can fly again after they try a new kind of surgery, so, yes, I can fly again real soon."

"Tell me again what they are going to do?" His begging and anticipation spoke through his eyes.

"Well, there is a new thing called a laser. So, to fix me they are going to stick a vacuum cleaner, a TV camera, and a death ray laser gun up my nose... and turn them all on at once!"

The boy's laughter was predictably loud as he tried unsuccessfully to repeat what the doctors would do to me. He always added the phrase, "then your head will explode," but his laughter made the last line impossible to say. Suzy laughed with him, and he reached out to her for a hug.

"I love you, Mom," he said, reciprocating her affection. Then turning to me, "I love you, Dad."

I hugged him with one arm and drew Suzy close to us. I could tell that he wanted to say more.

"Something else, Partner?" He nodded his head as his eyes brightened.

"Can we go flying today?"

7

TO BE A SUCCESSFUL MEMBER of the armed forces, you must be a risk taker. The first time I soloed in a jet airplane, I said, "Well, it's too late now!" as the aircraft left the ground—with me in it. Even a jet as small as the T-37 was exhilarating upon takeoff, giving you a sense of acceleration only felt in muscle cars. And people died trying to fly it, as I knew all too well.

The supersonic T-38 could kill you, too, only faster. When I soloed in this sexier machine, it was no different than the mission before. No longer did my heart pound a hundred beats per minute. I failed to tell myself after liftoff, "It's too late now." Instead, once cleared for takeoff, I planted my feet on the brakes with as much force as my legs could produce while winding the twin jet engines to full military power and calmly checking the gauges for any problems. With all gauges in the green, I released the brakes and plugged in the jet's two afterburners. I enjoyed the exhilarating takeoff roll and climb out in full afterburner of a jet capable of climbing nearly thirty thousand feet in one minute. I had progressed so far as a student that my instructor did not even supervise this first T-38 solo. He simply sent me on my way. That was the way it was for all of us. They assumed our competence to pilot a multimillion-dollar jet plane with complete faith in us. That was the risk they took, but it was a message that we all understood. They expected a lot from us in turn.

With this faith in us and with their faith in their own abilities to train us, we moved on to levels of training that required absolute faith. Formation flying is 25% skill and 75% trust. When you lead other aircraft in formation, the responsibility is enormous. When two aircraft take off in formation for the first time, it is fun because you don't know any better. If you are the wingman within a formation, your life is in the hands of not only the lead aircraft but the pilot on the other side of you. Formation flying depends upon all participants being reliable.

Bad things sometimes happen. To practice a formation pitchout and rejoin, you must first separate. The lead aircraft pitches out in a sixty-degree-bank turn away from the formation followed two seconds later by the wingman—or wingmen in the case of a four-ship formation. Occasionally, a student leading a formation tries to kill you with a pitchout the wrong way—turning into a formation. When that happened to me, I moved out of his way by aggressively pushing my own aircraft down, letting the solo lead pass over us. All of us instructors had those stories. There were guys we would never trust again.

The lead aircraft never flies at full power. It's necessary for the wingman to have the ability to fly faster than his lead if he gets behind. If you fly formation in the clouds or at night, staying close to the lead aircraft is mandatory. Standard close formation is three feet of wingtip clearance between aircraft. This distance requires the wingman to constantly watch his lead and not look elsewhere. If the formation is flying straight and level and the two aircraft run into each other, the blame goes to the wingman who broke that rule and looked inside his cockpit.

My scariest formation flying was landing in formation. Knowing that all aircraft crashes involve the ground, staying three feet from another airplane all the way down to the ground was not a pleasant thought. When an aircraft slows down, the controls of that aircraft become less responsive. So, imagine flying on the wing of a supersonic jet and touching down next to this airplane without ever looking at the ground. The idea of this exercise was frightening. When it was my turn to perform my first T-38 formation landing, I did it well on the first try. I owed all my success that day to trust.

One day I ran into my classmate Will, who flew B-57s for the Guard. It was the same day that a student accidentally put me into an inverted spin. I was wired, and my story topped anything he had to share in return. But that was about to change. These big twin engine bombers were flown solo. Will had his older brother, also a B-57 pilot, with him as his lead into Laredo AFB. After a visit, I stayed around to watch their formation takeoff. Any aircraft is fun to watch, but I knew that their formation takeoff meant one brother was trusting another. Two days later, I got a phone call.

"Hey Rob. Do I have a story for you? Remember when my brother and I left a couple of days ago?"

"I watched you take off. Did you lead, or was it your brother?"

"Oh, he always leads. He's older. You know how that goes."

"So, what's your story? What went wrong?"

"You saw us leave in formation, I assume? As we headed back to Wichita, I got a hand signal from Walt signaling that he lost radios, so he gave me the 'you-take-lead' signal and dropped back on my wing. We were IFR with no concerns. Our weather briefing had us clear and a million miles all the way home."

"Not so, I take it.?"

"We were in the heaviest clouds I can remember. I looked out on my right wing to see Walt's plane. It was barely visible. There we were with one radio between us, and everything was socked in for the next hundred fifty miles."

"Obviously, this story has a happy ending."

"Oh, yeah! Little brother got to save big brother, and I'm never going to let him forget it. He had to fly on my wing all that way starting in Oklahoma. These guard planes are old. T-37 training was useful. We have only one radio, one VOR, some have TACAN, but none has an ILS. We got a GCA coming into McConnell AFB, and I was hoping for a decent ceiling. They had earlier reported a five hundred foot overcast but soon reported it had dropped to a hundred foot ceiling and a quarter mile visibility. They wanted us to divert, but I convinced them to let me make an attempt, since I had a com-out on my wing. The Ground Controller talked me down. I could only hope that my big brother could keep me in sight. I gave him hand signals for dropping gear, but I never was certain he could see me through the soup. I worried that if he was late dropping his gear, he would fly right past me."

"Was he able to keep up?"

"He said he saw me signaling something and assumed it must be gear coming down, but he didn't know for sure. I nodded my head to execute gear down. He told me later that his hand was on the lever but waited to see my gear doors open before he slammed the gear lever down. When I nodded my head the second time, he knew I was dropping flaps. He was good. Never lost sight of me and hung on my wing for dear life. Our GCA controller guided us down perfectly. When he told me to report the runway in sight or execute a missed approach, I couldn't see it. I pushed the mic button to declare missed approach when I spotted the first center stripe on the runway. I called the runway in sight and brought us down to the best landing I ever made. I looked over to the right, and there was old Walt still in formation with three-foot separation. It was the greatest experience of my short career, I'm telling you."

"Man, Will. You are one shit hot pilot."

"It might just top your inverted spins."

"You've topped me. Talk about a dangerous mission. I bet Walt was real nice to you after that."

"When we rolled to a stop, and the crew put in the chocks, he climbed out of the cockpit and ran over to my plane. I was still shutting everything down. I looked at him below me. He looked like a kid in the circus. When I planted my feet on the ground, he had me in a bear hug and wouldn't let go. I've never seen him so happy before in my life. I had a rough time of it, but flying on my wing in the soup for a hundred fifty miles had to be the most stressful flight he's ever had. I think I grew up in his eyes after that flight."

Trust was the key to survival. I learned that the lessons of formation flying would apply also to the civilian world. Trust my abilities and trust those who are worthy of that trust.

While living in Laredo in south Texas, a hundred times on television Eddie Chiles or his female spokesman ran commercials saying, 'If you don't have an oil well, get one. You'll love doing business with Western.' I never did business with Western Company of North America, but Eddie's idea stuck. When I got my unlikely chance to separate from the Air Force, I learned how your highest goals morph into something totally unexpected. My first plan after becoming a civilian was to use the GI Bill to return to Oklahoma State University and become a veterinarian. The more I looked at the prospect, the stronger became my conviction that my time had passed, and I had too many potential obligations to consider. Vet school is expensive. I'd been in the real world too long to deal with idealistic younger students. My last time on campus had not been a pleasant experience dealing with irresponsible student behavior.

I was in love with a widow and her child and concluded that my time to go back to school had passed. I had already experienced more than most men my age. I pondered what to do, so I took a brief semester's time using my GI Bill to take courses to help me understand the stock market, how to run a business, and who to consult to invest my twenty-five-thousand-dollar savings. I built up over time a sizable allotment from my pay that I stashed away each month. Prudent bachelors can do that.

I learned from history books how the smart men made money in California's Forty-niner Gold Rush. The winners didn't dig for gold. They sold the tools that prospectors needed to dig for gold. I viewed the Oklahoma and Texas oil boom as a chance to feed the oil frenzy with the things frenzy demands—and I made a killing. It was a crazy time when no one bargained over price, and everybody paid in cash. It wasn't far from the truth to say that I was one of the few people who reported everything on my taxes and never broke the law. Best of all, I lived frugally, continued to invest in suppliers, then cashed out when I sensed the stuff was about to hit the fan. It was the craziest time to be in Oklahoma. The strong didn't always survive, but the smart usually did. I had miraculously managed to more than double my investment on average each year for seven years. Twenty-five grand became several million. I switched from Oklahoma investments to the money at the national level. Except for oil, the nation was in a boom.

I pondered my good fortune from hard work and learning, then compared it to my first takeoff in a jet airplane and what I said to myself. I decided that it was time to venture forth with more risk taking, so I modified my investment premise. This time I wasn't thinking about money. I kept that sensibly safe in sound investments. I was thinking about an investment in my future—my health, my family, and my next contribution to society. My same comment applied. *Well, it's never too late.*

I skipped returning to the VA hospital for consultation and turned to civilian doctors for surgery to fix my nasal sinus problem that had made flying so often painful and bloody. It is good to picture in your mind a goal. I pictured Suzy and Sean at ten thousand feet in an airplane, trusting me to bring them down and home safely.

8

"I DON'T RELISH BEING A guinea pig again," I said to Dr. Schedel, my ear, nose, and throat surgeon. "I was that already in the Air Force. How many procedures like this have you done?"

"The procedure I would do on you? Oh... I would say several hundred," Schedel replied.

"That's good because I'm paying for this myself. I won't go to the VA."

"Why not? I go there once a week for their clinic in EENT." EENT stood for Eye, Ear, Nose, & Throat.

"Try the waiting room," I said. "We report at seven o'clock a.m. They take roll call at eight o'clock a.m. I will receive an exam time at nine o'clock. Then I wait for a nurse to call me to the back. In that two to four hours, I see scores of vets walk in with their day bags full of items. Playing cards. Checker boards. Lunch pails. It seems like all of them bring in a carton, not a pack, of cigarettes. They smoke in the waiting room for two plus hours. I'm there for my smoke related sinus infections. That's why I was going to the VA. I was grounded from flying because of cigarette smoke and an unpressurized jet plane. I think they are now calling it something, let's see...."

"Vasomotor rhinitis related to exposure to secondhand cigarette smoke," Dr. Schedel said to finish my thought.

"That's it! I came out of the VA worse than when I entered. So, I'm willing to pay. I learned early that free stuff is never without a downside."

Dr. Schedel surprised me with his response.

"I think you made the right choice, and, furthermore, I would not tell the VA that you had surgery... at least not until we know it's successful."

"Is that because I have a VA disability?"

"Exactly." He added a nod of his head for emphasis. "You never know what they will do. They might take back your disability and make you pay them back from the day of your successful surgery."

He raced through the implications, risks, and cost of such a procedure.

It may alter the tone of my voice. There could be infection. It would be a long recovery with some post-op discomfort. I couldn't afford to sneeze.

My conclusion—It's worth every dollar I spend.

"Okay, Doc. When can we do this?"

"I do my cases Tuesday and Thursday mornings, so pick a day next week if you want." He stood up and walked to the door. "My nurse will set it up and tell you what to expect and give you instructions to follow before the day of the event."

"Okay. Thanks Doc." I looked up to see an empty doorway. He was already gone.

Doc Schedel's nurse gave me her memorized lecture—no food after 8:00 p.m. the night before, stop aspirin now, no water before surgery, bring a responsible adult, and expect to go home that afternoon. That's all I could remember. Thank goodness I received instructions on paper. I'm a checklist sort of guy. Suzy would help me—or rather *make* me—comply. It's always easy for former military personnel to obey their wives. We're used to having a commander.

TUESDAY MORNING AT 0-DARK-THIRTY, I arrived at Deaconess Hospital for surgery. Suzy had arranged for Sean to get to school with a neighbor. At nine years old, Sean could be trusted to lock up and get home after school. We hoped to be back before he arrived home. I parked the car as near an exit door as possible, which would make it easier to stagger to my car post-op. I stepped out onto the parking lot, handed Suzy the keys, and nervously walked into the main entrance of the hospital.

We were quickly processed through the paperwork and into a pre-op alcove hidden by a sterile shower curtain. I stripped to my bare essence and unsuccessfully put on the gown provided. Suzy, sensing my nervousness, took it from me, put my arms in the right holes, and tied the back so visitors could only get a peek at my backside. It was a nice gesture of caring, without her making note of my brief fear that things could always go wrong. I turned to look at her and tried to give her a reassuring smile. A floral clip rested behind her ear. Dressed in comfortable blue jeans, tennis shoes, and a heavy yellow cotton V-neck tee, it was her smile that caught my eye. There is no more beautiful woman than the one who truly loves you.

Several aides and nurses came in to ask questions, take my blood pressure, and check my pulse—all higher than normal. A male nurse came in to hook up an intravenous line. I followed my orders not to drink water or eat before surgery, which made good veins hard to find. After a few pokes into rolling veins, he hung a bag of normal saline.

First, a nameless anesthesiologist entered our nook to go through his procedure and to ask questions related to any reactions or allergies I might have to medications. He was remarkably tanned for a specialist who must spend his entire life as a ghost in the hospital. I had never seen one in direct sunlight.

Dr. Schedel came into our cubicle to talk about what to expect. Shouldn't he be nervous? Afterall, my life is at stake here. Instead, he was calm and all business, just like a fighter pilot—and just as cocky! I relaxed.

"Any questions?"

"Yes," Suzy said. "How long will this poor baby be recovering at home?"

"I'll see him in my office this Friday. Then we will have a better idea. He'll want to stay home for a few more days after he sees me."

Our doctor walked out before Suzy or I could ask anything else. An aide came to wheel me into the hallway. Another nurse stuck a syringe into my IV catheter.

"What is that?"

"Versed," she replied, "to keep you calm and...."

THEN I WAS AWAKE. THEN I was not. Then I was awake again.

"The nurses told me to keep waking you up." Suzy spoke to me softly. "So, wake up... wake up."

I drifted off again. Suzy still softly implored me to wake up. Dr. Schedel quietly appeared. He must have eavesdropped on Suzy's wake up routine. He spoke in a loud voice.

"Missus Amity, I would let him sleep. Don't wake him up."

I wasted no time in complying, but a nurse interrupted my sleep once again, ordering me in loud resonant tones to wake up. She spoke to Suzy about her failed duty to wake up her husband.

"But Dr. Schedel told me to let him sleep," Suzy replied.

"Doctors need to learn my job. He needs to wake up soon."

Later, I concluded that Suzy followed the advice of the registered nurse in charge. I gradually came to a greater awareness of my surroundings, after Dr. Schedel entered the room to let me hear how things went. My eyes were closed when he entered.

"Good, you let him sleep," He sounded cheerful.

"Yes," Suzy said. "He was practically smoking hot when he came back."

"Yeah, the laser is hot." He laughed. "He'll smell a little burned for a while."

Dr. Schedel explained what he had done to and for me. It took longer than normal to stop the post-op bleeding. As a result, I had more packing in my nose. He warned us that getting the gauze out on Friday would take longer than planned. He looked at all my sinuses, including those above my eye, where I ruptured the left frontal sinus in a military training flight ten years before.

"I can't do anything but look at your frontal sinuses," he said. "They are too close to the optic nerve, but they look fine. Your surgery at Wilford Hall was well done."

He went on to say that he made a larger opening into each of my maxillary sinuses, the ones that often gave me moderate to severe tooth pain and bleeding when flying. He added his own opinion for my reassurance.

"I am glad you didn't let the Air Force do the old surgery that removed a quarter-sized piece of bone from each maxillary sinus cavity. It was not the best solution for the problem, we now realize."

He added that he lasered an enlarged cavity in my central ethmoid sinus, thus trimming the turbinates, those ribbons of bone in the nose that were clogging up all of my other sinuses. He compared it to a street's storm sewer grate, working fine unless clogged with sticks and leaves.

"Now you will be fine and ready to fly in no time." He walked to the door and turned toward me. "I'll see you Friday."

Even though Dr. Schedel confirmed that the surgery went well, it was hard to focus on the goal of flying again with twenty feet of nasal packing stuck up each nostril. The procedure had a name—Functional Endoscopic Sinus Surgery with Turbinoplasty. Put in lay terms, I had a new and large hole in the middle of my head that reduced the chances of a sinus blockage. Put in even better terms that a real man would understand, I was now truly an airhead.

AFTER THREE DAYS, DR. SCHEDEL pulled out the packing. Besides feeling like fingernails on a chalkboard, it reminded me of circus clowns that pull fifty feet of colorful crepe streamers out of each other's mouths. Except this came from my nose, or better described, from the middle of my brain cavity. The only good part about the experience was gladly knowing that I had only two nostrils, as he said, "only one more to go."

For two weeks I breathed from my mouth only. Because the scope used in surgery illuminated the optic nerve in each frontal sinus, I wore sunglasses in the dark for a week to reduce the pain in my eyes. I tried to watch television to fend off boredom, but even when Suzy dimmed the screen's brightness, it was too bright and painful to watch. Even donning sunglasses failed to help.

I irrigated my sinuses every two hours to gently clear out the dead tissue and normal slime associated with my nasal cavity. Blood was constant. Once a thin piece of turbinate bone washed out. I could not blow my nose upon penalty of bleeding to death, or worse, paying for another surgery.

Somehow over this time, I started to focus on my goal of flying once again and getting my money's worth out of that million-dollar education the Air Force gave me for free.

9

THE DAY WAS SUNNY, NO wind, and still cool as I taxied down the runway at Wiley Post Airport in Oklahoma City, ironically named for someone who died in a plane crash. A friend from high school, Brad Kilty, sat in the right seat. As a certified flight instructor, Brad was a seasoned pilot, who had done it the hard way, learning to fly on his own dime. He had a passion for flying that drove him to a high level of skill seldom achieved without financial support. He was a natural pilot who took any opportunity to leave the ground. Flight for him was like crack. Without his fix, he became agitated. Although his wife was supportive and loving, she would not fly with him—ever. She had missed out on a lot of enjoyment with one of the most skilled flyboys I knew.

We taxied to the north end of Runway 17 Left for engine runup. The Piper Warrior was only eight years old, which in civil aviation was practically a brand-new airplane. The throttle was similar to what I handled in military jets. Unlike jets, instead of a control stick, it had a yoke which I found awkward. The small Lycoming engine and propeller, oddly enough, were more complex than a jet engine.

I desperately wanted to fly after being grounded for eight years. I soon learned that it was not like riding a bicycle. We released brakes at takeoff when Brad yelled for the first time.

"Right rudder!" He shouted into my headset and stepped firmly on the right rudder pedal. "You're not flying a jet. Don't forget the torque on this prop. You'll be doing ground loops before we go a hundred feet."

What else have I forgotten in eight years? This is going to be a disaster of embarrassment.

Somehow, we got airborne in a straight line. The Warrior was flying at a relatively slow speed compared to a jet. We're going to drop out of the sky. We're too slow.

"Keep this runway heading until we climb to twenty-four hundred feet. You can level off there."

One minute later Brad mentioned that, because I had neglected to continue using right rudder on our climb out, my heading had already drifted left thirty degrees from runway heading. My eyes had glued on the inside of the cockpit. Not looking outside showed me to be no better than a beginning student pilot. It was a painfully humbling experience.

Flying out to a practice area, I was so busy trying to control the airplane that I soon realized I had no idea where we were or where the runway had disappeared. I was totally at Brad's mercy to get me back to Wiley Post and Runway 17 Left.

Then came my first traffic pattern, final approach, and landing. We flew west to the small C. E. Page Airport near Yukon, Oklahoma, one of hundreds of landing strips America built during World War Two. C. E. Page was also a famous pioneer aviator like Wiley Post, although Page lived to a ripe old age. Flying to Page's airport did not give me more confidence or improve my skill level.

Entering the pattern for the first time in years, Brad helped with my radio calls. This was an uncontrolled airport, which meant there was no control tower. Every pilot had to be his own tower controller and pilot at the same time. Courtesy was the key. Let other pilots know who you are and where you are. Entering downwind to the runway, I adjusted my spacing to the much narrower runway on my left, tried to judge the winds by a windsock at the center of the field, and held my altitude steady. I was doing okay—or was I?

"Watch your airspeed." He didn't take the controls from me. He was simply going to let us die with me at the helm.

I added power which raised the nose but kept the airspeed unchanged. It ruined my perfect altitude control. Low airspeed is what gets you killed in the traffic pattern. I lowered the nose slightly and kept the power steady. The altitude got better before I began my descending left turn to the runway. I was about to overshoot the runway, so I increased my bank angle and pulled the yolk back gently to pull myself around the turn. To my relief I rolled out well aligned with the runway center line. I told Brad what I was doing and why. I was too high for my comfort level, but Brad told me not to go around. Our runway was long and forgiving. I approached the runway threshold in a panic, not wanting to either stall out or go sailing off the other end of the runway. When I finally touched down with wobbly controls, I was ecstatic.

"I did it on the first try! Who's the stud now?"

"You're no stud, yet," Brad replied. "Let's see you do it again."

Even though no one died when I landed on my first try, I knew it would be a few more flying hours before I would solo. Brad whole-heartedly agreed with a laugh as we rolled down the runway. We added power to return to the air for another touch-and-go landing.

"Your final turn was one constant one hundred eighty-degree turn." He had to yell over the sound of our engine at full power. "That's how the Air Force does it. Next time I want you to do two ninety-degree turns to final. That's how we civilians do it."

And so, I did. The second landing was better, but my self-confidence was not. Brad demonstrated the third landing. I flew the remainder of landings in the traffic pattern before we navigated our way back to Wiley Post Airport for a full stop landing.

"Look across me to your right. Just past Lake Overholser," Brad said, giving me a brief landmark lesson. "You see the big airport over there?"

"That's Will Rogers." An American Airlines MD-80 was making a circling approach as I spoke.

"Another OKC airport named for a person killed in a plane crash."

10

I GOT HOME AFTER THE flight in a discouraged mood. I had been cocky but was humiliated. Now I wanted to crawl into a hole and hide. I was not even close to being a hot stick anymore. Military pilots used to make fun of civilians like I was now. I found Suzy and dragged her into my favorite nook in the house where I whined in self-pity. I was too humbled to share details. She listened to my depressing self-deprecation longer than she had to. The afternoon and evening gave me a chance to sit in my library and stare at my hero wall in solitude. Suzy kept Sean away for a while, but his excitement about my flying soon drew him to my isolated corner of gloom.

I joined them for dinner in silence and cast a pall over the whole evening. Suzy kept Sean in the kitchen to work on his homework. I went back to my place of solace until it came time for bed. Suzy waited up for me to join her. She was always there when I needed her.

"Suzy, I don't know how well we're going to do. I was terrible up there. Brad must think I'm a fraud."

"I doubt that."

I climbed into bed for the night and turned out the lights. She had Sean safely tucked into bed, after helping him with his homework. He relished my tale of an exciting day of flying an airplane for the first time in his memory. I disappointed him. We hoped he could sleep.

"You weren't there. It was awful," I said. "I couldn't even fly a straight line. I didn't know where I was. I couldn't even find the runway until I was practically on top of it. I didn't know how to use the radios. Brad did all that this time."

"We'll do better tomorrow. I know you. You will sleep on it and amaze Brad with how quickly we learn."

We remained silent next to each other, both of us thinking our own private thoughts and dreams. Suzy then summed it up properly.

"Look back and laugh. Don't look back and wish."

She truly was my co-pilot. It was hard to be discouraged when she cloaked everything in the pronoun, we. We were simply not going to let us fail. We only needed to be patient and focused. Flying for us was a common goal. We needed to share this experience of flying. It would be unique to us. No other woman had ever flown with me. No other man had ever taken Suzy aloft. It would be ours alone. Then Sean would go up with us. That, too, would be ours alone. It was our passion to build memories that were ours only. Each experience brought us closer. Each new experience further bonded us from two into one—from you and me into us. I dared not fail her. I dared not fail us.

I whispered in her ear. "Suzy, I love you."

She turned to me in the dark to whisper, her lips to mine, "Rob Amity, I love you. We're going to be sierra hotel tomorrow, aren't we?"

I pondered that for a moment, visualizing how flying used to be in a much faster airplane. We can do this. I drew closer to my wife, wrapped my right arm around her waist, and kept our lips lightly pressed.

"Sierra hotel. I like that. You will be sierra hotel, too, okay? We're a team."

"Always a team." Within seconds her breathing hinted of sleep that can only come with peace of mind.

Suzy was the most intelligent person I knew. I was smart enough to be grateful. Most of my success came after surrounding myself with people smarter in many ways than I was. Laying my head next to hers, I smelled the hair on her head that framed such a beautiful mind.

Continuing to hold gently to the softness of her skin, I savored the smooth feel and the warmth it radiated. I had long since mapped every inch of her body from head to toe. I knew every perfection, every flaw, each mole, and each dimple. Every childhood scar and scrape that brought her tears seared into my own memories as if it were my own childhood hurt. I cringed at each memory those marks revealed. I viewed her nakedness with awe and reverence. Even her imperfections were the essence that uniquely aroused me most. Whenever I viewed a woman who reminded me of Suzy, I perked up. But always my thoughts and my ardor remained reserved for her.

She continued to breathe softly in the moon's faint glow entering through our bedroom's French doors. Her face, silhouetted against a pillow, shown like a work of art, soft full lips, a gentle curve of her nose, and eyes peacefully closed in happy dreams. I glanced below her slender neck to her womanly form rising from the sheets and marveled at my fortune to know her intimately. Placing a hand upon her hip, she rustled slightly before returning to the rhythmic respiratory rise and fall of two breasts.

In a recurring dream I fantasized that I had to rescue Suzy in a totally dark room among a hundred other naked women. I could always find her with a single touch. But in my slumber the search required my going down a line of many women. With each strange touch I recoiled at the unfamiliarity of the skin, then quickly moved over in dread to the next unseen body in line. I made rapid tactile checks because the wrong woman in my arms was a terrible notion. Then I found her. My single touch instantly became a full body embrace, feeling her skin, the shape of her hand, and the smell of her hair. I would lead her away with tears in my eyes and joy in my heart. My dream always ended there. I would wake up, gently feel her presence in our bed, and drift into deep sleep, after thanking God for His gift to me.

My memory of dreams soon bridged over to real dreams. Having drifted off into slumber, I was undisturbed in more vivid visions of turbulent flying, gleeful laughter of a fearless little boy and of a goddess-like form of a woman who rewarded me every night with her loving and sensual presence.

11

ARRIVING AT THE WILEY POST Airport, I drove my prized Porsche 911 onto the taxiway and ramp and to the hangar housing the rental Piper Warrior. Brad was already going through his own preflight check of the aircraft. He would expect me to do the same, which I proceeded to do.

"Good morning, Mister Brad, sir," I was determined to sound cheerful. "I hope you're ready for your new pilot. I fired the old one for you last night."

"Good! It saves me the trouble," He gave me a stern look before breaking out in a smile. "What makes you so cocksure this morning?"

"Suzy and I talked last night." I walked around to the empennage, checking the position of the trim tabs and the free movement of rudder and ailerons. "I've been trying to fly like a civilian. Take my radio calls. That worried me a lot. What if I make a mistake and use Air Force jargon? Then it occurred to me. They might like hearing that language. So, I'm going to talk on the radio like I'm used to talking."

"That works for me. Are you going to square your turns for me in the traffic pattern?"

"Absolutely. Pattern discipline must be uniform. But I think if I quit worrying about what to say on the radio, I'll be better at keeping my head out of the cockpit."

I shared what my first flight instructor said to me in the Air Force after my first two or three poor performances as a student in the T-37.

"'You need a flight surgeon to install a bay window in your stomach. That way you can see where you're flying with your head up your ass!'"

Brad looked at me with an inquisitive look of amusement. I would not allow any sarcasm from him today. He would never have the chance. I was checking the tires and the landing gear strut under the left wing. Next, I pulled out my fuel tester and drained a few tablespoons full of fuel from the tank to check for water in the avgas. Upon standing up from under the wing, Brad spoke in a business-like tone.

"Okay, then, Mister Pilot. You take me out to Page, we'll shoot as many landings as you need to do, then you take me back here to Wiley Post and shoot a couple more landings. You do that and you're saving a lot of flying hours for yourself."

"It's a deal. I flew a lot of hours last night in my sleep. Most of it came back to me overnight."

And so, it did. I called Ground Control, giving our aircraft type and tail number, location, intentions, and coded proof of having checked the current weather conditions. We taxied out to Runway 17 Left. Arriving at the runup pad at the end of the runway, I turned into the wind, set my brakes, ran up the propeller to the proper RPM, and checked the two magnetos for effective current to the engine's sparkplugs. With everything acceptable I taxied to the holding point at the end of the runway and made my next radio call to Tower in military terms.

"Wiley Post Tower, Cherokee niner-eight-seven-two-Kilo, is number one for the active."

The tower controller cheerfully cleared us for takeoff. Away we went straight down the runway, lifting off, maintaining runway heading, and turning to the west for Yukon, Oklahoma, and C.E. Page Airport. No need for instructor-assisted right rudder today. Spotting the runway was at first a challenge. Runways are hard to find until your mind gets around the idea that they tend to blend into the hazy terrain before you acclimate your eyes to them. Once my search spotted the distant runway, I turned the radio to Page's Unicom frequency and listened for the chatter on the radio. It was silent, so I flew beside the runway at a reasonable altitude to look for the windsock that told me what runway to use. This morning I could focus on my position to the runway, check for other aircraft in the area of the pattern, and fix my proper place in altitude and airspeed with a clear view of the runway. I squared my turns to final and, for the first time, rolled out on final approach at a good angle of descent and at the proper airspeed. The touchdown was good enough. I added power on my landing roll and took off again, climbed to pattern altitude, and checked for the presence of other aircraft. Turning a hundred eighty degrees to reenter the traffic pattern, I repeated the approach and landing another dozen times. After that, we departed traffic to fly home to Wiley Post Airport. I repeated the same process of checking for current weather, then entered the pattern after alerting the tower of our position and current weather code. There was other airplane traffic with us in the pattern, which was good practice but routine. After a first touch-and-go landing, Brad took the yoke from me and asked if he could please make a landing by himself. I was more than happy to let him. More than a dozen successful touch-and-go landings wore me out. I was pumped by the excitement and the realization that it had all come back to me. All it took was one humiliating initial flight, a good night's sleep, and my use of familiar military radio chatter. What an epiphany it was. The airport personnel perhaps recognized my military background. Maybe it was my imagination, but their replies were different—respectful. And I didn't need that bay window in my stomach to see clearly.

12

"I THINK WE'RE GOING TO make it, after all," I said. My enthusiasm, lacking the evening before, was back with a hyperactive vengeance.

Suzy and Sean grabbed a hug as I stepped through the twin doors of our welcoming home. I was happy and relieved. Footsteps can reveal the pace of our souls. They could tell I was successful, even before I opened the door. I glanced down at Sean, who gripped my leg with both arms and legs. He was at the age where I needed to talk to him about stopping the practice. It would be painful for him, but it's part of growing up. I would assure him that the pain in my leg far exceeded his emotional pain of ending this means of affection.

Suzy's affection on the other hand would not be curtailed. She wrapped herself all over the top half of me. First planting a big fat kiss on my lips, she then pressed her forehead and nose against my own.

"We did it, huh?"

"We did it. Brad wants me to fly again, but I'm not worried. It all came back to me. It was like I never left… well almost like it."

"Any sinus problems? Headaches? Bleeding?"

"No. None at all. Remember, I'm an airhead now."

Suzy laughed aloud. Sean heard my joke for the twentieth time and laughed louder than any of us. Suzy took my hand while I shook Sean off my leg with considerable effort. She walked us into our family room off the kitchen. We dragged ourselves over to the room's wet bar. Waiting on the drink cart was a bucket of ice with a chilled bottle of Veuve Clicquot Yellow Label Champagne.

"What's the occasion?" I asked.

"You're back. I could tell this morning when you got up with Sean that you were not going to fail. I know you too well."

"And if I had come home after a disastrous day of flying?"

"You would've never seen the Champagne at the bar... but I had a feeling."

Suzy looked as good as ever, dressed to kill in her white tailored slacks, medium heals that matched a thin navy belt, and a gauzy tan silk blouse adorned with ribbon and lace.

"I felt good about it this morning. I'm glad you had faith in me, too."

"And I've never slept with a civilian pilot before. We may have to have a check ride soon."

"I'm for that." I laughed, then looked down at our rapidly growing boy. "Just as soon as our junior flight examiner gets sent to bed."

Sean smiled. He had no clue what we were talking about, but we were saying his name and looking at him. That, coupled with his hope to fly with me soon, was cause for more laughter.

"Until then," Suzy said, "sit down and rest your weary bones. I'll pour each of us a glass, and I've got ginger ale for Sean. We all get bubbly tonight."

Sean's cheer was a little too loud, but deep down inside, I found myself screaming for joy with him. I sat down on our well-worn and comfortable red leather sofa, adorned on the arms with small Navajo rugs, bought at the Chimayo Trading Post in New Mexico.

Our family room was the most used room in our large home, accented with warm dark wood wainscoting and crown molding at the ceiling. An original-style Hunter ceiling fan continually turned to keep the air fresh and the temperature constant. Across from the wet bar was a solid wall of bookshelves to which we often added new books. I collected histories while Suzy added her favorite American and English classic literature. We voraciously read each other's books, not just our own. In the corner to the left of the books was a lamp and table sandwiched between two comfortable easy chairs for reading. They remained little used because we preferred a sofa on the far side of the entry for sitting close to each other, with Sean often sandwiched in between us. That still left enough room for the inevitable dog that Sean kept begging for. Rustic wooden beams supported the ceiling and drew the eye to our special place. On the wall to the right of our books was what I called my hero wall. Every veteran has one as a badge of honor and a source of pride. I hung several framed photos of me as a reminder that I had once done something special. There I was by my T-37 Tweet jet in a color photo. From my pilot training days at Laredo Air Force Base, I hung a photo of me standing on the ladder of a T-38 Talon, the supersonic trainer considered the most enjoyable jet to fly of all time—the same jet that astronauts flew. The focus of my hero wall was a shadowbox holding patches of my numerous student pilot classes that I trained to fly. Along with my own squadron patch, the shadowbox held my captain's bars and a patch of the T-37 aircraft I flew as a rated instructor pilot. Randomly hung on the wall were several black and white photos of different training groups from Basic Training, Officer Training, Pilot Training, Survival School, and Instructor Pilot Training. In a prominent spot in the center of the wall was an oversized color photo of Captain John Alexander and me as a first lieutenant in our flight suits. Suzy stood between us. Who could have guessed it would turn out so different?

I didn't intend to have a hero wall. In the beginning I wanted to forget about my time in the military. First, there was my bitterness over John's death. Also, it was the animosity I brought out in those who were more gung-ho than I chose to be. I went through a series of epiphanies in the eight years since, going from antiwar to anti-defeat. I went from hating war to believing that war would be less horrible if it started out with victory as a goal. My thoughts went to the more than fifty thousand deaths in the Vietnam War. John's accidental death was not even in that count. But surely our nation would have had fewer deaths if we had only chosen to defeat the enemy, not just contain our foe. Instead of a knockout punch, our politicians chose to count bodies. It turned into a game of Whack-A-Mole, not a war to win. But then one day I chose to be proud of my efforts, however inconsequential they may have been. It was dangerous work to fly, certainly not like flying in combat, but people could still end up just as dead. My opinions, even as I changed them, seemed ever more clear to me with each new year. So, I put out my mementoes, including wooden models of the airplanes I flew, and made sure any visitors to our house couldn't miss them. Perhaps I was daring someone to utter something disparaging.

Suzy joined us on our red leather sofa, handing a crystal glass of ginger ale to Sean, then a green champagne flute to me. Suzy was generous. I almost spilled some of the precious nectar of the gods in the handoff. She was soon back with her own more reasonable pour in another green crystal flute.

"Now, Sean, be careful like we said." Sean nodded his head in acknowledgement and raised his glass with hers. "To our flyboy and to our many adventures to come."

We slowly moved our glasses toward Sean's, anticipating what any nine-year-old was capable of doing in a moment of excitement. We all touched glasses without damage while chanting Here-Here!

"What adventure do you have in mind?" I asked. "It's still a few more days or weeks before I will feel comfortable taking you two up."

"What about the YMCA camp in Davis. You and Sean are in the Indian Guide program. I read that they are going to Camp Classen this spring. You could fly us there."

"Bad idea. Indian Guides is for sons and dads only. They want it to be a bonding experience away from mothers. You can't go with us."

"Well, then, bond away. That will be good for you two."

I pondered the prospects of spending time away from Suzy. There had not been many. My dad was always fond of saying, "Business trips away from home are good for a marriage. The reunions can be spectacular."

So, we made plans for a flyboys' weekend adventure. I looked down at a grinning Sean, who relished sitting between us.

"You ready to go fly with your dad, Partner?" I expected another scream, but he was too busy not spilling his bubbles. "I'll have to change your name from Partner to Junior Birdman."

I regretted saying it immediately. He exploded in laughter spilling ginger ale on the both of us from his glass, then spewing more as he tried to suppress a mouthful of laughter. We reflexively stood up to dodge the spray. I grabbed hold of his glass with my free hand and deftly stabilized it with the light touch of a hand flying a precision approach. Suzy was already out of range and running to the kitchen for towels. She returned in time to see me with a Champagne glass in each hand and futilely attempting to dam the flow of Sean's ginger ale from my lap. She couldn't stop herself and broke out in tension-releasing laughter that quickly became contagious. We stood in a family triangle, looking and laughing together until Suzy grabbed Sean around his shoulders and gave him a wet, sticky hug.

Sean giggled. "I don't do bubbly very well. I'm going to try something else."

We quickly mopped up Sean's ginger ale and assessed our own need for a clothing change, while Sean went back to the kitchen to drink milk.

"You want any more champagne, dear?" I asked.

Her glass was still half full. She had hardly sipped from her glass. The mess had apparently diminished her thirst.

"No, thank you. We're still working on this one. You better have a second, so it doesn't go to waste. It's mighty good though."

I refilled my glass and sat down next to her again, this time with no competition from our boy between us. She laid her head briefly on my right shoulder, then asked me a question.

"Speaking of a mess. When are we getting a dog?"

It wasn't a new question. The subject had come up many times before. This time I surprised her with a different question. "Are you going to take care of the dog?"

"Of course not."

"Okay. We know that the dog will be Sean's." I began the recitation we had discussed already a hundred times. "He needs to be old enough to be responsible for it. Feed it. Water it. Brush it. Play with it. Right?"

"And learn to be nurturing like all good fathers should be nurturing."

"Okay, I'll add disciplining the dog to the list."

"You're a mess. You know that?"

"It's Sean's ginger ale." I removed my wet and sugary shirt. "With Sean and me going to Camp Classen, are you going to take care of his puppy while we're gone?"

"No."

"Then the only alternative would be to get him a puppy for his tenth birthday, after we get back from our flyboys' weekend."

"Deal!"

"Dang! You got me."

I feigned a posture of defeat just to tease her. We both already knew what we wanted to do about a dog. We both knew that giving a companion to Sean would teach him vital nurturing skills. Many of life's lessons begin when we take on the responsibility of another's life and wellbeing.

"But now, I want a concession from you."

"Oh, boy! What is it this time?"

"I want to buy an airplane."

13

BRAD KILTY'S ENTHUSIASTIC VOICE, COMING out of the telephone's earpiece, was so loud that Suzy heard what he said from the next room. *"You want to buy an airplane? I'm sure you will never forgive me... but let me help you!"*

Like most people, Brad was happy to help someone else spend their money for something he loved.

"I need your help to do this right, but you're so nitpicky, we'll probably never find one to meet your standards."

"How much do you have to spend?"

"I don't know. How much do they cost?"

"Spoken like a true rich guy."

"Says the guy who already owns his own airplane."

"Okay, so we need to find out what type of airplane you need.... Do you know what you want?"

"I know I want it to be a single-engine with plenty of horsepower and retractable gear. Something that could comfortably carry a family of three… or four if that happens… and our baggage with ease... and safety! It has to be safe."

"There are lots of heavy haulers you can choose from out there. Cessna 182 RG or the Piper Cherokee Sixes... the Saratoga RG and the Lance. You can get them with retractable gear. That would fit the bill."

"Safety?"

"You can't beat the 182 safety record."

"How about a Beech Crap Banana? That was the first airplane I fell in love with as a kid that caught my imagination."

"Go ahead and pick the most expensive airplane right off the bat. Just maintenance alone for a Bonanza can break the bank. Beechcraft is proud of their parts. That's why I fly a Cessna."

"You told me before that this may be a great time to buy an airplane."

"To buy an airplane, yeah, but the parts won't be cheaper."

"Suzy wants our plane to go fast."

"If you want to go fast, a Mooney fills that need. But the cockpit is cramped... narrow... that's how it goes faster than other airplanes. The way to recognize a Mooney is its tail. The vertical stabilizer tilts forward, not back like all other aircraft."

"I want speed AND comfort, so Mooney's out."

"Well then, you're back to your Bonanza. With the right engine, you'll get both. And it has retractable gear, the best gear system of any airplane out there."

"How about safety?"

"A few of their V-tails had issues of weakness in the early years, but the straight tail version, safety wise, is tied with the record of the Cessna 182."

"How do you know what airplane is safe?"

"FAA just released their safety report for years 1981 to 1982. You do know, don't you, that the FAA headquarters are here in Oklahoma City?"

"I know that, but I didn't know they listed safety records for airplanes."

"That's what our taxes pay for."

"So, where do we find one of these to buy?"

"I know lots of brokers and sellers around the airport. I'll put some feelers out."

"I hate to put you to that trouble."

"Are you kidding? I love spending someone else's money buying airplanes."

On that note, we hung up.

EARLY MORNING TWO DAYS LATER, I parked my Porsche at the FBO hangar to meet my first airplane broker, whose office was inside. It was a clear and bright late spring morning. The temperature was perfect for those who relished quiet before the sun's heat triggered air conditioners to turn on all over the city.

Brad wasted little time ferreting out sellers who market by word of mouth or post For-Sale-Aircraft notices on billboards. He consulted with several dealers who advertise nationwide in various aviation magazines. This morning he was waiting for me inside the fixed base operator's lobby. Always gregarious, he had two other men in conversation. As was typical of him, these men were new acquaintances, flying in to refuel on their way to other cities. It didn't matter to Brad. His conversations were sources of added information that he had an insatiable appetite for.

Brad turned to look at me when I came through the door. Dismissing himself from his new friends, he walked determinedly over to me with his aura of enthusiasm on full display.

"You make me feel like a man on his way to judgement day," I said. "What have you done to me now?"

"Only good stuff," he replied. "I found you an airplane broker I think you will like. Have you met Terry Green before?"

"No. I don't recognize the name." Brad was rapidly striding down the hallway past a half dozen aviation-related offices. He wore faded blue jeans and a heavy cotton white T-shirt. His shoes were dark blue canvas deck shoes. It was the perfect apparel for flying before heading to work at his restaurant, the Great American Railroad.

"Here we are." He stopped, knocked on the door, then opened it before anyone could welcome him inside.

Sitting behind a desk at the back wall of the office was a man talking on his telephone. I presumed he was the Terry Green that Brad approached. They shook hands while Green continued to speak on the phone. As I stood by quietly waiting for the call to end, I amused myself with a look around the one room office. There was no secretary. It was strictly a one-man operation, with his office décor what I would call "aviation eclectic." The office appointments were spartan. His desk was second hand. A file cabinet behind him looked like war surplus. The barebones nature of the office did not reassure me.

Brad seemed to sense my skepticism. As our broker continued his telephone conversation, Brad nudged me. Pointing out of the only window in the small office, he drew my attention to the pristine new Chevy Corvette outside. I had noticed it when I came in. It looked freshly washed, with water still clinging in droplets along the bumpers.

"That's Terry's Vette," Brad whispered. "He buys a new one each year, and he washes it every morning before he comes to his office."

"That seems like overkill to me."

"Yeah, but if you want an airplane, this is the nitpicky guy you want finding it."

With his telephone conversation ended, Terry Green stood up from his chair. He was my height with at least twenty extra years and pounds on him. Dressed stylishly and casually, he was spit and polish from head to toe. I looked for a gig line on his shirt plaque and trousers. He was former military, no doubt. He reached his hand first to Brad's then to mine. His handshake was bone crushing.

"Rob, glad to meet you. I'm Terry," he said, not waiting for introductions. He turned to Brad. "And how are you, my friend?"

"I'm fine, having fun buying airplanes at Rob's expense. It's a good life."

I laughed as they continued to banter on. Terry had the good sense to size up his potential customer. He turned to me, inducing conversation about myself.

"Rob, I hear you are Air Force. Tell me a little bit about yourself. What did you fly? How many hours do you have? What airplane would fit your experience? Tell me everything."

The man was congenial while being all business. It was an approach that I preferred as a customer. Get to the point, then we can chit-chat later. I related the same issues I shared with Brad previously on the telephone. I wanted comfort, speed, and safety with a retractable gear. Gear up and down was natural to me. Not having that as a step in my checklist would be strange.

"Rob, if you want to go fast, you need to consider a turbo-charged engine," said Terry. "You can go a lot higher, too."

"The last thing I need is to go higher. That's what got me into medical trouble to begin with."

Brad leaned over Terry's desk. "Turbos have enough problems. For a first airplane, I would steer clear." He turned to me and added, "Rob, only recently had sinus surgery. I suggest to both of you to go easy on your airplane choices."

"We could go pressurized," Terry said.

I knew a lot about pressurized aircraft, since the T-37 was the Air Force's only non-pressurized jet.

"Pressurization only begins after passing through eight thousand feet elevation. I don't plan on flying higher than ten thousand feet if I can help it. For me it would be unnecessary."

It made sense to me. It was my first foray into a hobby with unknown factors to consider. I was no mechanic and never wanted to be. I wouldn't know a tick from a tock when it came to recognizing something amiss with the engine, much less a turbo engine. Pressurized cabins were a nightmare, so I had read. I knew how to fly airplanes, not how to fix them. I had a lot to learn, but I was wise enough to know there would be a lot of ignorance in me for a while. I needed to discover much more about general aviation before I upped the ante with a more complex airplane.

"For me reliability and safety would be high on my list. I'm not doing my own maintenance. What aircraft is safe, fast enough, and doesn't break down easily?"

"Brad told me you like the Bonanza. You can't go wrong with that airplane. It is rugged, reliable, and easy to fly. They are pricey, though."

I tried to cloak my next question in terms that didn't sound cocky. I didn't want to sound nouveau riche.

"What's a new one cost on average, then compare it to one maybe five years old?"

Terry gritted his teeth in angst before he spoke. He pulled out a binder and thumbed through several pages. "That is going to be a wild guess. Demand is off for airplanes, especially here in the oil patch. This is 1983. Five years ago, 1978, Beechcraft built 82 model F33 Bonanzas." He ran a finger down the printed sheet in the binder. It looks like they are forecasted to build only ten this year."

"Is that good for buyers?"

"When demand is down, they build fewer to keep the price up."

"So, we're talking about how much money for an F33… between new and five years old… with normal hours on it?"

"For a new one, you're talking definitely six figures, especially when you start adding accessories… and you will want to."

"And older models would be…?"

"Perhaps as low as eighty thousand dollars for an average one that is five years old. Of course, with oil going away, you can likely negotiate it down to a good price."

"Can I do my own bargaining, or will you be doing it?"

"I don't care," Terry said, "as long as we understand that my commission is the same. If you think you can do better than I can, well then, be my guest."

"I guarantee you there are doctors, lawyers, and oilmen out there looking to unload their Bonanzas. Everything looks like it's for sale these days."

"Terry, surely you keep your ear to the ground," Brad said. "You hear of any big spenders who would be happy to unload a Bonanza?"

"I know who owns 'em. I suppose I could put some feelers out. One just might pop up. For sure, I could use the sale myself. Lots of sellers in Oklahoma. Just not many buyers."

"I like the F33 models. I'm not that thrilled with the V-tail Bonanzas, at least, not since I was a kid. Let's limit our search to the straight tails, the bigger 285 horsepower Continental, and with a better laid out instrument panel."

Terry abruptly stood up. "I think I've got my marching orders. The prospects out there will not fit all your wishes, unless you choose to buy a new aircraft. But just remember, the Bonanzas out there can all be retrofitted with many of the items you may desire."

"Okay, then," Brad said as he reached for Terry's bone crushing hand. "We'll let you get to it."

This time I was prepared, gripping Terry's hand firmly to shake. "I appreciate your efforts. I'm ready to get back in the game."

“I’m on it,” he replied. “It looks like a good day to go hunting.”

“Definitely a Marine,” I said.

His iron grip did not let go after he heard that.

“Nope. Army Scout, 11th Infantry, back in the big war.”

“I’m sorry,” I said. “Let me correct myself. *HOOAH!*”

14

TERRY GREEN WAS A DYNAMO. A week later he called me on the telephone to tell me about the Bonanzas he had located that were for sale. These were not aircraft I would easily find for sale in the many newsstand publications offered for free. Instead, these were airplanes sold in the dark world of moneyed interests. The network of brokers was more customer friendly. Although the prices might be higher, the quality of the aircraft on average made it worth the added expense. By contrast, the dealers ran their business more like a used car lot, meaning there were good ones, and there were bad ones. I was in no position to know the difference.

"I've got five Bonanzas for you to look at. Now, if you would consider a V-tail, I can find a whole lot more than these five."

"I'll stick with the straight tail, Terry. It's more like the T-37 I flew."

"Okay, here's what we've got. There's a beautiful F-33A model out of Florida. 1971 model with the two hundred and eighty-five horsepower Continental engine. It should cruise at about a hundred and seventy-two knots. Original instrument panel, full autopilot with altitude control. It's an original owner airplane. That can be good sometimes. Sometimes not. The only thing to worry about here is that it's in Florida. You may find a lot of corrosion in airplanes near the Gulf and the Atlantic. Florida has both."

"Sounds interesting. How much?"

"He's asking eighty-five thousand dollars for her. That's the low end. My other four go up from there."

"What's next?"

"The next one is out of Carlsbad, California. She's about a quarter mile from the coast, but don't worry about corrosion. The air is dry as a bone out there. It's never an issue. This one is a 1981 F-33A, so you're almost getting a brand-new airplane with this one. It has a much better instrument panel and a beautiful interior of leather seats in a nice rich tan. I forgot to mention. The first one in Florida has about twelve hundred hours on it. This one has only two hundred hours. Like I say, it would be like buying a brand-new airplane."

"How much then?"

"You can double what the first one will go for."

I had money, but I wasn't about to be a fool and pay for what I didn't need. "Let's see what the next one on your list has to offer."

"Of the other three, you might be most interested in the one that is in the hand of a distressed oilman in town. He needs to sell it quickly. I don't know a lot about it. He keeps it at Will Rogers Field. It's a seventy-nine model F-33A, but I don't know its damage history or the number of hours on the airframe or the engine. The guy is trying to save his house. Believe it or not, no one is buying aircraft now, maybe because prices are high. I bet he will take a whole lot less. You'll want to check it out thoroughly, though."

"What about the other two?"

"The last two are worn out. One is an E-model 33. Those were good airplanes, but not when they've been treated poorly. It would be cheap, though. The other a is sixty-six model... C-33. It's a Bonanza, but until 1968, they called them Debonairs. It has the smaller engine. You flew jets. I don't think you would be happy with this one."

"Why don't you set me up to see the oilman's Bonanza? See if I would want to help him save his house."

The next morning Terry called me back. We drove to a large hangar at Will Rogers Field, now renamed Will Rogers World Airport. Although it was a big airport for Oklahoma, there was nothing worldly about it. Brad Kilty met us there by flying his plane six miles from Wiley Post to Will Rogers.

Brad was my most trusted aircraft examiner. Even when he was overly picky, I knew that someday his compulsive behavior would be an asset for me. This was the day. Terry introduced us to the financially strapped oilman.

He was a short, balding man in his early forties with horn-rimmed coke bottle eyeglasses and a mess of curly hair covering the back of his head. Calm and laid back, the man did not look like one who was losing his house. Men with steady nerves could be tough negotiators. Perhaps it was Terry who floated the idea to the owner to sell his Bonanza.

Brad, ever eager to help someone else spend his money, led us like a bloodhound to the Bonanza, one of a dozen aircraft crammed in the hangar. We followed him as he began his excited commentary.

"I see a Speed Slope windshield, three-blade prop, with the new back window configuration. That looks a lot better than the old C-models. No tip tanks. That's a shame, but you could always add them."

As Brad got closer his commentary morphed into observations inside.

"Oh, it has dual controls. That's a plus. Most only have one control, although I guess one control would give you extra room for your co-pilot. Oh, good to see the seats have sheepskin covers. You better check underneath. He has either worn out his seats, or he's trying to protect them."

"You'll find it to be pristine leather underneath," the owner said.

Brad was already diving into the passenger door and pulling off the sheepskin to see for himself.

"I see a lot of wear on these covers. How many hours does this airframe have on it?"

"A little over eight hundred hours."

"So, you fly it about two hundred hours a year. That is about right to keep all the systems running properly. Same time on the engine and prop?"

"All the same," Terry said.

"Any damage?" Brad didn't wait for an answer. "Oh, look! Rob, you have two King KX-155 NavComs with glideslope, DME, ADF. You can use the ADF as a wheel chock or listen to Top Forty radio with it. Wow! An S-Tec autopilot, let's see which one it... oh, it's an S-Tec 60-2 with altitude hold. Four-place intercom... hey, do these David Clark headsets go with the deal?"

"No damage," the oilman said, "and yes." He started laughing as he turned to Terry and me. "Where did you find this guy. He's acting like a young kid on his first visit to Boys' Town."

We stood and laughed. There was nothing else to do. Brad was in his own little world going through each minute detail of the aircraft's equipment, upholstery, even brake pedals. He checked the floor mats for wear. He looked for dirt. He wiped fingerprints off the windows, gauges, and even the shiny paint on the inside of the doors.

Brad next stepped outside, going slowly around the aircraft moving the control surfaces and listening carefully for strange noises or rubbing cables. He opened the cowlings on both sides to view the big Continental IO520BB 285 horsepower engine. Wiping his fingers along the engine, he checked his finger for grease. He shook all the spark plugs.

"Hey, this is good. It's got Gami Injectors."

I was afraid to ask him what those were for fear he would tell me. I wanted him to keep looking. I was getting the purchasing bug myself. He pulled a flashlight from his pocket to peer better into the innards underneath the engine. Soon he began mumbling with his face deep inside. He popped his head out with a big smile like a kid at Christmas.

He quickly moved around to the back, stopping to compulsively wiggle an aileron, on his way to the inspection port forward of the empennage. Pointing his flashlight and one eyeball inside, he checked the cables that went to the tail's movable rudder and elevators. When he pulled his head out, he called me over with a wave and handed me the flashlight.

"Look inside at the skin... see how shiny it is? There is absolutely no corrosion on this airplane. The owner has taken care to keep this bird out of the elements."

The inside skin of the plane was as shiny as a sheet of aluminum foil pulled off the roll. Lots of cables ran from nose to tail. Their integrity was the difference between life and death. I recalled a couple of brothers who were serial airplane thieves. Their last escapade was stealing a twin-engine Beechcraft Barron from a hangar. Not being the sharpest knives in the drawer, they failed to notice that the tail end was undergoing maintenance. They taxied at night to the takeoff end of the runway at Wiley Post and started their takeoff roll, only to discover that the control cables were disconnected from the empennage. With no elevators to affect liftoff, the brothers plowed the Barron through the outer fence and smashed into a multi-million-dollar Instrument Landing System at the end of the runway. Somehow, I think alcohol was involved.

"This is one beautiful Bonanza," Brad said. "If the logs look good, this may be as good as they come. I've not seen a used airplane this clean."

I looked over at the other two men. "How are the logs?"

"All maintenance performed on this Bonanza was done by Beechcraft at their facilities in Wichita."

"Even oil changes? Annual inspections?"

"Everything."

Brad bent to my ear and whispered. "You'd be a fool to let this airplane go."

"Brad and I will go through your logbook, then we might talk."

The oilman opened the passenger door and pulled out the maintenance log from a side pocket. "Have you checked yet about financing? That takes a while."

"For the right price, I'll be paying cash."

His eyes looked at me with keen interest. I doubted that he would be good at poker.

"If you need cash," Terry said to him, "this would be a good deal for you... and you might have it today."

After going through the logs to our satisfaction, Brad and I asked Terry to go back to his office and do a history check with Beechcraft and with the FAA. Since the Federal Aviation Administration was located in Oklahoma City at Will Rogers World Airport, I hoped he could do it quickly and in person. I wanted to waste no more time than was necessary getting confirmation. I was in an airplane buying fever pitch. Nearly ten years after getting grounded from flying, I was ready to feel cool again.

15

EARLY THE NEXT MORNING TERRY Green and his client had money in their hands. Brad Kilty continued to act like a kid at Christmas. Suzy was happy for me. Sean was as I expected—bouncing off the walls of the house. I remembered as a child when I would buy a large purchase, only to regret it immediately. That was often the only way I could know I got what I truly wanted. Fortunately, I remained excited about the purchase of what turned out to be a pristine Bonanza, just as Brad promised it would be. I felt compelled to write to Hal Freed from my Air Force days.

Dear Hal,

Well, we did it. Suzy and I bought an airplane. It's a 1979 F33A Beechcraft Bonanza straight-tail. I took it on one test flight before I forked over the cash, and I just loved it. I almost felt a wave of sierra hotel come over me. It cruises at 172 mph, so that's 198 knots. That's almost the cruise speed of a Tweet. That makes me happy. It has a much better range though. Suzy is excited. I can't wait to take her up. First, I might need to go through ten hours of orientation before the FAA will let me fly without a CFI. A friend of mine thinks they will waive the requirement because I have so many hours of retractable gear time in the T-37 and T-38. We'll see. I only bought it yesterday.

Let me know what you are up to these days. I hope this letter follows you to the right address if you are on the move again. I still want to try one more time a driving adventure on Route 66 without the stupidity of our last adventure. Perhaps we should include our wives this time—Mrs. Tod and Mrs. Buz on Route 66 in our 4-seat Corvette. They did it to the Ford Thunderbird.

I must ask. Are you encountering any hecklers since Reagan took office? I still run into some surprises out here. I might say more in another letter. I'm more worried about the college campuses. They still seem to want to protest. I thought the war was over, but apparently not for them. The peaceniks still want to keep fighting. It reminds me of jousting at windmills.

Please note my new address. More about that later.

Your old buddy,
Rob

As eager as I was to get a reply from Hal, Suzy requisitioned me for furniture duty. With a new house, I discovered that a house purchase was only the start of expenses. I was thrilled to let Suzy pick out the furniture that she wanted. She already knew what I like, so why shouldn't I let her.

While she spent our money, I took out my aggressions on a punching bag hanging in our garage. Furniture salesman, airplane brokers, and bad drivers were not in my images where my punches landed. Instead, I was smashing the faces of the trolls who spoke of baby killers, vets who didn't deserve respect, and fakers who bragged about imaginary heroism. The number of men who claimed to be North Vietnamese POWs already exceeded the actual number of 687 Americans who returned home alive. Almost 1,600 were still missing-in-action. The number of these frauds grew each year. I didn't trust anyone who volunteered their story until I knew them well. The others? I punched them every morning. I punched them for their lies. I punched them for the hatred of real veterans. I reserved head blows for Captain Military, Army Medic Phillip Snart, and even an old girlfriend who almost ruined my life. I threw low blows to the men and women who screamed "baby killer." I slapped young college protesters with the back of my glove. Only kid gloves for them. They were too young to hurt. They only needed sense knocked into them.

I could escape my worries and frustrations, using this surrogate of a foe. I danced around in the manner of a Cassius Clay, seemingly tireless as I circled clockwise around the bag, landing left jabs repeatedly, until landing a knock-out punch with my right glove. He crumpled onto the garage floor, only to have a different foe replace him. I circled around again with my therapeutic jabs to lure the next opponent into a false sense of security, then I reversed direction to trick him. Oh, I was good in my imaginary bouts. Down another one went. It was good to be so dominant—so intimidating.

I worked on my technique, like the twisting jab that Clay used against Sonny Liston. My goal was to knock out my enemy before I was too exhausted. It was the only way I could win. I punched like America should have fought the Vietnam War. Punch hard right up front or get weary and quit. Each day that I punched and jabbed was a day I became stronger. I punched and became more confident. I jabbed and grew more enabled. I circled and became more unpredictable. I didn't "float like a butterfly and sting like a bee." I flew like a fighter pilot and targeted like a steely-eyed killer. I could face anybody, fearless and focused. I was happy, cocky, and ready for anything thrown my way. My imagined weapon would be best if never used.

IT WASN'T LONG BEFORE I got a reply from Hal to my previous letter.

Dear Rob,

Wow! Good to know you are back in the game. I guess the surgery is holding up. That's good. You bought the Cadillac of single engine airplanes. Oilies obviously make more money than us fly boys. I hope Suzy gets the bug and feels comfortable in the cockpit with you. We could do a flying vacation together. Doesn't your Bonanza hold four people? Forget the Corvette. Flying Route 66 would be a whole lot more cool than driving. Also, there's less road rage up top.

I may be getting another promotion shortly. I guess they have forgotten my mythical past. At least the Old Man hinted as such. I don't think he would say that without reason.

I'm spending a lot of time now on college campus. It's crazy how you can't call things what they are anymore. Their philosophy seems to be "why use one word when I can use three?" The library here is no longer called the Library. It is now the Learning Resources Center. It took me two days to find the Library, until some haughty so-and-so told me the new name.

Lisa complains of what you mentioned. Everything she teaches in class gets challenged. That might be okay, but she receives such impassioned and viperous rejoinders, I feel the need to escort her each evening to her car in the parking lot. She can't mention what's happening with Reagan without protesters interrupting her class. They wouldn't dare do that to me. Let them try.

Time is short here. I see myself staying in the Reserves, but I want to teach also. It's a busy time for me. You and I have certainly gone in different directions. Still, it will be good to meet up with you in the future. You're not half as crazy as those students I teach.

All my best to Suzy,
Hal

16

I SAVORED SHARING THE NEWS of my new airplane with another military pilot. It turned out, one flight was all it took for my flight evaluator to clear me for good. The FAA had different rules for pilots with several hundred hours of retractable gear time. I didn't have to miss flying anymore. There was one question I had that was fundamental to a former jet jock. Would it be enough? Jets were fun because they could do loops, spins, and zooms. I couldn't go upside down with an airplane like the Bonanza. Perhaps I could come close. It was in that spirit that I took my first solo flight in my new purchase.

It takes time to become one with something new, whether it's riding a horse, living in a house, marrying a wife, raising a child, or flying an airplane. I wasn't about to take my family up until I was worthy of their trust. I wanted to know the instrument panel blindfolded. I needed to know the normal sounds it made when cruising, lowering and raising landing gear, and adding flaps. I wanted a feel for the engine. How much right rudder did I need on takeoff to neutralize the turning force of a propeller? What was my visibility around the aircraft? How well could I coordinate a left and right turn using ailerons with rudder? Jets, with their higher speeds and absent propeller-inducing yaw, required little rudder. I would sort out all these issues when I was alone.

It was 5:00 a.m. I was taxiing in the dark to the takeoff end of the runway, which was not yet open for tower control. I was on my own to inform any early morning traffic of my location. After going through my run-up-before-takeoff checklist, I radioed traffic that I was entering Runway 35 Right for takeoff. By clicking my radio button several times, I turned on the runway lights to my desired brightness. Applying power to the engine, along with the correct amount of right rudder, I began my takeoff roll. Compared to the Piper Warrior I had earlier flown, the Beechcraft Bonanza provided a more satisfying force of power and acceleration. The nosewheel came off the ground followed by the main gear. I immediately sensed the effect of a mild crosswind and crabbed the nose into the wind to maintain my direction of climb aligned with runway heading. I called my position over the radio and remained in the traffic pattern to log three night-landings that were required to carry passengers at night. I had done many night landings in the military—even night formation flights—but still managed to prove on impact with my first hard landing why we practice and must keep current. My second and third traffic patterns and touch-and-go landings were satisfactory, according to my strict standards.

I next climbed out and radioed Wiley Post Traffic that I was departing the pattern to the northwest to an area devoid of most aircraft on their way in to the several runways closer to Oklahoma City. It was there that I could do some rudimentary flight checks while waiting for the sun to rise at 6:15 a.m. I practiced a couple of turning stalls. To my private embarrassment, I once again forgot that as the aircraft slows to a stall speed, the rudder becomes less effective. I ended up unintentionally turning my heading ninety degrees to the southwest before I stalled and could recover to flying speed. My second stall was much better because I increased my rudder and kept my heading steady. I was learning by way of mistakes at a rapid pace.

On some mornings, the Oklahoma sunrise can be a spectacular red fire in the clouds. I had only seen it from an airplane once before when I was in South Texas. I had lost other opportunities because of mission requirements. The conditions looked favorable this morning. My back was to the sun. There was a thin scattered to broken cloud layer up ahead which would soon be below me as I climbed through five thousand feet. It was after 6:00 a.m. I knew at altitude the sun would be up sooner for me than for those on the ground. I was over the cloud layer, so I dropped the nose gently to affect a steady descent to skim the tops of the clouds, just as I had done ten years before. Levelled off and trimmed, I waited and hoped.

It was like I was on a boat racing on a windless lake, skimming the surface and pushing fog to each side. The first hints of pink on the thin clouds began its slow ignition into a brighter lake of fire. Flying away from the sun slowed the progression of the fire from soft pink to angry red. This was the moment to take my mental picture of a memory I hoped every pilot has had. I flew on the deck in this spectacle of cloudy fire for only a couple of minutes before the clouds grew hotter and turned into a blinding yellow light that signaled the real start of another bright and sunny, summer day in Oklahoma. I had seen for the second time in my life a brief glimpse of Heaven.

I climbed to a more visible altitude and made my turn toward home. The first coordinated turn in my Bonanza sent my inner ear to spinning as I rolled out level. I needed more practice. I now headed into the sun, which nearly blinded me. A few more practice turns on the way home cured my aileron-to-rudder miscoordination. All the rest was straight and level with a smooth landing and a routine taxi to the hangar. To my delight, I had only positives to share with Suzy and Sean. It was with zeal that I reported to Suzy that I wanted to introduce her to the fiery lake—that little bit of Heaven—that I had floated upon.

"I'M NOT GETTING UP AT four a.m. to go fly with you just so I can see a sunrise at six a.m."

Suzy was adamant. I was puzzled. I couldn't understand why a one in a million chance to see a sunrise atop the clouds wouldn't appeal to her.

"What if I check the weather and it looks more likely? Would you then?"

"What does it take to make it more likely?"

"Clouds and ideal stuff in the morning air."

"Stuff? What sort of stuff?"

"I don't know."

"That's all I need to know."

"I'll go to your library and look it up."

"After you find the answer, I'll still tell you no."

"You don't want to fly with me?"

"I do, just not while I'm asleep in the cockpit."

I took her hint to heart. Even though she was a morning person, 4:00 a.m. wake ups with a one-in-a-million odds of seeing a rare sunrise would not include Suzy Amity. But my efforts would not end just yet.

"How about a sunset?" This brought a smile.

"You just want to share everything, don't you?" I waited until she relented. "Okay, I'll see a sunset with you."

"How about tonight?"

"No! It doesn't get dark until nine at night in June. Try in six months when I won't have to stay out late."

I threw up my hands in frustration. "I give up."

"Rob." She said my name in that tongue-in-cheek condescending tone that comes with a couple who never take offense. "I'm ready right now. Sean's at the Goodwins with his friend, Jimmy. They'll watch him. Let's go now."

"They won't mind?"

"I'll call and let them know we'll be back."

"I'll meet you in the car."

It's funny how frustration can turn on a dime into elation.

IT WAS A DREAM COME true. I had Suzy in the air right after noon. The sun was blazing hot and at its peak. She complained of the heat in the cockpit, but I assured her that once we climbed above the haze layer, it would be cooler. She marveled at my correct prediction. We climbed through 8,500 feet and got the relief we both wanted.

"What would you like to see?" I asked.

"Anything but straight and level."

"Really?" Her request was unexpected. All pilots know that passengers want only smooth sailing.

"Do some steep turns. Also, it should be bumpy up here. That's a disappointment."

"You are indeed a strange wife." Without warning I pulled the nose up to zoom higher, then banked sharply left into sixty degrees of bank. I intended to bring us into a moderate dive, but it wasn't enough bank, so I increased it to nearly ninety degrees. The steepness of the turn allowed the nose to slice downward past the horizon into a steep dive. Then I pulled back up and to the right to reverse the process. The maneuver bled the airspeed off to the point that my climb was less impressive the second time, so I leveled off.

"You like that better?"

"Do it again," she replied. The grin on her face and the joy in her voice was a greater taste of heaven for me than any fiery lake of clouds at sunrise. I had indeed married well.

We continued with steep turns. My ability to avoid disorienting dizziness in the turns got better. She was unphased as I continued to practice steep turns, stalls, and whatever I could think of to amuse her.

"If you want bumps, we must descend into the haze layer."

Suzy abruptly segued into a different request.

"Do I get to fly the plane?"

"You've got it," I said and shook the yoke. She looked at me in surprise.

"Really?"

"You're supposed to say, 'I've got it.' Then I repeat 'you've got it.'"

"That sounds silly."

"You want to fly like a fighter pilot or not?"

"I've got it," she said and shook the yoke.

"You've got it," I replied.

As she flew, Suzy began asking what moving certain controls would do to the airplane. I told her to push gently on the rudder pedals. The tail of the Bonanza wagged left and right. She turned the yoke like a steering wheel and felt the response of a wing dipping in the same direction. Pulling the yoke back satisfied her, but pushing the yoke forward elicited her first negative response.

"Oh, I don't like going weightless."

"That wasn't weightless," I said. "You were maybe a half of your weight... half a G."

"I still don't like it."

It got me to remembering in a jet that we had the constant hazard of a vulture or a hawk gliding on a thermal. We would approach birds at 250 to 500 mph, depending on the aircraft. They would always fold their wings and dive. Most were at my altitude. I simply pulled up the nose and got above them as they dived below us. It made sense—if they go down, we go up. The problem was that sometimes they were above us. If we surprised them, they would still dive. Depending upon their elevation above us, I had to make a split-second decision—pull up or push down. As a pilot, I got comfortable pushing hard on the nose of the jet into a negative G dive and going under the also diving bird. The difference? The bird was only weightless in its dive—zero G. I was still one negative G of dive ahead of them. It got to be fun doing that, but we had many close calls in that situation. Bird strikes had killed a pilot or two.

"I don't like going weightless, either," I said. "Let's not do that unless we're forced to."

She continued to fly the airplane with a grin of happiness to go with it.

"Why don't you fly us back to the pattern. I'll talk you through it. I will do all the radio calls. It'll be fun. Are you game?"

"I'm ready. Point me in the right direction. Just don't let me kill us."

I told her to descend shortly after our turn to the correct heading. She pushed down the nose. I suggested she could descend easier by reducing power on the engine. She and I both liked that method better. Suzy brought us back to Wiley Post's airspace where I took the controls and showed her how to land the airplane. As we taxied to the hangar, she shared her thoughts.

"I want more. When can we go again? Tomorrow?"

17

NOW NINE-AND-A-HALF years-old, Sean was noticeably taller than even two months before. Over the same period, though, he became more hyperactive, probably a result of his aviation excitement. His enthusiasm overcame any lethargy caused by his growth spurt. Today he was totally wired as I strapped him into his seatbelt and shoulder harness and put on his headset in our Beech Crap Banana for his first airplane ride with his Old Man. Purchased only weeks before, I had barely been able to contain his frenzy and frustration. He asked me every day if we were going to fly.

This Bonanza was considered a high-performance aircraft with a 285 horsepower Continental piston engine, retractable landing gear, three-blade propeller, and the best instrument panel oil field money could buy. Like the crazy cars of the oil boom that now were worth pitifully little, this airplane had enticingly few hours and an owner with no money to pay for it since oil went bust. Like our house that Suzy and I bought at nearly half its original value, this valuable aircraft sold for pennies on the dollar. Airplanes, like houses, have constant bills that go with the property. Aviation fuel at inflated prices per gallon, yearly extensive and expensive inspections, hangar fees, and insurance all run up the tab. Brad warned me that "if your airplane gets more expensive than your house, it's time for a new hobby." But since we bought our house with cash, Brad's admonition didn't have any impact until I studied the costs. It was a close call whether to get another hobby.

Flying for me now was natural. The unconscious-competence I developed in the military was back. This Bonanza's handling characteristics were closer to the jet I flew years before. For me, raising and lowering landing gear in an airplane was second nature. The old joke about, there are only two types of pilots—those who have landed gear up and those who will, didn't often apply to military types. We used a checklist for everything. I had one strapped to my leg as Sean and I started our Saturday morning takeoff roll at Wiley Post. We were flying to the runway at Crazy Horse Municipal Airport in Davis, Oklahoma.

Becoming airborne in the Warrior, the civilian airplane I first flew with Brad, was more like flying a kite when it lifted off. By comparison, the Bonanza lifted off the runway with more authority. After raising the landing gear, this airplane punched through the air, not floated through the air. I didn't tell Sean about air sickness. The result was that he never was sick. He enjoyed the bumps and turns that are part of the flying experience. The first air pocket we encountered, that dropped our plane abruptly and sent us bouncing off the seat, caused Sean to look over at me with a worried look. But I smiled back at him and simply yelled, "Whee!" He returned my smile and relaxed the rest of the eighty-six-mile flight. My boy was fascinated with all aspects of our short journey but said little. Once we landed on this narrow and short airstrip, his questions poured out at an exponential rate.

"Dad, is there a parking lot? Why are we going the wrong way? I'm hungry. It's hot. Why don't we have an air conditioner? Cars do."

Sean shifted gears now to some old jokes we knew too well. He repeated his list of questions he asked when he was six.

"Is our airplane stronger than a train engine? If a tornado came by, what would happen to our airplane? Is a train stronger than a tornado?"

The interrogatory seemed endless, until we finished our back taxi up the runway to the parking area surrounded by hangars full of abandoned or seldom flown aircraft. The oil bust and legal costs hidden in each airplane had nearly destroyed civil aviation. A friend, Jay Goodwin, who promised to pick us up, carried with him a handheld aviation radio and caught our radio call as we approached the airfield.

"Hello, Rob." Jay greeted me in his deep resonant voice. "Who's your sidekick with you?"

"How's it going, Jay," I replied. I crawled out of the cockpit onto the wing. "This is my new co-pilot."

"Hello, Mister Goodwin," Sean said. "Where's Jimmy?"

"Jimmy is waiting in the car. He's not much of an outdoorsman, yet. I see you are a real pilot now."

Sean replied with a correction. "No, I'm a Junior Birdman."

"Should I start calling you Junior then?"

"Okay."

Jay and I had known each other for many years, but it was the first time we had ever met with our sons. Our wives had always been in charge of getting the children together. We were too busy working. A father/son gathering was new territory for us and far from our usual association.

Jay was a man who was most impressive when in motion. Once moving, his presence came to life. His walk was authoritative. His eyes were penetrating whenever he spoke to another person. It was hard to avert your attention at such times because you were afraid to. A weightlifter of many years, he stayed in great shape while working out in moderation. He learned, as I did later, that excess training turned into neglect in the long term. For a year we practiced martial arts together. Jay had gone through the training. I was simply his "tackling dummy." He would work me over on the mat, and I in turn would pick up a few tidbits of self-defense. Even while pulverizing me on the mat, his smile remained animated and genuine. He loved everyone. Without effort he possessed an ability to lead, even if he was not trying. Jay and I liked each other because we each had traits that complemented the other. I learned from him how to lead. He learned from me how to be patient and to recognize a load of bull when it came his way. Today and tomorrow would be a good test of our strengths.

"Rob, I have another father I just met waiting in the car with the boys. Let me help you with that gear while you secure your airplane. That's a beauty, by the way. I like the green and tan paint you put on that."

Jay helped Sean and me place the chocks under the wheels, secure the wings with tiedowns, put a cover on the pitot tube, and lock the doors. We headed to Jay's Dodge Caravan. Sean raced ahead and was already in the car with his friend. I headed for the back seat. The front seat was occupied.

"Rob, I don't know if you have met this gentleman. He just moved here from California. Interesting guy to talk to. Hop in, and I'll introduce you."

"Thanks for the pick-up." I stooped to climb into the back seat with three chattering boys.

I sat down after the boys made me some room then reached for and buckled my seat belt. With the anticipation of meeting a new friend, I looked up.

"Rob, this is Phillip Snart. He's a PA at one of those Mercy Hospital clinics. Phil, this is Robert Amity."

I stared for a moment in the darkened car waiting for my eyes to adjust before I spoke. My heart began to race. I held my breath. I wanted out of the car but then decided to advance on the attack instead.

"Phil, I think we've met already, remember? As I recall, you hate the Air Force... and wished my best friend a good time in hell. I'm really glad you're here."

18

I PONDERED MY OPTIONS AS we rode the nine miles to Camp Classen. This weekend trip was for my son. I did not want to ruin that. My boy did not need to know that the man in the front passenger seat was glad that his biological father died in a plane crash. The need to keep my composure was obvious. *He will talk to me until he finally finds out what he doesn't want to hear.* I would not be caught with my guard down, and I was not one to forget.

I turned my attention to the two boys with Sean and me in the back seat. Two mop-headed boys were already plotting mischief with my tow-headed son.

"Jimmy, how's it going over there? Who's your friend with you?" I asked.

"My friend here is Sean." All three broke out in laughter at Jimmy's not-so-original joke.

"Nice to meet you, Sean," I said and shook Junior Birdman's hand. "Now. Who's the kid who's not your friend?"

The three boys laughed again. At the same instant Phil Snart jerked his head around to look toward me.

"That's my son. His name is Tanner. And he is a friend of Jimmy's."

He's sensitive. When I was nine or ten, he was the kid we would pick on. My inner ten-year-old came out in me. Without time to think rationally, I said, "Tanner? Tanner Snart? That sounds like a funny name I would find in a *Batman* comic book."

The boys got the funny name part. It was fun to see all three of them laugh at my juvenile joke. I looked up to see that Mr. Snart was scowling. This was going to be either a weekend to tiptoe around or dive right in and have fun like an impish child. I relished the chance and decided to throw caution to the wind.

"How long have you four boys been here already, Jay?" I asked. "Have we missed anything?"

"Not much so far," Jay replied over the noise of his Caravan. "Your airplane is the most excitement we've had."

"Did you get all our food and drink, or do I need to stop at a store and pick up anything?" I asked.

"No, we got it all." Jay replied. "Plenty of food, plenty of drinks. More than enough beer."

"How much do I owe you?"

"Not a blasted thing, my friend," Jay said quickly. "We're all good."

"Thirty-five dollars," Phil Snart said, hurriedly countering Jay's offer. "Maybe forty."

"Phil, what are you talking about?" Jay asked. "I got Rob's stuff. He can't carry that much weight in his airplane. I already paid you for our beer."

There was an uncomfortable pause before Jay added. "Phil brought the beer… generic beer! You know the kind… well wait till you see… the cans are white with black letters that say *BEER* on it. That's it. Who knows where the stuff comes from?"

"Our cans better *not* say beer!" Jimmy yelled.

"Ours say *COLA* and *LEMON-LIME* and *ROOT BEER!*" Tanner replied.

"Beer! We've got beer!" Sean laughed at his own joke.

"Root Beer, you dope," said Jimmy.

"Beer! Root Beer!" Sean said, and they all went nuts in the back seat. I covered my jewels, just to be safe.

The ride to Camp Classen was a familiar jaunt, having been there many times as a child. Nestled in the ancient Arbuckle Mountains, it is a rockhound's paradise. According to geologists, the Arbuckle Range rivaled the Rocky Mountains millions of years ago. The oldest range in the United

States, exposed granite dates back 1.4 billion years. The mountains are no longer towering, but each layer of its enormous early life is pealed back like layers of an onion. From Interstate 35, cars can see row after row of sedimentary rocks exposed like tombstones in a graveyard. Each is rich with fossils exhibiting the progressive evolution of life on Earth. As Jay drove us up to the camp, it was easy to see the competition playing out between the established scrub oaks and the new and intrusive cedar trees that thrived on a terrain mostly composed of rock, not soil. There are many places where water springs forth from the rocks. The largest waterfall in the state is nearby. Uniquely growing, not eroding, Turner Falls continuously adds to the limestone rock under it with more calcium layers. There is a triple waterfall on private land that no one knows about unless you get along with the landowner. As we entered the camp, layered with cabins, trees, a field of short grass, and a small lake, you could see the excitement build in the three boys. It was the small lake that caught their attention first. Boats and canoes rimmed the shore. Many boys, with and without dads, were paddling or rowing in the water. Near the center of the small lake was a multiple level diving tower, that to a boy was both frightening and magnetic. A manned lifeguard stand was well placed for optimal surveillance. Horseback riding, archery, fishing, and rock climbing were among the opportunities for our boys. Opposite the lake was a large mess hall, an outdoor pavilion, and even an outside chapel with a prominent cross in the center of the chapel grounds. Jay's Caravan was hardly stopped when the three boys in the back seat with me were rolling out to disappear at lightning speed, leaving us to do all the work of unpacking.

Before afternoon we set up some chairs and camping stoves outside, then sorted out bunks in the cabins—kids on the top bunk and dads underneath. The mattresses looked and smelled like dead animal carcasses. They could easily be the original bedding from the days of the Civilian Conservation Corps. They were sticky to the touch as if they died years ago. Jay and I had slept on worse, but to see Snart squirm at the smell was a treat.

"It looks like someone died in surgery on this mattress," I said. "Phil, you ought to feel right at home."

Early arriving dads in the camp had already organized an event quite suitable for any veteran who made it through basic training. To be shared with our sons, the obstacle course was tough enough for a kid but easy for an adult male who may have softened some from too many years of married life. For Jay and me, it looked easy. For my friend the pilot hater, it looked to be more of a challenge. The object was to run the obstacle course with your son. Each father/son team was timed. The smart competitors never went first. We wanted to watch how it should be done and learn what not to do. I volunteered Mr. Snart and Tanner to start first. Just as I expected, at the go they ran to a log ladder that reached to about ten feet. They had to go over that and climb down the other side. The Snarts climbed together, and once over the top, they climbed down together. Before them were several similar climbing features, ropes, and tunnels that would be more efficiently traversed if you knew how. I looked at Jay and suggested he go next. When he and Jimmy headed to the start, I turned to Sean.

"Partner, do you want to win this race on the obstacle course?"

"Sure," he said, a bit puzzled. "Why?"

"If you will do what I suggest, we can double their speeds."

"How?"

"Those dads are slow, and the boys are climbing very carefully." I whispered my plan in his ear, my hands gesturing with each word. He was a quick study and smiled broadly.

I treasured the chance to make us look like the most cooperative and innovative father/son pair in the crowd. It could bond us closer together while he remained in his pre-teenage years. For now, he believed my ideas were sensible. Our turn soon came up. We approached the first obstacle and waited for the man with the timer to shout *"GO!"*

The first obstacle was a ten-foot-high ladder of logs. I asked Sean "are you ready?" and hoisted him as high as I could near the top of the obstacle. Once he was solid on the logs I let go and climbed rapidly to the top, swung my legs over the top, and dropped down to the ground. Then I was able to wait until Sean came over the top, where I could grab his arms and lower him to the ground. At first Sean was confused, but I pointed to the next obstacle, and off we went. There was a water hazard, not deep at all, that required a swing on a rope to get across. I quickly told him my plan, he agreed, and he grabbed hold of the rope. By grabbing him and pulling back, I was able to push him hard across the water. With innate understanding of physics, Sean knew the proper time to let go of the rope. I called to him to throw me the rope. As it came to me, I backed up and with adequate speed passed over the water hazard without difficulty. We next had to crawl on our bellies under some wires to the other end. Unlike infantry basic, there was no barbed wire and no machine gun fire. Another log obstacle came up, and we repeated the same process as in our first ten-foot challenge. We came to a dark tunnel that we entered together. Knowing that the tunnel would not have any real hazards, I had Sean hop on my back, and we ran the short distance without a problem. We traversed one last stacked log obstacle and were done in record time.

With times certified, Sean and I had won the competition by a wide margin. No one, including Jay and Jimmy, was even close. The Snarts had bombed badly. It was the best lesson I could have given my son. Cooperation wins the race.

"You cheated!" Snart said.

Phil Snart was the kind of twit, if he had been back in high school, we would have stuffed inside a school locker so tight that the teachers would have to extract him with a set of bolt cutters.

"Show me the rules," I said.

19

THE DAY WAS EXHAUSTING FOR the boys. Less so for the dads. We got a chance to pull out our baseball gloves to play catch after we found the ball diamond, with its chain-link backstop—a luxury for dads whose sons threw frequent wild pitches. We loved the exercise it offered. I loved playing catch because it gave us a chance to talk as we threw his Little League baseball back and forth. Sean had a good arm on him for being only nine years old. With a natural throwing motion using body, shoulder, arm, forearm, hand, and fingertips, I rarely had to chase an errant throw, unlike my poor father, who got more exercise chasing balls than he wanted to. As a kid, I had a notoriously poor aim at my father's ball glove. Sean, by contrast, had a gift.

We continued to practice strikes, grounders, and high fly balls. He was a master at trapping a grounder—much better than I was. He already had the judgement to get under a high fly and catch it with ease. But his forte was pitching. He already had the potential to be a star, especially because of his accuracy. I encouraged him to go easy on his fast curve balls and to go easy on his still growing bone plates, until his body matured some. He threw the baseball fast anyway, without evidence that it hurt him.

"You ready to face some batters?" I asked, crouching down in the catcher's stance.

This was a rare opportunity for us to pitch over an actual home plate. It had sunk slightly and had years of dust to make it half buried in the ground.

It still offered us a chance to gauge his accuracy with more precision. We learned about catcher signals, after going to a real ball game. For us it was simple, with only four hand signals. An index finger pointed down signaled a fastball. Closed fist meant a knuckleball. Two fingers pointed down called for a curveball. Three fingers pointed down signaled a screwball.

I signaled a knuckleball for starters. He shook his head. I signed a fastball. No again. Two fingers for a curveball. NO. It had to be a screwball. I signaled three fingers down. He shook his head.

"You don't have any other pitches," I said. I was ready for his silliness.

He wound up and sent me an unknown pitch. I stepped to one side as his curveball nearly brushed the buckle on my belt as it passed and slammed into the chain link backstop.

"Come on, Sean. You're going to hurt someone with those antics. Do we quit now, or are you going to behave?"

He started laughing at his not so surprise pitch. Every kid thinks he has invented a new practical joke.

"I'll behave," he replied.

I signaled another fastball, but Sean was still giggling and sent his pitch high and outside for his imaginary right-handed batter. I stretched my glove high across my right shoulder, barely snagging it with a pop in the pocket. I threw it back to him and noted amused embarrassment on his face.

Another fastball landed in my glove with hardly a movement of my hand. The impact of the baseball dead center in a ball glove is a sound of beauty to another ball player. One pop of my glove after another kept us fired up for the next hour. It was uncanny the endurance he had. His throw was so fluid that it looked like he was throwing in slow motion, which added to the difficulty of judging the speed of each pitch. If Suzy had known how long I let him let loose with this baseball barrage, she would have grounded me from parenthood. Ah, the beauty of fathers and sons getting away together—and distant from motherly disapproval.

After we tired of throwing the baseball, Sean asked me a silly question. Silly at first often becomes insightful.

"Dad, why don't we call it throw, instead of catch?"

"Ha!" I pondered this. "From now on, let's call it throw."

"Okay. Can I go run the obstacle course by myself?"

"Sure, Partner."

"By myself?"

I nodded.

"Will you time me?"

Where a boy gets that energy is the mystery every dad ponders. We secretly wish we could play like a kid well into adulthood. I knew the answer to why? It was physics. The smaller a person is, the easier it is to do things like a child. The ant can carry a hundred times its weight because it's small. The same principle applies to a child. Sean's energy was not yet expended. A stopwatch was a dad's salvation.

We ran to the obstacle course, where Sean blended his run into the start of the course. I hardly had time to check my watch before he scaled the first obstacle. I wasn't about to follow him. Instead, I took a seat on a nearby bench, hoping I could steal a few minutes of rest and relaxation. It wasn't to be. To my surprise, he finished the course earlier than I planned. His time was excellent.

Later that afternoon we dads sat around sharing stories, occasionally stopping a boy from committing some infraction. But we mainly enjoyed being in the company of other men. It was good for the boys when they came up to us to listen to the banter of fathers being men. Not being a beer sophisticate, I found Phil Snart's generic variety acceptable. All beer tastes the same to me. The other men couldn't say enough bad about it, until a seasoned camp counselor came up to us unexpectedly and ordered us to get rid of our beer.

"It's a violation of Camp Classen policy to have any alcohol on the premises," the man declared. "I like beer, too, but it's gotta go."

The dads nodded their heads in unison in a look of contrition. The counselor stared back at us, then had a surprise question.

"Who in hell brought generic beer? Who would ever do a thing like that? Is it any good?"

Jay came up with the best answer.

"Well, sir, it tastes like crap, but since you say we can't have it, one last beer would taste pretty darn good."

The camp enforcer let out a laugh and turned to leave the circle of dads. Looking over his shoulder, he added, "Help me keep my job men. Get rid of the crap, or you'll be leaving. Thank you."

We discussed for a moment what we should do to comply. Employing manly logic, our consensus was to hide it. Since it was Phil Snart who bought it, I suggested that if our stash got discovered, we could simply point out the owner. Snart was just too easy to pick on.

That night after the boys were in bed and the lights were out, we complied with the counselor's demand and got rid of the beer while trying to outdo each other's tall tales. A few fathers could relate to my experience after graduating from Officer Training School. Before the ceremony of graduation, where the newly commissioned officers toss their hats in the air, our instructors told us to have a dollar bill handy. It was customary for new officers to give a dollar bill to the first enlisted airman who saluted them. After we located our hats that we had launched skyward, we newly minted second lieutenants scrambled en mass from the parade grounds. The only exit was a back gate, where a dozen airmen stood lined up rapidly saluting each new officer emerging. Stuffing bills into their pockets as fast as they could, it looked like a uniformed male version of a strip club. As I came out, I didn't know which airman to reward. They were all saluting at once. Some new officers donated more than one bill. Nobody told us we would be ambushed.

Another father began with tales of scout campouts gone awry. One dad remembered how he learned as a kid to pack his own clothes into his pack, not to leave it for his mother to do. The January campout to the Chisholm Cattle Trail near Dover, Oklahoma, was a lot tougher after he learned he only had a T-shirt and a light jacket to keep warm. With the temperatures in the teens in the daytime, his hard lesson was finding out that the fathers in the group cut him little slack. Men can be brutal to each other. After that weekend he never forgot the Boy Scout Motto, Be Prepared.

I learned the names of several veterans in the group. Except for the Coast

Guard, the dozen of us fathers represented every branch of service. Marine training carried the most interesting stories. Army and Navy tales topped the Air Force. One Marine told a tale of boot camp, where their training was about survival in a hostile environment. The drill instructor had a small lizard in his hand and told the recruits that if they were hungry enough, they would eat anything. One squeamish recruit commented that he "would never eat a lizard like that." An officer passing by overheard the comment and stormed into the group. Confronting the recruit, he took the poor lizard from the drill instructor.

"Would you follow me into battle?" asked the captain.

If they engrain anything into those thick Marine skulls, it is that an officer is god and you obey them without question.

"Sir, yes, sir!"

He put his face one inch from the recruit's face. "Would you eat this if I ordered you to?"

"No, sir. I wouldn't eat that thing. That's a live lizard."

"I'm ordering you to eat it." He held up the lizard to the youngster's face, who began to whimper and cry the wail reserved only for men with an aversion to snakes.

"Would you follow me into battle?"

The recruit's eyes were wild with fear. His sounds turned guttural and animal in nature.

"Are you a Marine... Or are you *a coward?"*

While animal sounds emanated from the poor recruit, he bit the lizard in half and swallowed. The other recruits were silent. Probably smart. Otherwise, they would be next. The officer, still holding the back end of the lizard, stepped back and spoke.

"Never forget. While you are a Marine, you will always follow your officer because he is your god!"

As he let that sink in, he brought the poor animal to his mouth and took his own bite, then proceeded on his way.

It was five minutes and another round of beers before anyone had anything else to contribute.

SUNDAY MORNING WAKE UP WAS tough—not for the boys but for the dads. The boys were climbing down from their top bunks, often stepping on their dads, and randomly stumbling around like ants. One boy looked at his father and after a pause asked the fatal question.

"What did you do with the beer?"

His father looked up at the boy with the bleary eyes of a man slightly hungover and gave a perfect reply.

"Well son, it took a while, but we poured it all down the toilet."

"Okay," the boy replied, turned, and burst out the door to follow a friend. No doubt the beer answer would spread like wildfire.

We all were soon dressed and headed to our camp stoves to prepare our boys' breakfast. I'm convinced that fathers should never cook anything. Go camping and you will find there are fifty different ways to cook bacon and eggs. They are all wrong.

It had to happen. Our favorite camp counselor returned to our cabin, and he had to ask again how things were going? Watching all the weary looking dads, he asked the expected question.

"Did you boys remove your beer like I ordered?"

The response was instant, but not from us dads.

"They put it all in the toilet," a boy replied.

There are times when something is unexpectedly funny, but you can't afford to laugh. That was the response all the dads had in our Indian Guide contingent. Our friendly counselor looked us over, sighed dramatically, and chuckled in resignation.

"Chapel is at eight a.m. sharp," he said. "Boys, I expect that you and your daddies might want to go."

The man turned around to leave, then looked back to point the direction to go to Sunday services. And so, we complied.

We arrived at the outdoor chapel arena ten minutes early. The tiered wooden benches were still plentiful. We managed to get seats center stage about five rows up. Sean and I sat down and waited. Small talk was minimal among the men and their sons. As Sean sat there staring at the arena, I wondered what he was thinking. Was he thinking about flying? Playing throw? Did he do something adventurous yesterday? Was he reliving our fun on the obstacle course?

"Dad?" To my regret he used his loud voice. "What's that big wooden thing down there in the middle?"

He pointed to the center of the chapel arena, and I wanted to be alone in my airplane where no one could see me. Sean looked at me, waiting for an answer. I was almost too ashamed to speak.

"Son," I said, guilt swelling in my soul. "That's a cross."

20

"SUZY, WE NEED TO START going to church." Sean and I were back home Sunday afternoon. "We have failed our son, and I had to suffer that public embarrassment to finally realize it."

Suzy looked at me from our favorite leather sofa, where she sat seductively barefoot in sinfully short cutoffs and a short-waisted lavender tee. Her understanding of what I said was visible in her own green eyes. She bent her forehead to mine and put her hand on my shoulder.

"Oh, Rob. What have we done? That's so embarrassing."

"We take action... starting right now. First, we need a church."

"Where do the Goodwins go?"

"I can ask Jay, or we can first figure out what denomination we want. Remember the three options we discussed before we got married? You grew up Baptist. I was a Presbyterian. We could go to one or the other. We could find something that is a compromise choice."

"We need something that is good for Sean first of all," she replied. "We may need to start trying different churches near us. Next week, for sure."

"Then we take option number four... we find one together for our boy."

"Good. That's done. Now, what else did you boys do while you were away?"

"I think our boy is a natural in the airplane. He makes a good copilot. He enjoyed Camp Classen. We may want to join the YMCA. And you'll never guess in a million years who I met in Jay's car."

"And who would that be?"

"Do you remember a while back that I told you about a conversation I had with some jerk who hated pilots?"

"You mean that Army medic?" Suzy was showing more interest.

"That's the one. Medic? I'm not so sure. You remember he said… well, of course you know what he said."

"You were in a car together?"

"Yes. We also shared a cabin with him. Not just him. There were several fathers with their boys in our cabin."

"But you had to spend the whole weekend around him. How awful!"

"It turns out that Snart, that's his name… Phil Snart… he's very much a prig. The kind of guy that even a decent kid would have bullied in grade school. Talk about a killjoy. He bought the beer, but it was some generic junk. He asked me to pay something like thirty dollars for my share. Jay had already paid him for it for both of us. What a piece of work."

"I hope you said something."

"I went into my ten-year-old mode and picked on him all day Saturday. I found out that if you break a rule or make a new rule, he gets all nitpicky."

"Like what?" Suzy was now keenly interested in knowing more about this stuffed shirt.

"Well after the counselor tried to ban our beer…." Suzy looked at me in surprise. "Okay, we didn't know it was not allowed in camp. I guess we should have known, but I told Phil the Prig that if we got caught, I would tell the counselor who bought it."

"So, what did you do with the beer?"

"It took some time, but we poured it in the toilet last night."

Suzy lowered her head in a fashion only reserved for a bad joke.

"Oh, Rob! You men are so bad."

I could have taken on an expression of contrition, but after a men and boys retreat, I didn't feel anything but happiness.

"Suzy, let me tell you something. I haven't enjoyed myself so much since my days in the Air Force. Men getting together for a little orneriness is a necessary part of being a man. You need to understand that."

"I have no doubt of that. I didn't say I wanted you to be a milk toast."

"Breaking rules is part of what makes us men. The beer was wrong, and we won't do it again, but I wouldn't change how we handled it. It ties in with what I want you to know. I miss those days, but not for reasons you may assume. I could honestly live without the flying, but what I really miss nine years later is the comradery. I didn't know what esprit de corps meant until I joined the military."

"Rob, you've always been good at making friends."

"But this is different. When I entered pilot training, I already had a taste of how important our squadron members were to my own wellbeing. In OTS we did PT together. We ate together. We marched together. We got in trouble together. We shared problems together. Sure, it was tough going through the stress of training and the exhaustion of constant demands on us physically. The crazy thing was that we all began to enjoy doing it together. Then came pilot training. As we know, there were real risks involved. I understand why friends of mine who were in real combat feel so close to their buddies in combat. Their lives depended on each other."

Suzy took on an impish grin. "This doesn't mean you're leaving me, does it?" She got the laugh from me I knew she wanted.

"I grew close to the men in my squadron. Men form a special bond that is hard to understand. Now that women pilots are part of that esprit de corps, my friends who are still on active duty tell me it's just not the same. No reflection on the women. They make good pilots, I am sure. It's just that, weird as it might sound, you can't step out of the shower after PT and pop a gal on the butt with a towel. You can't body block a girl in a game of football. You can't have a girl as a roommate. The men talk about the lone girl in their squadron that has to do everything alone. They feel sorry for her and want her to have another female to pal around with, but still, it changes the whole dynamic of the squadron's comradery."

"So, you liked Indian Guides and taking Sean with you."

"Sean needs to be around men sometimes... to get away from his mother and see what men do when no one is looking. Think of it this way. Half of the great achievements in history would not have happened if the achiever hadn't broken a few rules. Boys need to see that happen and learn that, aside from breaking the law, rules are meant to be broken if it results in the right and good outcome."

"Are you sure that's a good idea?"

"Why did we start dating the first time? What convinced you to go on a date with me?"

"Okay. You're right. You were kind of wild. I found it interesting."

"To you I was an element of danger."

"I wouldn't go that far, but, yes, you did seem to stretch the rules and get things done."

"Suzy, I think women like a man like that more than a man who is rules driven and never takes a chance. Ever see anyone who fails and handles it poorly? It's much more appealing to fail and demonstrate how to get up and go right back at it."

"So, let me summarize this for us. You like doing things with the dads."

"Yes."

"I think that's good. You have my permission."

"None needed, thank you."

"I wouldn't want it any other way."

"Well, I love you, too, Suzy."

She stood up from our library sofa, heading to our kitchen to handle her daily chores. That left me to sit for a few moments in silence. Sean was already outside sharing our experience with his friends. My mind wandered from the comradery among men into flying. I recalled the day I took Suzy up for the first time. She was not reluctant, but I sensed flying was not the passion for her it might be. Perhaps John's death almost ten years ago made flying too much of a reminder. I daydreamed the question of where we could go in our Bonanza on a family trip for three. We could go anywhere we wanted, only limited by the capacity of our bladders. The flying would be fun, and the scenery would be different than when inside a car. A vehicle operator, if it is an airplane instead of a car, can pause to stare at things without flying off the side of the road. My places to see included the Grand Canyon, Santa Fe and Taos, Florida along the Emerald Coast, Minnesota, and the Great Lakes.

I could go on, but realistically, an in-state trip would be the first trip to take. Start small, then go big.

"Suzy, are you there?"

"I'm here," she said, stepping back into our favorite room.

"Where are we going on our first flying vacation?"

"Oh, I don't know. Maybe Canada or Mexico."

So much for in-state trips. Suzy was definitely not picking our destination for a while.

"Let's keep ourselves in the United States for now. What if we went out West to start with? Arizona or New Mexico. That's almost like flying to Mexico."

"We could do Santa Fe, then go to the Grand Canyon. I've never seen the Grand Canyon."

"Sean would love it. You would, too. The Grand Canyon is bigger than you can comprehend. There is an excellent airport right outside the National Park entrance. Every time I have been, it surprises me that my recall cannot fathom how big the canyon really is. It's like my brain's memory bank isn't big enough to hold it all."

"Then let's plan a trip before it's too cold. Name your date, and I'm ready."

21

WE TRIED NEW CHURCHES OVER the next few weeks. Suzy was comfortable with the Southern Baptist Church. Sean liked the preacher. When we asked him after the service, he could always summarize what the message was. I tired of hearing the sermon's message repeated ten times each Sunday. To my amazement, Suzy did not need a hymnal. She knew nearly all of the hymns by heart. Every Sunday morning in church, Sean would look up at her, then at me as I held my hymnal, and display the most delightful grin as we sang. He found joy in learning of his mother's newly discovered talent. She claimed her recall of hymns came from years of going to church every Sunday morning, Sunday evening, and Wednesday night for the first sixteen years of her life. It sounded like too much of a commitment for me. Then there was the alter call and the hymn, "Just as I Am." I admit it was a religious experience. I would never answer the alter call, but it did cause me to pray that someone would step forward so we could go home and stop singing that hymn over and over.

We found a Presbyterian church, but it was different from the one I grew up in. I had been part of the same Presbyterian congregation all through childhood. I know about the monthly votes after church, hence the name Presbytery. Each church in the denomination had its own way of doing things. Preachers were chosen or dismissed by the congregation, not by higher authorities in the faith. My church had picked some doozies, like the self-appointed exorcist to every parishioner in the congregation. He lasted a year.

We checked out a couple of Methodist Churches. Both elicited the same comment from us. We were comfortable, and Sean liked their Sunday Schools. In the smaller Methodist Church, Sean met some of his school chums in Sunday School. We returned there for a second visit and were hooked. At nine years old, Sean was a sponge for all knowledge. No longer would he ask, "what is that cross?"

I WROTE A LETTER TO my River Rat buddy, Hal Freed, now a Lieutenant Colonel in the Air Force Reserves with the 507th Tactical Fighter Group based at Tinker AFB, only thirty miles from our house. Now flying F-4 Phantoms, Hal was still living his dream of flying fighters. The Phantom was every pilot's plum assignment. When he wasn't flying fighters on weekends, he taught political science with his wife, Lisa, at the University of Texas in Austin. Having only recently completed his PhD from the same school and considering the post-Vietnam War climate, I was curious how that academic assignment was working out. Students remained antagonistic activists in many parts of the country. I could imagine how Hal would react the first time a student tried a face-to-face verbal assault over his military accomplishments.

Dear Hal,

I hope all is going well with you and Lisa. It's been an interesting year so far. I ran into what I think is another make-believe veteran the other day. This time he claimed to be a medic, then said the most vile things about John Alexander. Needless to say, I remembered how much my knuckles hurt the last time I slugged someone, so I restrained myself. He will still be on my target list.

Suzy is fine and watches out for our son. It's funny how I slipped so easily into the role of father for Sean. It came naturally from the very beginning. We started going to a Methodist church nearby, which may be a shock to you. Remember, we have a lot to repent over. I highly recommend it.

We are settled into our new house, which has been a Godsend for Sean and me. We have a large area in the front and in the back to practice pitching and even batting without fear of breaking any windows. You wouldn't believe the arm on that boy. I have to remind him to hold back on his fastball for fear he will tear up his shoulder or elbow. The kid has a talent. I can see a baseball scholarship in his college future. He even throws curveballs and screwballs like a pro. It took him some time to realize why I needed to know what pitch was coming. I took him to a game at Eighty-Niner Stadium. I showed him how the catcher signals the pitch and why. Now I'm chasing only a few pitches thrown over my head.

Suzy is pitching a trip to the Grand Canyon this summer and wants Sean to hike The Canyon with us. He is almost ten years old, so I think he can stand the rigors of the trail. I'll wear an Air Force cap as bait for any peaceniks I encounter along the way. I'll have Sean pitch a beanball at them. As a first trip, I want to talk Suzy into a day trip, like we took to Indian Garden. That was tough enough for me. I want to enjoy a bit more relaxation than we had on our hike.

Suzy enjoys owning an airplane. She has an iron stomach like Sean. She loves flying our Bonanza as my copilot. I've let her take a few lessons from me, but I think we would do better if someone else took her up. We have a friend, Brad Kilty, who I think might give her a few lessons. She would be a very competent pilot—nerves of steel.

I started this letter with the intention to ask you how teaching is going. Idealistic and know-it-all college students surround you all day. Teaching political science has to be tough with all those naïve students who are likely to object to everything you say. It would drive me to distraction. Sort of like my fake veteran (see above). How are you handling it?

Work is good here. I almost feel guilty. My time at the office or in the field is required less and less. Probably things go better when I'm gone. I'm finding that consulting with my old company pays better than owning it. They pay for my knowledge, not my hands-on work, which means I am free to take off anytime I want. Pretty good for someone not yet forty.

In truth, I'm going a little stir crazy. Suzy works part time as an Oklahoma County librarian. Sean is older, so she's thinking that going full time would make her feel like more of a contributor to society. I feel the same way. I need a cause. And not to boast, but I don't need the money. I need something where I can make a difference. Oh well, enough of the mindless thoughts of a societal slug. My love to Lisa. Write soon.

Your old buddy,
Rob

22

WE DIDN'T WAIT LONG TO plan and execute a trip to the Grand Canyon. With Sean in the back seat and Suzy in the co-pilot seat, we rolled onto Runway 35 Right at Wiley Post Airport, went to full power, and headed north on takeoff. Compensating for the excess baggage, I held the nose down until we had extra speed before liftoff. I confirmed a positive rate of climb on the vertical velocity indicator. After raising the landing gear, I confirmed the wheels were up and locked. With a sufficient rate of climb to altitude, I changed the pitch of the three-bladed prop from 2,700 rpm to a cruise setting of 2,500 rpm. The aircraft's speed increased to add more to our rate of climb. We leveled off at 10,500 feet heading west. We were on our way to new adventures in the Great Southwest.

It was my habit to prepare for all possibilities, including having to land unexpectedly in inaccessible places. My theory was simple. If you plan for the worst, it never happens. Forget to plan? It will happen. We carried an extra aviation radio, tiedowns for windy conditions, extra oil for the engine, and water for the passengers. That was the first pack. I packed another bag in the small luggage space with flashlights, extra batteries, emergency blankets, and first aid supplies. Anything I forgot was bound to make things happen, so I was methodical with my flight-packing checklist.

Weight is always an issue with civilian aviation. Thus, my emergency kit had to be minimal. I made everyone weigh before we left on our trip to ensure we would not have an accident caused by my poor weight and balance calculations. Sean, as he got older and heavier, was someday going to cause a problem. My airplane also had an uncommon problem because, as fuel burned, the balance shifted aft of the centerline. Too far aft and the plane would become unstable. When weight shifts forward to a reasonable degree, that usually presents no problem. Civil aviation, I discovered, is maybe more complicated than flying a fighter. In the civilian world there are no airmen to help you. I quickly developed a new appreciation for the work that the Air Force crew chiefs did for us before each flight. It was demanding work for me trying to do jobs that took a handful of personnel in the military.

From the air it's obvious the reasons for the boundaries of states. Each state has its own terrain and distinctive colors. The Texas Panhandle of the high plains is flat and intensely green from the well irrigated croplands. New Mexico has a salt and pepper appearance from the air while Arizona to the south becomes almost frighteningly barren and inhospitable. More forested land emerges as you go north to the Grand Canyon, but it is still hot, dry, and dangerous for those who get stranded.

As we approached Grand Canyon National Park Airport, seven miles south of the canyon's South Rim, I was inspired by the view of a flat plateau of land suddenly cut off in a one-mile plunge in depth to our north. It was hard to comprehend the amount of work the Colorado River managed to do in a few short millions of years. Sean and Suzy were glued to the Bonanza's windows and chattering away. I concentrated on the chatter of the radios as I contacted the tower for clearance to land. Several private jets sat parked off the runway. It was a busy place. Grand Canyon Tower instructed me to make a left-hand pattern to Runway 21, which meant I would make my final turn on the canyon end of the airport. This gave Sean and Suzy a better chance to view the South Rim of the canyon as I circled for a final approach and landing. Our landing was uneventful, but the low fuel level after such a long flight forced me to taxi while using my brakes to keep the nose wheel on the ground. I asked Sean in the backseat to lean forward. With the same request of Suzy, our taxi to the parking ramp with a more forward center of gravity became easier. We were soon in the parking area, the aircraft tied down, chocked, and locked.

We closed our flight plan inside the terminal of the fixed base operator or FBO. Stepping over to the small terminal desk, we arranged transportation into the park. While waiting, I directed Suzy to the interesting people you see from different states, especially near the national parks. I always found hitchhikers in such areas, but now in the 1980s there were fewer since the decline of the hippie culture. The Reagan national reinvention changed people in many ways. I directed Suzy's attention to the four men in their mid-thirties dressed in pristine jeans, identical crisp shirts in four different colors, and new unblemished caps reminiscent of the French Foreign Legion with the sun blocking black duckbill and a neck drape in back.

"I don't think they have ever hiked the Grand Canyon before." I said. "It looks like they had their wives shop for them."

"They look a little odd, don't they?" Suzy wore comfortable and unsexy hiking clothes. "Although, that one with the long dark sideburns and the light blue shirt looks kind of cute."

"I'll buy the same outfit and wear it if it will help."

"I don't think that will help."

"I wonder where they're from. I bet their story is interesting."

"You can find out. They appear to be waiting for the same transport van that we are."

The FBO shuttle, with *Grand Canyon Airlines* stenciled prominently on the doors, pulled up. We grabbed our small bags and filed aboard to sit on three scalding hot vinyl seats in the back. From there we headed north to the last remaining Harvey House in existence. With a rich history, Fred Harvey built the El Tovar Hotel as a destination resort, the showplace lodge in the soon-to-be Grand Canyon National Park. Opened in 1905 to provide meals and lodging to the northern terminus of the Santa Fe Railroad line, it soon expanded to meet the growing need of rooms for tourists. Rail traffic continued to increase on this Santa Fe Railroad spur, later renamed the Grand Canyon Railway. The hotel had stunning views of the canyon without having to leave the hotel's breakfast table.

We were lucky to be checking in since most reservations required booking up to a year in advance. We had called the same day that another family cancelled. The hotel was glad to help us both and to help their own bottom line. First, we unpacked our lightweight suitcases, then headed outside to get a better look at the canyon rim. To add fun to the experience for Sean, I asked him if he would play a game with me.

"Will you let me cover your eyes and walk you up the rim before you have a look?"

Sean pondered that idea for a moment. I added a selling point.

"It will make you feel like you are flying."

"Okay," he said.

Suzy and I each held a hand of Sean and walked him with his eyes closed the short distance from the back of the hotel to the low stone wall that would give him the best view in the park.

"Okay, Sean. Are you ready?" Suzy asked.

"Yeah," he said as he opened his eyes, pausing a split second to adjust to the light.

Sean's scream must have covered the bottom of the canyon with his sounds of sheer terror, elation, and astonishment.

"Wow! Ooooh! This is *HUGE!*"

The small crowd of tourists, who had seen what we were attempting, laughed in delight. The wonder of a nine-year-old boy had brought joy to a whole lot of people and to two doting parents. Among the group gathered were two of the four oddly dressed men we had seen earlier. I approached the one that Suzy had pointed out with the light blue shirt and long dark sideburns.

"That was an excellent idea you had for that boy," the man said as I approached. "We enjoyed it immensely."

"Glad to entertain you," I said. "You guys looked like you had a story to tell when you first caught my attention. Is this your first time at the canyon?"

"Yeah. None of us has ever been here before."

The man in his blue shirt was my height with an engaging smile to go with his relaxed, yet animated, conversation. His friend, at first glance, was scary looking. I was glad he didn't talk.

"Oh, man! You're in for a treat," I said. "Are you hiking down tomorrow?"

"We were but didn't plan very well. I guess you have to have a permit for staying overnight in these places."

"You can still hike down, but you'll have to come out, even in the dark."

"We do something poorly planned together at least once a year," he replied. "We don't really care. It's just good to get away."

"You guys must be close if you do this yearly." I hoped he would feed my curiosity.

"We're the old gang from high school. Those three know all my secrets... and vice versa. We can do a lot of stupid stuff on these adventures, but we always have each other's six."

"Ex-military?" I asked. The check six reference caught my attention.

"We all joined the Marines. What a cluster foxtrot that was. We did our time and got out."

"Thanks for your service. I know you gave up a lot to join up."

"Yup," he said curtly.

Sean came up at this opportune time to grab my hand, pull, and wave his other hand in a come-this-way motion.

"I gotta go. Duty calls." With a nod from the blue-shirted Marine, I was on my way.

23

IT WAS LATE IN THE evening before we got to our table at the El Tovar restaurant. Sean was already sleepy, slightly grumpy, but hungry. We sat patiently for our food order while watching the sun go down in the canyon. The evening was clear skies, which meant the bottom of the canyon might be a bit cooler for our early morning hike down the Bright Angel Trail to our destination at Indian Garden, a tortuous 9.8-mile round trip. It would take us most of the day to get down then make the slow climb back to the top. I had hiked the canyon rim to rim twice before, so this short jaunt was not a challenge, I hoped. After all, I was older now. Time would tell how the rest of the family would feel about it. Hal Freed and I hiked it together in my bachelor days. I hoped we would have a less troublesome experience for Suzy and Sean.

"What was the story with the blue shirt hunk you were talking to?" Suzy asked. Sean was lost in daydreams while gazing out the window.

"He was interesting," I said, "but I think he may have not told me the whole truth of why they were here."

Suzy gave me that go on look. She loved a mystery. I continued.

"He looks to be about my age, but he was the only one who did any talking. He had one of his buddies with him with the ugliest beard I've ever seen… he's kind of scary looking. There was not a peep out of that one."

"That's not unusual," Suzy said.

"That may be true, but he gave some bull about making an annual trip together. Then he said they never plan well but have a good time. Surely, one of those guys would plan better than that. Someone had to organize the wardrobe. Guys just don't coordinate those things... not real guys anyway."

"Did one of their wives do the shopping?" Suzy asked.

"One maybe, but not four. Definitely someone gave them those outfits at the spur of the moment. I would have already exchanged them for something less uniform."

Suzy had that look when she pondered something. I, too, was puzzled by this strange riddle. Then the piece of the puzzle I left out came to me.

"Mister Blue Shirt said they were high school buddies, and all joined the Marines together. If I guess their age right, they may have been in Vietnam in the period of the Tet Offensive. He certainly became less vocal when his Marine time came up. Sean grabbed me about the time that it was starting to become interesting."

The waiter brought our meal. We shook Sean out of his daydream so he could eat his meal of a hamburger, french fries, and a generic cola that our boy didn't like. The generic craze had hit the park service. Knowing that the hike in the morning would be demanding, we took the approach that long-distance runners take before a race—pasta by the bucketful.

We soon had our fill and packed up the rest of Sean's meal and guided our exhausted son to our room by the stairwell on the second floor. With no way to keep his leftovers cool, I took our ice bucket down to the ice machine. I put Sean's burger and fries in a plastic bag, put the sandwich and bag into the ice bucket, and surrounded the food with ice. With that done and Sean collapsed, we were in bed early for our sunrise descent into the oven called the Grand Canyon.

Yet, I couldn't sleep. I kept thinking of the four men, who seemed on the surface to be quite normal. They were not as dorky as they tried to look. I climbed out of bed and stared at the darkness in sleepy frustration. I picked up one of our small bags where Suzy had stuffed last minute items before our departure. I found the mail that Suzy had picked out of our mailbox before we drove to Wiley Post Airport. Stepping into the bathroom, I closed the door and turned on a light to read. There in the middle of the stack was a reply letter from Hal Freed. To my surprise a second much thicker letter from Hal was underneath. I pulled them close to determine the post mark. I wanted to read them in date order. Both envelopes bore the distinctive block letters of Hal's meticulous handwriting, a product of early computers and the requirement for exact lettering on data cards we filled out for students after each flight. I put the second letter back on the stack and carefully tore open the envelope. The second letter I promised myself I would read after our canyon hike. It was heavier and thicker than the first. I didn't want to spend all night reading something potentially time consuming.

Rob,

It was good to get your letter. You mentioned the challenges of teaching today's college students. With the experience I am having, which is a culture shock after life in the Air Force, dare I suggest a "cause" you might pursue? Start a career of kicking the ass of every fake vet you encounter. You appear to be a magnet for them.

Teaching political science to freshmen in college is not going well. There is a total lack of respect for civility on campus. I encourage discussion in my class. The anger in some students was unexpected. Now I feel like a referee more than a professor. The vets are good enough, but the young ones are going ballistic over Reagan's actions. One group is thrilled at the prospect of our national defense budget growing. I'm thrilled, too, but I try to keep my opinions neutral. Most of the vets in my class prefer to keep their opinions to themselves. I am an educator, not a propagandist. The other group is ticked off and shrill about the president bringing us to an "inevitable nuclear" war with the Soviets. It's a mess if you are really trying to teach them something.

Lisa teaches some higher-level political science subjects and has a few graduate students in her class. She has real problems because some of her PhD track students were protesters during Vietnam. They are either pacifists or frighteningly radical thinkers. The pacifists are OK. A couple in her studies are veterans. The ones we both worry about are aggressive in their opinions to the point that Lisa only goes to the parking lot with other faculty members. To make it worse, some of the faculty are radicalized. She's afraid to introduce them to me, for fear of what they would say in my face. They might be surprised at my own opinion, but I keep quiet.

We still have a few Iranian students. I thought they would be history after Reagan took office. In previous years, Lisa would have a dozen in her classroom. They were overly aggressive in response to poor grades in her class. Two or three would come in with their graded papers and raise all sorts of hell. When she sought help from her department head, his answer floored her. He told her to give them what they wanted. The tuition revenue was more important than academic integrity. I took a more back-at-you approach with my Iranian students. The result was that none enrolled in my classes after that first semester. That was a win for both of us.

What really has me concerned are the faculty who were in graduate school when the war was going on. They got their deferments. Never had to serve. They have a sense of intellectual superiority that is both laughable and frightening. Once it got out that I was bombing North Vietnam in the war, the news spread rapidly. I swear there were some members who would kill me on the spot if they could get away with it. I've been shunned by many. Others are condescending when they must talk to me. There are a few supporters, but they are too intimidated by the atmosphere on campus to be of much help. I worry about what in hell is happening. And all because of the Vietnam War. I think America would be a lot better if it had not ever happened. It makes me want to go on another road trip and kick some ass again. I bet if we took our wives this time, they would enjoy joining us boys in a little retribution.

Seriously, I would be careful. Crazy things are happening in the country. Remember the Symbionese Liberation Army when they kidnapped Patty Hearst? That was back in 1974. It's my humble opinion that there are more nutty groups out there waiting for their chance to be crazy. Add to that what I glean from my students. Most appear to be little Patty Hearsts, turned into mindless robots by their radical professors. Lisa and I both see it in our students. Since we don't follow the radical doctrine, we are ostracized—or worse.

Well, enough of my uplifting rhetoric. I'm glad you've got your own little Tom Seaver to play catch with. Tell Sean that he can pretend your catcher's mitt is some professor's head and that I would like to see it beaned. That should improve his accuracy.

All my best to Suzy,
Hal

I folded the letter and placed it back in its envelope, chuckling to myself. I could imagine Sean throwing beanballs at an imaginary bad guy. That's how children learn to be civil to each other. Venting my anger at a surrogate was how I learned as a child—never take out your real aggressions on the real thing. Baseball umpires certainly would agree with me. The one time I slipped up, my fist took forever to stop hurting.

I was disturbed by Hal's comment concerning life on a college campus. In the following years, I learned to expect the vilest comments from the antiwar crowd. Now, with Vietnam in my past, the peace crowd was devoid of a cause and seemed hell bent to find something else to scream about. Some were going ballistic because our president was building up the military. Others went ballistic at the patriotic wave of a flag. Closet peaceniks expressed their displeasure at this patriotism with a scowl or a condescending sigh. Now, according to Hal and reading between the lines, those early Vietnam War opponents were sending their children to college, and these kids were not rebelling against their parents. Their indoctrination came from their parents. Professors and teachers reinforced the belief and the behavior. Now, respect for authority, even in high school and elementary school, was going down the toilet. All because nobody was willing to win the stupid war.

24

"IT'S FIVE O'CLOCK," A VOICE whispered in my ear. One eye was still glued shut, but in my other eye the image of Sean came into near focus. He obviously was no longer tired. He held up our ice bucket. "Can I have my hamburger and fries now?"

"Um… go for it, son," I whispered. "Eat it before Mom says it's not safe."

As I pried open my other eye, I looked at Sean. He had turned his gaze to his mother lying face down next to me.

"It's safe," Suzy said in muffled tones. "Eat away."

Sean smiled and pulled the cold remnants of his evening meal from the ice bucket of cold but iceless water. He wasted no time polishing off the cold fries first, then the remains of his hamburger.

"Where's my Coke?" he asked.

"You mean your generic cola? It's right here where I'm pointing."

That, too, was gone in seconds. Sean was acutely wired as we quickly dressed for our hike. Our light packs had to carry a gallon of water apiece. The other most important item was gorp, a collection of M&Ms, granola, oats, nuts, raisins, small crackers, pretzels, and any other junk we normally would avoid because they tasted good. The stresses of a roller coaster descent into the canyon for nine miles sapped blood sugar before you expected. The demand for carbohydrates that were immediately available to boost blood sugar was important. We dressed in clothing that covered us head to toe and could get wet in the frequent streams we would encounter. Getting wet to cool off was often necessary. I elected to carry our airplane's emergency kit as insurance, knowing that accidents only happen when you are not prepared. From experience we always forgot something, so we went through our mental list until convinced we were ready. The El Tovar breakfast hours began at 6:00 a.m. We were right on time to be first in line as we walked from the door of our room. Sean, distracted by some unknown daydream, came out the door last.

"Be sure that door is closed," I said. He was old enough now to understand responsibility, but we still double-checked him. Suzy looked at me with a question.

"Did you mean to carry your pack to breakfast?"

No, I had not, but it was too late. Sean had closed the door. I didn't want to undo our trust in him. "I'll just take it down with me. If I have it, I can double check what I brought."

We weren't the only early risers. There were many with their own backpacks, but we still got a table by the window looking out at the canyon in morning light. We ate our breakfast at a rapid rate both from necessity and excitement. With our coffee, orange juice, eggs, bacon, and toast now devoured, we headed back to the room to grab our other packs. On the way out we got some other food items in the gift shop that we could enjoy if the gorp ran out. We took the stairs to the second floor to find our room's door slightly ajar.

"Sean, you didn't close the door," I said with some irritation.

"I did!" He protested strenuously, then lowered his head. "It was closed when we left. You saw me do it."

"We did see you close it, Honey." Suzy was quick to defend her son. "We know you did. Rob, don't go in there."

"Stand back." I pushed the door open further, much to Suzy's irritation. "Maybe it's the maid. Anyone here? We're coming in."

I waited outside the door, waiting for my eyes to adjust to the relative darkness in our room. There was no rustling inside that I could hear. I turned to Suzy.

"Do you hear anything?"

"No."

"It couldn't be housekeeping. She wouldn't work in the dark."

I proceeded to step inside when a familiar voice spoke behind us.

"Is something wrong? Can we help?"

It was our still blue-shirted Marine, this time with the whole group in tow.

"Our door was open… not a lot, but we are sure we closed it when we left for breakfast. I was about to go in."

The man turned to his three friends, then back to me. "Let's all take a look."

I hesitated briefly, not knowing exactly what to do. Suzy was paralyzed with indecision as Sean held her hand.

"We can be your backup if you like. By the way, my name is Bob. We'll stay here a minute while you take a look. They can't get by five of us."

I gave him a nod and stepped in, turned on the dim lights, and looked around carefully. After checking behind the door, checking under the bed, and looking past the shower curtain, I pronounced it safe to come in.

The four men stayed politely outside in the hallway as Suzy and Sean went into their room.

"Bob, I sincerely thank you. My name is Rob. That is my wife Suzy and our son Sean. I can't thank you enough… all of you."

After shaking Bob's hand, I turned to the others. Each one gave me their name when I reintroduced myself. The first two were my height. Jack was clean-cut, lean, redheaded, and already sunburned. Randy, uncomfortably intimidating, was the quiet one from the previous night with balding hair, a full beard which covered his throat all the way to his chest. Chet was the tallest one in the group with curly grey hair cut short on a stocky body composed of more muscle than fat.

"Are the four of you headed down into the canyon today like we are?"

"That's our plan," Chet replied. "We have to eat first. I keep hearing that climbing out of the place is a beast. I'll need all the energy I can store."

"Well, perhaps we'll see you down there at Indian Garden," I said.

"All right, let's go, men." With a polite nod to Suzy, they were off.

It seemed prudent to get Sean to use the bathroom before we headed out. It was four and a half miles to Indian Garden, but the relatively level walk to the Bright Angel Trailhead took time also. We hoped he would make it all the way down before he needed another pit stop. Sean was taking his time. Resigned to the delay, Suzy and I sat back down to wait. That is when our room phone rang. I assumed it was the front desk but was surprised to hear a familiar voice.

"Rob, thank God I got you," said a deep male voice with Top Forty radio quality. "Are you all right?"

"Jay?" I asked. "What are you doing calling here?"

"Are you all right?" Jay repeated with more emphasis.

"We're fine. We're all here, in our room, just headed out to the hiking trail to go down."

"Okay, you must listen to me and do exactly as I say." The leader in him was making the point strong. *"The emergency kit that you keep in your Bonanza. Where is it?"*

I looked down at my right hand, still holding my backpack. "I'm holding it. I stuffed it in my pack."

"Pull it out and look in it." Jay directed. *"What do you see in the bottom or back of it? Is there anything that looks about the size of a pager?"*

I pulled open the emergency kit, sifting through the bandages, sponges, iodine tablets, ointments, emergency blanket, and many more items than I realized it contained. And then, there it was. In the right corner of the kit was a small circular device lightly attached with adhesive.

"I found it," I said. "Who put that there? What do you want me to do with it?"

"I want you to make it go away. Put it in a pickup driving by, tie it to a dog. I don't care. Just make it go away and out of the park."

"Jay, you have to tell me what's going on."

"One question for you, Rob. About Phil Snart? What did you do to piss off that wussy little prick?"

It took me a moment to grasp the meaning of his question.

"You're kidding me! How the hell should I know? I never touched the guy. I won't even shake his hand."

"I'm sorry, Rob. I thought he was only joking. I just found out this morning that

he's tracking you, and he left for the Grand Canyon the day before yesterday. You get rid of that device, and he'll never find you."

"He can't track me from Oklahoma. How can he know I'm here?"

An uncomfortable pause ensued that made me dread what Jay hesitated to say. *"I might have told him, Rob. I'm sorry. He let it slip that, when we were at Camp Classen, he tried to slip a device into your emergency kit at night. Your airplane locks must be working well. He couldn't get it in the plane. He said it was a prank."*

"Is he alone?"

"Maybe not. He mentioned he had some friends from his Vietnam days who owe him a favor. Army, I think."

"Could they be Marines?"

"I assumed Army, but I could be wrong. That could all be BS, too. I don't see him having many friends."

"Okay, Jay. First, I had the bag with me at breakfast. We just got back to our room to find someone broke in while we were eating. I'm guessing it was either your buddy Snart or his helpers." If he was looking for the device, he failed. It could be him or someone else simply trying to steal stuff."

"Anything missing?"

"Not that I can tell."

"Then assume it's Snart."

"Copy that. I'll get rid of this piece of junk, and I'll take your word that he can't find me once it's gone."

"He must have tried to replace that thing this morning or replace batteries. Using weak batteries is not a great way to trace you in the canyon. Once you dump it, you'll be free of the twit."

"Out of curiosity, Jay, did Snart say what he intended to do once he tracked me down?"

"I'm not sure, Rob. Let me see what I can discreetly find out. I'll leave you a message if I learn more."

With that we hung up. I took the mystery device down the stairs, out through the lobby door, and into the parking lot. Spying a man who was checking out of the El Tovar and putting bags in his car, I asked him one question.

"You look like you had a good time. Where are you headed from here?"

"Headed to the North Rim," he replied. "If I was a crow, it would be eleven miles. Since I can't fly, we take the highway, and from experience, it takes forever to get around to the other side."

The departing traveler bent down to pick up another suitcase and some shopping bags full of souvenirs.

"Well, you enjoy the cooler side over there," I said cheerfully and tossed the tracking device deep into his trunk.

25

SUZY LOOKED AT ME WARILY. "Should we cancel our hike?"

"Jay seemed to think if we sent that device on its way, he couldn't find us," I said, hoping to reassure her.

"What about our four friends? Are they part of this mess, too?"

"I don't know, but I'm thinking it would be wise to try an abbreviated trail, perhaps to the three-mile station."

"Think of this," Suzy said. "If those men intended to harm us, they had plenty of other opportunities. And if they were the ones tracking us, why would they need to break into our room? They already knew where we were."

"Maybe they were looking for something else. Was there something else in our packs that they were looking for?"

"Maybe they found it, and they will leave us alone."

"Don't forget. Jay got the information about the device directly from that dope, Phil Snart."

"I can't believe he would come all the way out here to find us. We're just not worth the time and money. Maybe Phil's accidental sharing of his plans is part of the practical joke. We are scrambling around with worry for some demented person's lame prank."

In my worry I forgot that Sean was in the room with us. He was on the floor with his pack in his lap, fidgeting in anticipation that we were still leaving on our hike. I looked at Suzy.

"Let's not change a single thing. We'll leave for Indian Garden, return this afternoon, and have a good time."

"Agreed." Sean jumped to his feet at her words. "But for the whole way, I'm still going to check your six."

Loaded up, we locked the door of our room again, headed out of the El Tovar, and hiked west to the Bright Angel Trailhead.

It was already 7:30 in the morning, the sun warming rapidly. Suzy dutifully reminded us to put our hats on and turn our collars up to prevent sunburn. We were already covered in long-sleeved shirts, jeans, and light hiking shoes. Suzy donned her floppy, wide-brimmed, straw hat embroidered with bright red hibiscus flowers. Sean wore his favorite kelly-green ball cap from his Pee Wee little league baseball team he played on. I adorned my head with my cryptic ball cap that displayed only my Air Force pilot's wings but no words. Underneath my cap I draped a white linen handkerchief down the back of my neck to block the sun. It was a homemade version of the four Marines' own dorky-looking foreign legion hats.

It would get hotter as we descended more than 3,000 feet from the trailhead to Indian Garden. Climbing back out would have us returning at temperatures twenty degrees hotter than they were currently. More than a half-mile down and another half-mile back up, and hiking 4.8 miles, park rangers considered this down and back up trek to be a relatively easy day hike.

Reaching the trailhead from the El Tovar was a significant uphill day hike by itself. The entrance is relatively obscure and easily missed if you are not paying attention. For being a canyon of incomprehensible enormity, the trailhead is surprisingly narrow.

"Here we go," I said, stopping to collect all three of us before staring down. "Bright Angel Trail to your right."

"That's it?" Suzy said, a little anxiety in her voice.

From where she stood it looked as if her first step onto the trail would result in a fall of hundreds of feet. Switchbacks begin at once. Suzy's heart came up in her throat immediately when Sean ran down the trail at breakneck speed.

"Sean!" Her shout was panicked.

She hurriedly followed him. No longer afraid of her own death, she led the way to catch up and grab onto him. Sean skidded to a dusty halt at the bottom of the first switchback, turned around to face us, and waved his right hand frantically. He waited impatiently for us to methodically plod our way down the trail.

"Sean, Honey, you have to wait for us," Suzy said. "Don't scare me like that. You must stay with us. Do you understand?"

"But you're slow!" He yelled in excitement and charged once more to the end of the second switchback.

"Sean!" Suzy was frantic.

"Let him go. Right now, it's pretty safe. We'll corral him when we need to." I was unconvincing.

"Are you sure?" Suzy asked, more in protest.

Before I could answer, our boy yelled at us from the trail visible below. He had already lapped us.

"Come on! Come *on!* You're going too slow! *Hurry!"*

Now we had a need to corral him. I caught his attention before he could charge off again. I yelled at him through cupped hands.

"Sean. *Sean!* You can't go farther ahead of us than that. Wait until you can see us round the corner."

"Ah!" He was whining, then perked up. "But *hurry!"*

We continued our deliberate steps over the fine dirt pulverized by millions of hikers over previous decades. It was wise to check the path. Frequently we stepped over a log in the path, designed to stabilize the trail from erosion by wind or water and to provide a rudimentary step. Nothing on the trail was flat. If we missed tripping over logs, we would soon find the trail disappear into bare rock. The trail was usually paralleled by rows of stones or less often cut timbers, which were useful on the switchbacks to see the direction ahead. Other times the trail was discernable only by watching where the seasoned hikers went. That was a good reason to keep Sean within eyesight.

We rounded the corner to begin the third switchback only to find Sean waiting for us there.

"Sean," I asked. "Why did you come back up?"

"To make you hurry."

"Well, you go down...." I abruptly cut off my sentence. He was already running down to the next turn.

Sean tried to lap us again. That's when Suzy and I in unison yelled, "Stay right there!"

Groans or not, it was obvious to us that at nine years old our boy needed a leash. We admonished him, when we caught up to him, and ordered him to go no more than twenty paces ahead of us. That obstacle was quickly surmounted with irritating ingenuity. He took long strides and counted to twenty repeatedly until he had violated any reasonable interpretation of twenty paces. We encountered our first tunnel carved out of the rock, which briefly fascinated Sean. The descent steepened more for a half mile where we went into another tunnel cut into the rock. Switchbacks became steeper still. Suzy and I were laboring hard now to keep up with Sean, who was so far inexhaustible. We approached a plateau on the trail, suitable for taking a pause in our hike to look down at the bottom of another mini-canyon one thousand feet below us. Then another heart-stopping act happened, and Suzy put her foot down on the whole enterprise.

"Mom, *look!*" Sean said. With excitement he broke away from us and ran full speed to the edge of the canyon's cliff. He hit his brakes with his shoes and skidded to the edge. With his feet less than a foot from the drop, he turned in a most enthusiastic and carefree manner saying, *"Come here and look!"*

We hadn't gone even a mile, yet, when the family's leadership passed to Suzy by sheer force of will. I could not repeat what Suzy said to our boy, and to me, because it would take too long. The temperature was rising already, and this did not help.

We continued our way down with a less than contrite son in tow, eventually coming to the last switchback before reaching the Mile-and-a-Half Resthouse, 1,100 feet below the rim.

The pavilion, built of stacked stone corners, supported an open-air roof with bare pine joists. Timber and rock were the only materials used. A thermometer hung above the pavilion's side entrance to the small, shaded shelter. Steps behind the resthouse descended to an open and flat area where we were able to pause and enjoy the best scenic vista.

We lingered in the shaded area behind the structure to check out the view and to observe the better conduct of Sean, now too preoccupied to recall frightening his mother at the cliff's edge. We pulled out our gorp for the first time, finally realizing why it was important. Low blood sugar was already causing us to shake. A light day hike proved to us how out of physical conditioning we had plunged.

Our next destination was Three Mile Resthouse, another thousand feet below. The farther we descended the more the vegetation changed around us. Rock formations changed as well, revealing hundreds of millions of years of geologic history in just the first mile and a half. Only the Arbuckle Mountains in Oklahoma rivaled such a rich geologic story. We encountered our first mules after leaving the Mile-and-a-Half Resthouse. The narrow trail meant the right of way always went to the mules and their riders. We politely backed up to the wall side of the trail to let them pass, holding still so we would not provoke a cranky mule. A joke going around concerned a rider's question asked of the mule team leader. "Have you ever lost someone on a mule while riding along these steep cliffs?" The leader's answer was classic. "We've never lost a mule."

Our other surprise was seeing the runners along the trail. Many were running in pairs and intent on making it to the North Rim, which was nearly the distance of a marathon. Some runners would even run back—all in a day. On one of my previous hikes across the Grand Canyon, I encountered a pair of hikers who were simply walking rim to rim and back. They made it three quarters of the way on their return before one of the hikers experienced leg cramps. He stayed the entire night in the Cottonwood Campground's outhouse screaming in pain. The canyon was no place for the meek.

Another half mile past the first pavilion the trail grew even steeper. Now our legs, knees, and ankles were getting an increased workout. We continued under a hot sun and even hotter rocks all around us. Rapid flowing streams frequently paralleled our trail. Once we stopped to luxuriate in the cooling effects of canyon water on our bare feet. We watched closely as Sean removed his shoes and socks. Suzy snatched them out of his hands and secured them safely in her lap. Sean, being hot and being all boy, walked to the edge of the water. Turning around to face us, he sat down and let the flow of water lap over his shoulders. Smiling impishly, he reached up with a wet hand to check that he still had his ballcap atop his head. Inspired, I stepped into the cold water up to my knees. I knew that my water-soaked pants would keep me cooler for mere minutes when we resumed our descent. That was fine. There were more streams to come.

After hours of hiking, we arrived at the Three Mile Resthouse, 2,100 feet below the rim. The shaded pavilion was smaller, and the roof was lower than the previous resthouse. The presence of a tap water faucet was a welcome sight to us. Sean was running out of steam. I had forgotten to make Suzy and Sean drink water along the way. They had used some of their water but not enough to prevent dangerous dehydration. While normally you drip sweat, in the canyon the air is so dry that most hikers never get sweaty. The sweat leaves your body as vapor, not water. Your clothes never get wet, so you don't think about the water you are losing. We were quite hot both from the exertion and the increasing temperature. We sat down and drank all our personal warm water. It had to be as hot as the canyon itself, which by now was above 100 degrees. Then we pulled out the food we had packed and ate ravenously. At the pace we were hiking, we calculated that the return trip could end quite late. For the first time I worried that we had not brought enough food to power us back up. The hike back up to the top takes twice as long as going down. Not to worry. We had a mother and wife with us, who brought everything except the tablecloth. Her backpack would be much lighter on the ascension. From our vista, Indian Garden was visible to us, but 1.8 miles away by trail and another 1,000 feet below.

After refilling our water bottles, we headed for our final destination. More mules passed us on the next leg of our hike. Sean had renewed energy and once again challenged our rules to rein him in. Suzy and I were more cognizant of the need to get back up in a reasonable timeframe. We would not waste a lot of time at Indian Garden. Time was already getting ahead of us.

Indian Garden was an oasis in the desert. Cottonwood trees by the score surrounded the area. Not matching the vegetation outside of it, Indian Garden had lush greenery in an otherwise dry environ. A campground was adjacent. It also was home to pump houses that supplied water to campsites and resthouses nearby. Many pavilioned picnic tables were testament to its description as a must-see destination. We were tired. An area to sit down gave us a first chance to unload our packs. We found a picnic table in the shade of those many trees. While resting, we hatched a plan to move with the shade to other tables as needed. Looking among the other shaded tables, we realized then that we would have competition for the shade. Our four Marines were already there and occupied the best shade in the house.

"We can't get away from you," I said in greeting. "You might need to carry us out of here. Any takers?"

They were clearly in a good mood, having rested up for a long time. Bob, still their group social leader, spoke on their behalf.

"We were just getting ready to leave," he said, "otherwise, it's going to be dark before we get back."

"How long do you think it will take you?" I asked.

"I'm not really sure. If we're in this hole, it gets dark before it does on the top at the El Tovar. We figure we need to get out of here... *way* before the official sunset."

I glanced worriedly at Suzy and at Sean.

"I hadn't thought of that. I didn't think that we would need a flashlight."

"You might want to leave now, then," Randy said. What a shock? These were the first words he had spoken.

"I just might take your advice," I replied. "We need to get back for dinner before we starve to death."

"If you need a flashlight," red-headed Jack said, "why don't you take mine? I can pick it up after you get back to the El Tovar."

I pondered his offer for a moment, then Suzy whispered in my ear. "Take it. We may need it to get out. We are late already."

"Thank you, Jack. I'll accept your offer."

Jack pulled out a large Kel-Lite that I had seen policemen carry because they are virtually indestructible. I took it gratefully as I looked at Suzy. Her relief was obvious. I looked at Sean, who was too busy consuming enormous amounts of gorp to look up. He would be fine.

26

TIRED AS WE WERE, WE left soon after our four friends departed for the top. After refilling our water bottles from the tap at Indian Garden, it was off on the long slog back to the top for us. We knew our pace could not match the four Marines, which made for some worry.

"How much food did you bring?" I asked Suzy.

"Plenty. Here. Have a bag of peanuts."

She removed her pack and pulled out a bag each for Sean and me, grabbed a bag of M&Ms for herself, and threw the pack back on her shoulders. The sun overhead was even hotter, as we expected. That meant that the sun would set later than we feared. As scorching as it was, the sun was our friend. Darkness was not. We needed all the daylight possible. The peanuts, then M&Ms, and my own stash of gorp kept Sean leading once again by much more than the agreed to twenty paces. The ascent for me was much easier than going down. Descending was hard on my joints that were pounded by each down step I took. Ascending was much tougher on my leg muscles, but the reduced impact with each step was a welcome relief. We paced ourselves, knowing that the climb out would take twice the time of our descent. Again, Sean started admonishing us to hurry up. Irritating as it was, it did force us to pick up the pace. Suzy was noticeably fatigued, as I'm sure I was, too. We still had more than half of our water after passing by the Three-Mile Resthouse. The sun no longer was overhead but much lower on the horizon. Long shadows cast across the distant rocks. A pair of park rangers making rapid time passed us as we paced up one of the many switchbacks.

"You need to be out by dark," one of them said. "You can't stay here."

"We don't plan to." I tried to assure them. "We're making good time. We have plenty of water."

"If not, we'll be back to chase you out," said the other.

Taking one step at a time, we plodded along behind Sean, who kept an irritating pace both forward and backward on the trail, probably doubling his distance hiked. As we passed the Mile-and-a-Half Resthouse, the sun was missing. I turned on our borrowed Kel-lite. The trail grew darker by the minute. To add to the stress, Sean persisted in getting ahead of us. Suzy, in her anxiety, paced ahead to stop him. I shined the light in her direction, fearful she might stumble on the trail. The further she hiked ahead of me, the less my light could help her. I called to her, but she was out of range. The idea of our separating too far was not a good idea. At least the trail was clearly marked with stones and timbers. In mere minutes the trail would be illuminated only by the stars. I had a flash of fear and pictured Sean and Suzy falling off the edge of the trail.

From out of the darkness came a blow to my head. I fell hard onto the dusty path. Briefly stunned by the impact, I lay still. *Did I just fall off the trail?* The ground was too flat and dusty. No, I was still on the trail. I called for Suzy once more but was unsure if my voice was worth much. I called out no louder than a mumble. I was out of breath. An unfamiliar male voice spoke to me.

"I'll take that light from you now."

I DIDN'T LOSE CONSCIOUSNESS, BUT I was not good for much of anything else. My body would not let me do more than muddled thinking. I stood up—or was I lifted? I couldn't tell. A rag went in my mouth, and a hood went over my head. My hands were behind my back. When I tried to move them, the sharp pull of a restraint around my wrists brought me to more awareness of my situation. Someone rifled through my pockets. One or two people were carefully walking me over rocks, turning me one way and then the other. The walk was smooth for a while, then it became treacherous. I was off the trail. I tried to count my steps to keep myself aware of what was happening. The rough terrain was slow and hazardous. I lost count of how many times I stumbled and they lifted me back up. Clearly, two men were handling me, maybe more. My involuntary escorts seemed to take a long time—perhaps fifteen minutes. Eventually, I came to a stop, and my kidnappers forced me to sit on the ground and lean against an irregular surface. A lock clicked. My captors left me alone.

I had never been restrained like this before. I couldn't move my arms or stand up. The panic of claustrophobia took hold. My heart raced, and my breathing became rapid. I restrained an urge to struggle against my bonds, knowing that my efforts would only cause my panic to increase.

I trained for this. It was in the Air Force when I went to Winter Survival School near Spokane, Washington, at Fairchild Air Force Base. Winter training seemed ironic, since my base of assignment was in hot South Texas. We had prisoner of war training. They tortured us in clever ways that would not leave a mark. I learned quickly that the safest route was to go into the deep recesses of my mind and stay there. Back then, I did algebra problems and prayed to God for patience to wait until it ended. We all knew that in training it would end at some point. Now it was different.

My algebra this time was a bit rusty. So, I asked God to remove my panic. Having returned to church, I didn't hesitate to ask God for help. After some effort I managed to spit out the rag given me by my kidnappers. Slowly, my position and my fetters escaped my mind, allowing me to think what to do next. I had no way to determine the length of time I waited. I did not know where Sean and Suzy were. I had to fight that panic along with that of my own captivity. Were they looking for me? Were they in a panic? Perhaps they fell off the trail. They could be hurt, or they could be safely hidden from these men. A third wave of panic grabbed me. They would be frightened for me. Would they reach safety without me? Did they need help? I prayed more, restraining my urge to ask God for vengeance—right here on this spot.

No one talked to me. The bag placed on my head was still there. Was it darker still? Were Suzy and Sean lost in the dark? I noticed my hot moist breath inside the bag. It was stale recycled air that I kept breathing over and over. I nodded my head several times to scoop fresh oxygenated air into my bag. It helped only a little. My makeshift legionnaire's cap was now heating me up. It, too, was captive in the bag over my head.

I tried to remain calm, even dozing off briefly, but startled awake to familiar voices. Suzy urgently hollered my name, not far from where I was. Sean frantically called his mother. Suzy loudly hollered in reply. A male voice interrupted her. Suzy was not one to raise her voice. To cry out as she was doing so was alarming. Her voice suddenly changed from threatening to fearful. She was defending Sean to the limit, but in the dark her voice quickly ceased. Only the cries of Sean were left in my ears. They were approaching deliberately because suddenly another a body blow triggered the strangely agonizing cries of a mature male voice. There was a brief silence, then the cursing began in earnest—words Sean had never heard. Then more shouts from Sean, another body blow, and more screams of agony and colorful cursing.

Sean's kicking the crap out of him in the dark... defending his mother.

Sean protested, until Suzy again raised her voice. Their voices drew nearer, until I recognized the steps of a grown man, who dropped them on the ground beside me. There was the familiar click of a lock and all was silence, except the footsteps of a kidnapper leaving us to our darkness.

"Rob, is that you?" Suzy whispered between panicked breaths.

"I'm here," I whispered, trying to sound as calm as possible. "Sean?"

Sean's hand reached out to my tethered arms. His hand trembled. He was too terrified to utter a sound.

"That kid *better* be here," a male voice said, then uttered a string of curses to describe our son. "I've got plans for you, you little brat!"

Suzy shouted at him. "You wouldn't *dare* touch my son...!" The man smothered her voice with a sudden grip on her face. I futilely struggled to break loose, enraged by the man.

"One more word out of you, lady, and I will take it out on your precious little darling here. I hate little children, and I hate you. It will give me pleasure to make you wish you had kept quiet."

"What do you want?" I asked.

The blow to my head was instant. Thankfully, in the darkness, the impact glanced off my head without real affect. I wasn't going to let him know that and fell limp to fake unconsciousness. As I did so, I quickly extended my right foot against Suzy's leg. I tapped with my shoe toe the familiar movement we so often did at night in bed. She quickly and subtly moved her knee toward me.

"You will shut up and do as we tell you. You understand, Amity?" he said, angrily pausing for my reply. Impatient, he yelled again, *"Answer me!"*

I rapidly tapped Suzy's leg in the hope that I could avoid another blow. She was always a quick learner. She didn't fail me this time either.

"You've *killed* him!" Suzy screamed. "What do you *want?"*

The man appeared startled by the sudden assertiveness of this mother and wife, who was seemingly unafraid to defy his demands. Suzy's response so sufficiently shocked him that he turned on the flashlight and pulled the hood off my head to get a better look. My fake unconscious state had to end at some point, but I held my breath as long as I could to continue my charade. I opened one eye to take this opportunity to see what surroundings we were in. The man's back was to me, so I opened the other eye. His flashlight gave me a quick mental picture of where we were. Our confines were underneath a rock shelf that cantilevered over a bit of flat ground made softer by dirt and rounded river rocks. It appeared to be a spot selected for shelter from the weather with nearby access to water. Did that mean we should plan on an extended stay? I hoped not. The river rocks suggested to me that we were in a place subject to eons of intermittent rain flow. *What genius thought of this spot?*

I looked at Suzy in the flashlight's rapid movements. She was strapped down as I was. Sean was clinging to his mother's right arm and trembling in fright, still not uttering a word. The man held the flashlight to our faces, which made it hard to see the next time I dared to reopen my eyes. With one movement of the light toward Sean, I identified the creep. He was tall, stocky, with a long stringy ponytail.

"Hello, Phillip," I said. "What in hell do you think you are doing?

Just as I guessed, he did not strike me again. Because he could see me, and I could see him, he no longer had the guts to hit me. This only confirmed my first impression that Phillip Snart was a cowardly weakling. Thoughts raced through my brain. *He said he had friends out to help him. Were they as gutless? The four men we met were Marines. Was that their job—to do the dirty work he couldn't do with his own hands? Why did he care about us?*

Just as suddenly as I popped the question and stared into his cowardly face, Snart turned off his stolen flashlight. He no longer had to look me in the eye. I braced for what would come next. The Kel-Lite to my head did not miss this time.

27

STARS SPUN IN MY HEAD but not like in cartoons. These were the stars of a dream from my childhood, returning to my unconscious. When I was five years old, I suffered many hallucinations in my sleep. Not knowing the difference, I related them to my Kindergarten chums as normal dreams. I found them interesting, not nightmarish. Years later I discovered that what my friends called nightmares were nothing like my frequent hallucinations. One such experience returned at this moment.

I was in outer space as a child. Immune from the hazards of a vacuum, my dream suddenly thrust me into a scene of the most serene beauty. I could only describe it years later as a glimpse of Heaven. I slowly drifted in a large circle. Within this circle was the most beautiful spiral galaxy cluster of millions of stars. Bright against the dark void of space, the stars glowed a haunting combination of blue and red. They did not blur into purple. Instead, each one of the millions of stars shown individually in their distinctive color of red or blue. I could pick out each one. As I circled this galaxy at a rate much like the second hand on a clock, a voice began to speak to me. Her voice was calming and soft as it repeated the same words.

"Keep going. Keep going."

As a child her words did not calm me but distressed me. I woke up from my dream very disturbed and depressed. I shared with my mother the details of this vision. She listened and comforted me. I went securely back to sleep and chalked it up to another interesting dream that doesn't happen in real life.

A year later, my pediatrician recommended that I have a tonsillectomy. My parents, obedient to the suggestions of physicians, scheduled me to undergo the procedure popular among all the second graders at my school. With promises of getting to eat ice cream all day long after giving up two tonsils and some adenoids, we got up early in the morning to head for the hospital. Soon I found myself on a table in a strange room surrounded by men and women wearing surgical masks. A large bright light blinded me from above, before a nurse told me to close my eyes. The nurse was holding a common kitchen strainer which contained a surgical sponge. In her other hand she held an eye dropper.

"Hi, Robbie. I'm your nurse. I'm going to put you to sleep. Okay?"

I nodded my head. My eyes were wide open to make sure I would know what she did next.

"I'm going to put some drops in this strainer here. I will hold it close to your mouth and nose, and I want you to blow, over and over. Okay?"

I blew. Without air, I inhaled and smelled the interesting effects of ether. My nurse kept slowly talking to me.

"Keep blowing. Keep blowing. Keep blowing...."

I was back in outer space and orbiting my galaxy in my little piece of Heaven. A female voice kept softly speaking to me, but I was unable to tell if she said, "keep blowing" or "keep going." It didn't matter. I was in Heaven, and this time it was peaceful, familiar, and comforting to be back with God. Looking back, it was the most wonderful dream of my childhood.

Now my dream was back as I lay unconscious on the rocky and dusty floor of our canyon hideaway. I was now orbiting my heavenly galaxy of blue and red stars as an adult. I did not need protection from the void of space. I knew I was with God again. That voice calmly called to me.

"Keep going. Keep going. Keep going...."

Suddenly, my galaxy went away, and I was left floating in a room with all sorts of household objects floating in suspension before my eyes. I reached to grab a windup clock, but my hand only passed through it. I grabbed at a fork, but it stayed out of reach. A hundred objects floated in front of me but remained unreachable. I was not in control of anything around me. My frustration caused me to cry out in fear.

My fear grew when the objects disappeared and in their place a wall came into view with paisley teardrop-shaped motif repeated a thousand times. It was all I could see in any direction. Puzzled by these interesting shapes, I stared at them for too long. Then the horror began. First a single teardrop grew teeth and began to flip its tail. It began a horrendous screeching growl, now spinning counterclockwise. It continued a further metamorphosis as it spun itself into a little dragon. The dragon continued its growl, even when I willed it to stop. Soon enough, a second teardrop began the same transformation, and two were screeching at each other. The cacophony grew louder still. Eventually all the teardrops were spinning, a growling mob of angry paisley dragons, which turned their cacophony into roar of a thousand. The dragons one by one lifted off the wall and became three-dimensional threats. Like the household items that floated in the air before my eyes, they were unreachable. As I feared, because I was unable to grab them, they began coming aggressively closer until all hope was lost.

I must be in Hell!

The hell ended abruptly in an unending void of dark nothingness.

28

DAYLIGHT WAS SLOW TO COME to Snart's hiding place. I'd drifted into real sleep at some point. I knew I needed to rest if I had any chance of getting us out of this inexplicable captivity. My hallucinations were still fresh memories. Thinking back to the blow to my head, I spotted a small pool of blood on my right arm. It was enough to show that Snart hit me hard but not enough to worry about a gash in my head needing stitches immediately. My headache was less when I sat still. I was able to communicate in whispers with Suzy and Sean.

"Suzy? Sean?"

"We're here," Suzy replied. "Are you okay? I tapped on your leg with my foot and called to you all night. That man must have hit you solidly."

"Yeah, I guess he did."

"Why is Mister Snart doing this, Dad?" Sean's voice spoke of worry.

"Sean told me who he is, Rob. Why does he want to hurt us?"

"I'm not sure, except I know Snart didn't start any close friendship with me when we first met or at Camp Classen."

"He's the man who said those vile things about John?"

"Yes. I hope he doesn't wish me dead, too."

Immediately, I regretted my words. The renewed look of worry on Sean's face broke my heart. I could add it to the list of words and actions in my life that I would regret for a lifetime. I had to start thinking before I acted. One mistake while we were tethered could indeed be fatal.

Our best stroke of luck was that Sean was not tied up. Snart, figuring correctly, knew that a nine-year-old boy would not run away from this mother in need. As big as the canyon was, there was nowhere to go anyway. I guessed we were far from the trail. If we got loose and escaped, we had no idea which direction to start. They could hold us captive just as easily without tying us up, although we might be able to kill them before we died ourselves from heat stroke, dehydration, and starvation.

Although yesterday had been a hot and sweaty experience, and we had sweated more than enough water to be dehydrated, we were all still needing relief. We told Sean to go outside and to do whatever he needed to do. "Mister Snart will be out there to stop you but tell him you have to go pee really bad."

Before he reluctantly went outside, I remembered to give him one more request. We needed some information.

"Sean, until we find out where the trail is, you come back inside," I whispered. "It's easy to get lost out here. But when you are out there, look around and tell me what you see. Is there more than Mister Snart outside? If so, do the others look familiar? Where are they outside? Look for the trail."

I feared I had assigned him too many jobs when all he wanted was to relieve himself. Sean crept cautiously to the edge of the rock overhang. He looked to his right and his left, then stepped to the left. By the sounds he made, he did not go far. When he was through doing his business, Sean took the initiative to return to our location and proceed to the right. Our first question was answered immediately.

"What's this twit doing out here?" an unfamiliar voice asked. "Hey, kid. Get over here."

The voice was clear as a bell, seemingly in the overhang with us. The rocks, I knew, could play tricks with sound, so I hoped Sean could report to us the voice's proximity.

Come on, Sean. Look around. Who are you talking to? Be careful.

"I had to pee," Sean said in a raised voice. He started to cry, which was unusual. He rarely cried except when he cut or bruised something. This had to be nerves or the child's art of manipulating an adult.

"Okay, kid." The silence that followed hopefully gave Sean a chance to provide us with more useful information.

"Are you done, then?" A second voice asked the question. This meant there were at least three men to contend with.

Keep talking, son. Keep it up.

"No," he said. I could practically hear the tears running down his cheeks. "My mom needs to pee really bad, too."

"Well, go back and tell her to go," the first man said.

"She can't," said Sean. "She's all tied up."

A string of curses erupted, further educating Sean as to the ways men can get angry.

"What did you do?" the first man asked in a loud voice, but he wasn't talking to Sean. "Did you leave them staked out in there? So why is this blasted kid out here running around?"

Then the other man directed his anger at Sean. "Get your business done, kid, then get back with your mom. We'll take care of her later."

Keep going, Partner.

There was no more conversation for two or three minutes, until the second man spoke up.

"Toilet paper? Why do you need toilet paper? You're on a camp out. You don't need any toilet paper."

"Come here, kid," the other man said. "See that cottonwood tree over there? Use the leaves on that tree for toilet paper."

Keep your eyes open, Sean. You're doing great.

Sean knew nothing about using leaves as a substitute, so I wasn't sure if this would end well. Suzy and I whispered as much to each other as we could between listening opportunities. We studied each other's restraints and determined it required a knife to cut us loose from the zip ties. The morning sun revealed that we were locked to spiral tiedown stakes. The weakest link we agreed was the zip tie, but the tiedowns could also be our ticket out. With our hands still behind our backs, the leverage to do anything was in short supply.

Their voices began again. Every word gave us clues. "Are you done, kid?"

"Yes." Sean whimpered. "Can I go back to Mom?"

"Get outta here, kid. Go!"

Sean appeared around the corner of our hideaway, a look of relief on his face. He ran over and sat down between us. I wanted to put my index finger to my lips, but being tied up, I instead made a silent shushing with my lips. Sean nodded and put his lips to my ear.

"I saw the road," he whispered. "I saw it when I went to the tree."

"Good, Partner. Were they the four men we met again yesterday?"

"There were only two... and really big, Dad."

"And Mister Snart?"

"I think they talked to him, but he was somewhere else. I couldn't see him."

"The two men were big," I said, turning to Suzy. "That doesn't sound like our friends from yesterday."

"No, Dad, these were new."

"What are they wearing?"

Sean thought for a moment. He was struggling for a way to describe it.

"They look like G.I. Joe."

Suzy and I were amazed at his powers of observation. He had been fearless, likely because he had no idea what was at stake. We remained puzzled trying to find any reason we would be targeted for anything. Perhaps my chance meeting of Phil Snart months ago was arranged. But what for? It could have been something I teased him about. But it couldn't be enough to have two goons helping him out. Was it some sort of exercise of a militia group gone rogue? And where was Snart? Sean heard him but could not see him.

"Hey, kid!" one of the G.I. Joes said. "Come get this for your mom."

With urging from us, telling him that it was okay, Sean cautiously stepped out into the morning sunlight, then returned with an empty beer bottle. Suzy looked with horror at the worthless article in Sean's hands. These men we either clueless or purposely mocking her plight.

"I understand the concept," she said in loud frustration, "but how in blazes can I use it tied up?"

From around the corner came a chuckle of a reply. "Make do, darlin'."

Without hands it would not work for her. It wouldn't work for either of us. Suzy raised her head suddenly, a look of a breakthrough in her expression. Suzy asked the most brilliant and obvious question to Sean. In a whisper she asked her boy.

"Sean, did you bring a knife? Is there one in your pocket?"

"A little one," he said sheepishly.

Suzy had scolded him many times for playing with his grandfather's boyhood jackknife. It wasn't a little one. She motioned him to lean his ear to her lips. "Can you carefully cut the straps on my hands?"

Sean, visibly upset to get busted for breaking a rule, slowly pulled the folded knife from his pocket. He tried repeatedly to open the blade, but the age of the knife and the small size of Sean's fingers worked against him. Each time he tried and failed meant a greater chance that Snart or one of his goons would make their presence known. Finally, with a good hook on a fingernail and a little side move of his tongue, Sean pulled the blade open. I knew that Suzy's father had always worked at keeping the knife sharp, but with Sean's clandestine use of it, I wondered how well it could now cut an industrial-sized zip tie. Our boy quietly moved behind his mother.

"Sean, make sure the sharp end is away from my wrist, okay?" she whispered, while leaning forward to expose her bound hands.

The warnings from his mother unnerved him, causing his hands to tremble. The zip tie left little room to get a knife blade under her skin.

"Sean!" I said urgently. "Don't cut there. Go between Mom's hands."

He moved the blade, then looked at me for approval. I shook my head. He moved to a different spot. I nodded the go ahead. Much to our surprise, the knife sliced clean through with little effort. Suzy carefully took the pocketknife out of Sean's hand and quickly moved to cut my wrists free. In turn she folded the knife and put it in my right front pocket.

"Thank goodness," she said and grabbed the relief bottle, then glanced at it and dropped it in disgust.

She made a bold move to exit to the left where Sean had previously gone unnoticed. A long minute later, she quietly returned. Sean stood uncomfortably near us until I was finished using the bottle. Fearful of someone getting suspicious, I directed Sean to empty the bottle and return it. I wanted him to tell me again what was going on.

"Gross!" he said as I handed him the heavy bottle.

Our boy exited to the right, carrying his package gingerly by the neck. No one spoke for nearly a minute, which gave us hope that they had gone. Then Sean began talking, but it was too far from us to understand.

Was someone grilling him? Would he inadvertently give away our secret?

"Maybe they're feeding him," I said, no longer whispering. "I could use some water."

Suzy took the chance to get into our packs, still nestled next to us. We each took a long drink from the bottle, then replaced the water in our pack along with the cut ties to hide the evidence. It was hard to remember to keep our hands behind us. We needed to look tied up until Sean returned to us safely.

We lost all sense of time, likely because Sean was still missing, and we did not hear a sound outside. We needed to eat something, or the chances of an escape would be cut short. Suzy again decided to get into our pack and pull out our gorp and a package of salted peanuts. We quickly wolfed the gorp down, chewing frantically. I stuffed the peanuts in my left pocket, only to discover another bag of peanuts there. I grabbed the bottle of water again, filled my mouth, sloshed it around to minimize evidence of our gorp feeding frenzy, and swallowed. Suzy did the same. She once more stashed the water bottle in the pack. Sitting back down, we waited for Sean and prepared to pounce.

29

OUR PLAN WAS SIMPLE. SUZY said that Sean's rescue had to be our priority. I agreed but suggested that she should be the one who would get him out of harm's way. I could then either bring back help or come on my own to get her.

"Sean has to be on the trail with another family or a park ranger before any other plan, okay?"

I spoke softly into Suzy's ear. "We'll know more of what's possible when Sean gets back." An unanswered question came to mind. "Have you seen any weapons on them?"

"No, just a flashlight and the hood they put over your head."

What is with these guys? No weapons. They seemingly want to kidnap us, but planning must have gone awry. And where is our buddy Snart? Did he screw up? And where is our son?

The sun rose to a much higher angle before Sean abruptly appeared in our shaded hideaway. Suzy started to reach out to him, but I quickly turned and said sternly, "Don't move!" She stopped, then hurriedly moved her hands again behind her back. A large man in camouflage, wearing a bandana as a mask, stepped into our space. From around the corner the camouflaged bandit pulled another man into view. He was similarly bound with his hands behind his back and a hood atop his head. Without fanfare, his captor pushed the man to his knees and kicked him to the ground at Suzy's feet.

"Got a present for you," the man said in a deep voice. "Enjoy the company."

The big man left as quickly as he arrived. It was hard to tell if this new victim at our feet was unconscious or not. His designer jeans and khaki shirt were a contrast to camouflage of the captor who delivered him to us. We spoke to him and waited, but he gave no response.

"Sean," I said, "can you take that hood off his head, please?"

Gingerly, Sean removed the light nylon cover from under his head where he lay prone on the dirt. Sean jumped in surprise, which answered another question.

"Mister Snart!" Sean looked at me with surprise and trepidation. After all, this was the man he kicked in the shins multiple times less than a day before.

"Well now I know where old Phillip went." I couldn't help laughing. "The original kidnapper himself. Kick 'em, Sean!"

Obediently, Sean laid a toe into the side of his leg as hard as he could. The scream that came out of the hood was not normal. Primitive sounds of human agony only emanate with severe wounds. Snart's cursing followed immediately. Suzy had had enough. She jumped from her fake bondage onto her knees so she could look down on Snart's face. His face was drawn tight in agony, but nonetheless, she grabbed it in sweet revenge.

"Shut your filthy mouth!"

Snart responded exactly as she demanded. In the silence that followed, we four captives could hear the laughter of men around the corner. If they had been friends of his, it was now in the past.

"Have you guessed that Phillip must have FUBAR'd this?" I asked Suzy. I leaned over to a now alert Phil Snart. "You picked on the wrong child and mother… and right now I'm the only person standing between you and my family. No more screw-ups, or I'll kill you myself."

We looked each other in the eye for a prolonged time before he averted his gaze. I continued, enunciating each word clearly.

"You're going to tell me what's going on, and then you'll tell me who and what your ex-buddies are. If you don't, we all three will kick your leg until you do. It's obvious your ex-buddies would enjoy that. Tell me why?"

I waited in vain for a response. This was a bizarre turn of events. Our original captor was now ours to do with as we wished. The two other kidnappers, who didn't want to be unmasked, were unaware we were untethered. Our primary goal to ensure the safety of our boy was now more likely to succeed. Suzy and I knew, without ever saying it, that it meant we would die before we would let harm come to him. Our problem was that we couldn't plan our escape when we had this little prig of an excuse for a man in our presence.

I turned again to face Snart and repeated my question. "Tell me!"

I still got no reply.

"Sean, kick 'em again."

That was all it took. As Sean took his stance to deliver another blow, the prig of a man started talking.

"I screwed up," he said.

"Tell me something I don't know." I motioned Sean to be ready with another kick.

"No!" Snart said preemptively. "I'm talking, okay? I wasn't supposed to take your wife or this brat of yours. Don't kick me again, please!"

I looked at Sean, who seemed to relish this kicking a little too much now. I motioned him to take a step back. I moved closer to my new informant.

"So, why did you take these two? You already had me locked up in this pretty lousy hidey-hole here."

"I was afraid they would alert someone, and I panicked. Now I'm toast… just like you."

"What does that mean? Toast?"

"They want to hide the evidence of killing you."

"Killing me." It was the burning question I finally got to ask. "Why me?"

"I think I identified the wrong man for them. It's not you they're after."

"Who's this *they* that we're talking about?"

"I can't tell…."

"Sean…." I said.

Our son jumped to his feet immediately and stepped forward, cocking his leg.

I held out my hand to stop him. "No!"

"Sean, stay back," Suzy said. The anger in her voice would scare anyone. "The next kick is mine."

"Remember the Weather Underground?" Snart asked. The question kept Suzy's shoe away.

"Sure, I do," I replied. "The antiwar creeps who bombed the U.S. Capitol and the State Department. Killed three of their own people when they accidentally blew themselves up. They sucked at terrorism. Go on."

"These guys say they're former Weathermen."

"And how do you fit in?"

"This was my initiation to join. I had to kill a war criminal."

"You weren't really an Army Medic in Vietnam, were you?"

"No." He lowered his gaze downward in shameful confession. "I made it up to get inside veterans' heads."

"Veterans' heads? What can that achieve?"

"My recruiters said it was a way to get veterans to talk... and help identify a target."

"You're pretty lousy at it, don't you think?"

"Maybe so," Snart said, downcast again. "How did you figure it out?"

"You hardly knew me, and you were spilling your guts with boasts. Medics don't do anesthesia or surgery. That was a lie. Then you bragged about being such a life saver while belittling me for my service. Who among veterans does that? The real giveaway was when you said *OORAH!* That's what the Marines shout. The Army's is *HOOAH.* Subtle difference, but an Army Medic would not have made a dumb mistake like that."

"I hate all you warmongering fools. You're a loser."

"As losers go, your efforts suck just as much as the Weathermen. Be glad you haven't blown yourself up like those other boneheads."

"I'm not feeling good," he said abruptly. "I'm going to be sick. Please untie me."

"Not a chance, you little prick!" I was growing angrier. "If you call out a warning to those cavemen out there, they will never get the pleasure of killing you."

I pulled out Sean's old jack knife and put it next to Snart's throat. He flinched at the blade's close proximity. He squirmed over his whole body, but his throat did not move out of fear of the knife's sharp point.

"I learned how to kill a man with my bare hands when I was in Air Force Survival School," I whispered, "and we practiced on live animals. But don't worry. This knife will be much faster."

30

ONE QUESTION STILL HAUNTED ME. Why weren't the men outside keeping an eye on us? They seemed conflicted about what they were doing. These giant creeps were perfect examples of people who sucked at terrorism and had no military experience. They needed a checklist of emergency procedures because, for them, the stuff had definitely hit the fan.

We let Snart lie still on the dirt, keeping him tied up. The two creeps outside failed to lock him to the tiedown anchors. I read once that it is difficult to stand up without using your hands, so I decided to test Snart's threat level.

"Phillip, old buddy," I said, "if you can stand up on your own, while tied up, we can let you stretch or whatever you need."

At first confused, he looked at me quizzically before deciding he understood my suggestion correctly. He began flailing in the dirt, struggling to put himself in a position to lift himself up by his legs. He flinched at each movement of his battered leg. Sean's kick alone would make it impossible, but he could never position himself to where he could attempt to stand up. He was fortunately tethered to the dust on the ground.

"Help me up, will you?" he asked, rolling around on the floor struggling to get to his knees. "Your son kicked me in the shin last night. My foot's purple this morning. It hurts when I'm standing. It feels like all the blood in my body's going down there."

"Well, Phil. I'm afraid if you can't stand yourself up, you're screwed. I'm not going to help you."

"When I get home from this, I'm going to sue you and your wife and your son. That brat did serious injury to my leg."

"You were better off before you grabbed me," Suzy replied. "Sean loves his mother. You have a son."

"Yes, Tanner."

"Tanner's a sweet boy, I'm sure," Suzy said. "I sure hope he would defend his mother from you."

"Tanner Snart," Sean said with a giggle. "It sounds like a funny name."

"Don't you make fun of my son," Snart said.

"I'm sure he is a fine boy... who's not overly proud of you right now," Suzy replied.

"Not to change the subject, Phil," I said, "but why are those two not watching over us?"

"You have no place to hide," Snart said with smug satisfaction. "You can't get out of here going left. It's a steep wall there with no outlet. You come out to the right, and we're right there to block you."

"But they don't want us to see their faces." I pointed out.

"It's a fad, I guess. They never told me to cover up," Snart replied.

"So, who's the target you meant to kill? What's his name?"

"I don't know. Your name is all I got. The pilot I was supposed to kill flew a B-52. He was chosen at random from a list we have. He flew a lot of bombing runs in Vietnam. I think they called it Operation Arc Light. He killed a lot of people, and we want to kill him. Sorry for you, you're now included. What do you baby killers call it? Collateral damage?"

Snart was odd in the way this conversation was going. He vacillated between going to the confessional to seek forgiveness, then giving his blessing to committing mortal sins. I pictured him as a boy bullied in school, ignored for summer jobs, and deserted on dates. I never asked him if he had a wife. Perhaps Tanner was the only family he had. The poor kid, despite his priggish father, seemed nice enough—and Sean liked him. I asked him one more critical question.

"So, they're going to kill you and me. What will they do with Sean and his mother?"

Phil Snart's true stripes came out with one last callous answer.

"They're going to kill us all and leave us out here to rot where no one will ever find us."

"Well, that's never going to happen." Before he could react, I pulled out a washcloth from my backpack and stuffed it into his mouth. He registered a panicked claustrophobic expression. I had no sympathy for him, as long as he kept on breathing. I didn't wish to smother the prick.

"Now we can plan our escape," I whispered.

The sun quickly warmed us up even in mid-morning. I judged the time by using the shadows as a gauge. I took the liberty to go out of our hidey-hole and scout out the left side. It did indeed look impassable, but I remembered that Snart had chosen it himself. I concluded that he probably had often gotten in over his head in many things. He likely didn't know diddly squat about terrain or selecting hide outs. For hours in our dark captivity, I assumed that he knew what he was doing. Then when two more men showed up, I based my caution upon the principle that there were two men who knew more about what they were doing. Instead, it turned out to be the Grand Canyon equivalent of the three Weather Underground members who blew themselves up. Suzy and I discussed various options and came to one overriding strategy. Although we agreed about their incompetence, we had to be correct in our actions, or we would not get out alive.

I checked occasionally on our friend Phil. He remained panicked but was still breathing. Every time Suzy got soft-hearted and wanted to help him, I reminded her that he wanted to kill Sean, not just us. That did the trick for about an hour before I had to repeat the words "kill Sean."

Things we had on our side were in plenty. Our adversary was incompetent. They had displayed no weapons. They believed the left side of their hideaway was impassable. We had rocks as clubs, which at least made us even, since they had them, too, and surely, they knew how to use them. I learned a great deal of defensive martial arts from my sparring buddy, Jay Goodwin. I learned how to kill live animals with my bare hands, which I prayed would not come in handy. Lastly, they planned to kill our son. That was never going to happen.

Just after we assessed all our strengths, I glanced at the steel tiedowns that our captors had screwed into the rocky soil to hold us down. If we could remove them, they would be formidable extensions of my fist. Swinging a heavy coiled piece of steel like a mace could give us an advantage in a first assault. I was mindful of the warning about any weapon. Don't ever let your enemy take your weapon from you. That was why baseball bats and other clubs so often did more harm to the good guy. Firing a gun from ten feet away was a safer way to defend yourself. Sadly, we had no option. I weighed the merits of using this tool with some reservation.

31

ONE CRITICAL ELEMENT WAS NOT on our side. I didn't know what I was doing. My plan was an untested prototype. Our whole plot was predicated upon their being more stupid than we were. People tend to be predictable. They hadn't returned to bring us anything to eat or drink. My guess was that they hadn't planned on an extended stay any more than we had. Perhaps we had one other advantage. If they were out of food and water, we had the advantage of Suzy's last-minute addition of snack foods. Water was another issue, which prodded me to get our whole plan going before we became delirious from dehydration.

I stepped outside with Sean, turning left into the high rocks in front of us. I guessed that it would not require much of a climb to get a vantage point to see the men. Hopefully, there were only two, but we hadn't confirmed that. I turned to Sean in a whisper.

"Partner, remember our obstacle course at Camp Classen?"

He nodded his head.

"Do you remember that we also like to play throw, not catch?"

He nodded once more and laughed quietly.

"Sean, I want you to do both today." I pointed up about twenty feet above to a ledge of sedimentary rock with about four feet of depth—big enough for a boy to stand on comfortably. "Climb that wall to the ledge and then play throw. We don't need to escape from this place by climbing up to that flat spot. What we need is artillery. Can I load you up with some good throwing rocks? I won't ask you to hold your throws today. I want the hardest fastest that you can throw a rock. Look at those two men and think of their heads as catcher's mitts. Knock 'em out or at least knock 'em down. And keep throwing rocks as long as you can see them moving."

Sean looked again at the short climb. To a nine-year-old it was high.

"Remember how I lifted you up at the obstacle course to speed you along? I'm going to do that again to get you up there fast."

"Okay, Dad. Do we do it now?"

"Not just yet but keep an eye out for any good rocks. When we are ready. Pick them up... as many as you can fit in your pockets."

We quietly went back to the hidey-hole where Suzy sat untethered and unconcerned about Snart lying on his side. He was still breathing, which was all I cared about. Suzy already knew what her job was. Once the artillery was successful, she was to help Sean climb down from his ledge and head toward the trail that was somewhere beyond the cottonwood tree. This plan would require some fluid thinking. Just because the trail was visible didn't mean we could get to it directly. At least at this point, if things worked as we planned, our boy would be out of harm's way.

My job was to spring out of our hidey-hole, turn right, and stun them with a single assault reminiscent of a counterintuitive Nathan Bedford Forrest charge. We assumed that the men still believed we were bound and held by steel anchors. They would not be prepared for a sudden assault. Two against one was not to my favor. I would have to neutralize the first quickly. *Please Sean. Don't miss.* I didn't want to kill anyone unless I had to.

I removed the exceptionally long and strong laces from Snart's boots. Putting one in each pants pocket, I assembled our team of three Amitys to execute the mission. Suzy and I led Sean to a reasonable spot where his climb to the ledge had the best footing.

"Sean, this is the same height as that obstacle course." I was lying. "What I need you to do is get on that ledge up there but keep your head low so they can't see you."

"Do I lie down?"

"Yes. Keep as low as possible." Sean started gathering round river rocks to carry in his pockets. "They are close by but wait until I yell the word 'NOW' before you stand up. With your best pitching arm, I want you to throw bean balls at the men until you run out of rocks. Then, I want you to come down from that ledge as fast as you can. Mom is here to help you down. You do what she says after that. Okay?"

"Okay." He stepped over to the rock face.

He had grown since Camp Classen. I was weak from our ordeal. I relied upon his natural climbing abilities more than I anticipated. I managed to boost him by his rear end and then his feet to get him above the halfway point. Suzy and I huddled underneath, uncertain of his chances of making the next ten feet on his own. The location we selected paid off because the rock face angled at that point. Sean could lean slightly forward, adding assurance to his discomfort of the height. After taking a nervous breath, he secured a couple of good footholds and reached the ledge to his left. He confidently looked down at us and pointed beyond the ledge, then put his finger to his lips. He had spotted them already. With his stealthy moves like a pursuing snake, he slithered his way further onto the ledge, turned his head to us, and gave us a thumbs up.

With Suzy watching from below, I left Sean to begin my assault. I stepped over to Snart, who still lay prone in the dirt. I had made up my mind. Looking behind Snart's head, I reached down to a tiedown anchor and began unscrewing it from the rocky ground that had held it so firmly. The tip of the screw came to a point that looked promising for doing some major damage. I turned the handle and re-gripped it, so that when I took my first swing, the sharp point would be the first contact on my opponent. I turned around to see Phillip Snart struck with fear and looking at my newly discovered weapon. With a big grin, I walked over and straddled his upper torso to stare into his frightened eyes.

"You won't need this anymore," I said and pulled the rag out of his mouth. He gasped for air but made no other sounds as I put the wet rag in his shirt pocket. If he cried out now, it wouldn't matter because I was already running around to the right and toward my captors.

I expected the path before me to be a gentle slope. To my surprise, it was extremely steep. It delayed my timing. I could not build up the speed I needed to tackle the first man I encountered. The incline leveled off just as the first man came into view. The man that I was about to tackle was the size and look of a Sumo wrestler. My adrenalin was pumping. His had not started. On the fly I yelled out to Sean.

"Now!"

My voice echoed off the towering formations, causing Mr. Sumo's attention to turn in the wrong direction from my voice. He confused my actual location, which gave me another two seconds of unseen approach before impact. A rock suddenly ricocheted off Mr. Sumo's shoulder, causing him to turn his eyes further away from my approach. I swung my steel weapon at his head, making a solid impact with the tiedown anchor. The steel point hit him on his temple, tearing a nice gash forward of his right ear. When my whole body made impact, I learned that the man was even bigger than I earlier imagined. The pain of steel's impact caused him to stumble as I collided with him. My body fell with him to a hard impact on the ground. He landed face down, thanks in part to my own strategically placed position on impact. To my horror the tiedown anchor broke free of my grip and rolled a few feet away. For a moment he was stunned. I reached my stronger right arm under his thick neck and around his throat, locked my wrist with my other arm, and applied maximum pressure. As expected, the thickset man instantly objected. Flailing his arms and feet franticly, he first rolled left. The jagged rock bore into my back for a split second before he rolled the opposite way. I took advantage of a slight downward slope and let this rolling motion carry his inertia full circle. This allowed me to remain atop him in the struggle. He rolled again in the opposite direction. This time the slope in his roll worked against me, ending with him on top and our backs toward the ground. His size was frightening. To make it worse, I could feel the steel coils of my tiedown anchor pressing into my back. His weight was slowly squeezing the air out of my lungs. Rocks gouged into the muscles in my back, as he ground me into the jagged surface. Still kicking and grabbing me with his hands, I held my strangle hold secure. At some point one of us was going to run out of air. He was definitely going to be running out of blood to his head soon. His head wound copiously dripped bright red blood onto my shoulder, chin, and throat. He got a solid grip on my stronger right arm. I held on for dear life. To my relief his grip weakened, and my arm went free. I continued to keep a tight grip on his thick neck while attempting to roll out from under him. I was desperate for a breath and making little progress in extricating myself from his limp mass.

Another man appeared above us. Without saying a word, the second man clamped onto my arm and wrenched my death grip from his companion. In lifting me off, my other arm ground its way out from under the neck of a large and limp head. Then the other attacker extracted the rest of me from under Mr. Sumo's enormous and limp body. He lifted me to a standing position. This new Goliath raised his fist to finish me off when another rock came spinning into his temple and left eye. Another rock flew harmlessly by, but the blood was already flowing down his cheek and onto the rocky ground. I looked for Sean and couldn't believe what I saw. As Sean wound up for another unrestrained pitch, his target was only thirty or forty feet away—closer than I supposed he would be. Sean's next rock left his fingertips, raced the short distance, and struck his target. As teeth landed at my feet, Goliath fell in a heap across his unconscious pal.

I stood, gasping for air. My mind was not clear. I saw another rock impact the head of the Goliath. The last rock whizzed by me to strike the back of the Sumo's head. My brain was shocked back into action.

"Get going! Go! Go!" I watched Sean move to the far end of the ledge and carefully crawl his way down on his belly. I quickly surveyed the terrain. The trail that Sean had spotted was just beyond the cottonwood tree, which promised to be a possible escape route. I pulled out the two boot laces that I borrowed from Snart's footwear and tied Goliath's hands behind his back. He looked to be less unconscious with every second I bound him. Turning to Mr. Sumo, I rolled him on his stomach after considerable effort. Because of his lifeless dead weight, I feared he might be dead. Frantically, I tied his hands behind his back, while keeping a cautious eye on his tethered partner. Less than a minute passed before I left the two men to their own fates. It

would not be long before they would return to consciousness and unbind each other. I headed back down the short path to Suzy and Sean.

Suzy called out to Sean. *"JUMP!"*

He made a last leap from the rock wall into the arms of his worried mother. We turned toward our hidey-hole to grab what we could. I searched for my favorite ball cap, quickly concluded it was lost in the ordeal, and shouldered our packs. Suzy glanced at me in horror.

"Rob, are you all right? You've got blood all over you."

It shocked me when I looked to the right at my chest and arm. Mr. Sumo had shed more blood than I first realized. Then I cursed myself under my breath. I left my curly steel weapon with the two kidnappers. I took precious extra seconds and unscrewed the other tiedown and handed it to Suzy.

"Hold that for me. I need to do something else."

Although in a hurry, I pulled out our lifesaving pocketknife and cut the zipties off the wrists of our nemesis, Phil Snart. He looked up at me with angry eyes.

"I hope you rot in Hell!" he said ungraciously.

I stared back at him in confusion. How could someone, in his current situation and as vulnerable to our family as he was, have the gall to spew such vitriol? I am a compassionate man. I didn't want him dead, but I was no fool. He needed to be restrained until we escaped to safety. Even untied, he would not be a problem.

"Phil, with that leg," I replied, looking up at the hot sun outside his chosen hideaway, "I hope you can get out of Hell."

32

WE COULDN'T RUN BECAUSE WE had no level path to follow. I recalled some of the movements I went through the night before when I was hit in the head, hooded, and dragged into this nightmare. It was not level terrain. It often required some turns to avoid obstacles. Yet, it was near darkness for my kidnapper. It had to be easy enough to still navigate in the dark. We had the advantage of daylight.

"I think it's this way," Suzy said, pointing to a path that hinted of a faint hiking trail seldom used. "Remember, they dragged Sean and me literally kicking and screaming. They didn't hood us."

"Another clue that Snart didn't know what he was doing," I said.

We increased our pace as the trail improved. Out of the corner of my eye, I spotted a familiar object. I bent down, picked up my Air Force wings cap off the ground, and put it back on my head.

"We're on the right path," I said, tipping my cap.

It seemed evident that when my kidnappers put the hood over my head, my cap got dislodged and eventually fell out of the hood as I stumbled on. For the first time, I realized that my head ached from the blows of Snart's Kel-Lite and my tussle with the two mystery men. I had no idea what shape they might be in. They were not stirring when we escaped. As good as I worked over my man the Sumo wrestler, it was nothing to what our Sean had done to the Goliath he beaned more than once. Our son had been deadly accurate. From experience Goliath was likely through for the week. So, too, was Snart. I wasn't as certain about Mr. Sumo, despite his blood loss.

We continued forward in faith that we were on the correct course to intersect the Bright Angel Trail. The improving trail we used suddenly disappeared into a rock formation that forced us to decide between going around right or left. We paused for a moment, recollecting in reverse order how we left the trail when first kidnapped.

"Right!" I said.

"Correct!" Suzy replied.

"Hurry!" Sean was already ahead of us and looking at the trail.

In fifty yards we stopped to celebrate our return to the Bright Angel Trail and its relative safety in numbers of other hikers. Several parties passed us. With blood all over me, it was easy to stop each group and ask them to alert park rangers that we needed help. An elderly gentleman with his granddaughter in tow stopped and offered us some of their food. Our adrenaline had abated, and we found ourselves starving for energy. We gladly accepted the gentleman's offer, since the climb out of the canyon would be a big calorie burner.

His granddaughter looked in her middle teens and stood back behind him in shyness.

"This is my granddaughter," he said. "She's the only part of my son I have left." Turning around to look at her, he said, "We make a good team, don't we, Honey?"

She smiled and held out her Peanut M&M-filled hand to Sean. "Could you use some?"

"Sure." With a smile on his dusty face, he took the handful she offered and put them all in his mouth. The man and his granddaughter realized that we were famished and in need of more than polite chatter. They pulled more snacks out of their packs.

"Your cap caught my attention," the gentleman said, while handing Suzy a bag of peanuts. "Are you a pilot?"

"Yes, sir." The Peanut M&Ms he gave me were delicious. "South Texas during the Vietnam War. I never let the Royal Mexican Air Force get north of the Rio Grande."

"Well, thank you for your service," he continued. "I lost a son early in that war. I never fail to thank all of you boys who served."

"Thank you for recognizing our veterans," I said.

"And we are so sorry you lost a son," Suzy said. "You never get over something like that."

"I do miss him," he said sadly.

"Did you also serve?" I asked.

"Yes. The Second World War... Pacific... Navy. I didn't do anything special. Mostly ducked."

"I bet," I said with a chuckle. "Well, thank you for allowing us to be here today. It might have been a lot different without your service."

The old man could still stand erect like a brand-new sailor. His floppy hat did not hide a deep and wrinkled face that bore the marks of hard work and determination. He held a walking stick, beautifully carved into a twisting vine. Carrying a light pack, he wore clothes indicative of a seasoned hiker.

He pulled out more gorp from the backpack at his feet. He handed me a couple of paper bags filled with nuts, raisins, M&Ms, pretzel sticks, and more.

"Tell me exactly what has happened here. You look absolutely exhausted... all of you." He extracted a one-gallon jug from his pack. "You need water, too, it looks like. Is that your blood I see or someone else's?"

"No, sir. It's not mine. You'll know him if you see him. He looks bloody like me, only bigger." I took the water jug from his hand. "Thank you. We definitely need the water especially. I can't thank you enough."

I reached for Sean's empty water bottle, filled it full, then handed it back to the man. He waved his hand. "No, you keep it."

I started to protest but thought better of it. Never turn down an offer of food or drink.

"Don't worry," he said. "I always carry two gallons on me—one gallon for me and my granddaughter here and one gallon for stranded hikers such as yourselves."

"You're a lifesaver, sir," Suzy said. "We've had a rough two days, and it may not be over, yet."

The three of us paused to take long drinks from our refilled water bottles. Sean volunteered, he had been so determined to get up top, he had forgotten how thirsty he was.

"This is the best water I have ever drunk."

Suzy and I looked at our son. We had to agree with him.

"If you don't mind, I'll ask again. What happened to you?"

"We were kidnapped," Suzy replied, "about a half mile from here."

The three of us sat down with our new friends off the trail in the dirt where the rocks could shade us from the afternoon sun. Our sailor and his hiking companion listened to us describe the details of our captivity and the threats hurled at us by the two oversized mystery men and the mental pipsqueak, Snart. We described how the three men tied us up and told us we were to be eliminated forever. Sean chimed in with his own colorful description of cutting the restraints off our wrists, spying on the men who held us captive, and his rock throwing heroics.

"They are still out there and looking for us," I said.

"Rob, I don't think they will be worrying about us," Suzy said. "They'll be lucky to get out of the canyon without help."

The conversation eventually lapsed into contented pauses as we watched the shade creep away from our resting place.

"Well, I don't want us to keep you," the old sailor replied. "You need to get back up to the safety of your quarters. We're headed down a ways more."

"We enjoyed the brief rest," I said. "Your food and water were blessings to us. Thank you."

After taking another drink from our water bottles, we all got to our feet to gather our gear. With a last handshake they restarted their slow descent, while we gratefully scarfed down their donations of food as we commenced walking. Returning to our slow plodding climb back to our El Tovar oasis, we were keenly alert to any surprise arrivals to block our path. Would the three men catch up to us and take any opportunity to do us harm? Were the four Marines part of this Weatherman wannabe group? This time Suzy promised she would not fail to check our six o'clock. We hiked in such intimate proximity that people might have guessed we were on a frequently interrupted honeymoon. My guess was that we entered the trail with about a mile and a quarter to go. We might be at the top in two hours. The walk from the trailhead to the El Tovar would be another half hour. We would stay close until we reached our room. Where was a park ranger when we needed one?

Finally reaching the last wall of the canyon, we began the steep ascending switchbacks that would bring us finally to the end of our odyssey. Another family of hikers ahead of us stopped to look up as people at the top recognized them and hollered down. The family shouted back in reply. It served to inspire us to keep up our steady pace. It was no longer an up-then-down hike but a steady ascent, which was a challenge for exhausted leg muscles. We paced ourselves to avoid cramping. Only I knew that in the morning, when Sean and Suzy got out of bed, the hike would be there to remind them with muscles sore beyond description.

An hour later we reached the trailhead for Bright Angel Trail. A shuttle, that could have taken us to the El Tovar, left minutes before we arrived. It was now a mile long gentle downhill walk to the civilization of Grand Canyon National Park with all its amenities.

The next half hour dragged along. It was a welcome sight as the parking lot of the El Tovar came into view. We checked in at the front desk, and to our surprise, the hotel clerk informed us they had missed us and began a search. After we failed to return for our restaurant dining reservation, the maids had checked our room to confirm we were gone. The hotel alerted the park rangers to look for a family of three.

"A man came by asking about you right after you left on your hike yesterday morning," the female clerk said. "He was nervous... wouldn't leave a message for you."

"What did he look like?" I asked.

"Not like any other tourist," she said. "He was tall, stocky, had one of those hippie ponytails. A man his age looks terrible with grey hair in a ponytail. Don't you think?"

"Especially him."

I looked at Suzy and Sean, who were dirty, tired, and sweaty. I was a bloody mess on top of that. I turned to our desk clerk again for a request.

"I need you to do two things for us," I said. "First, we want someone with security responsibility to escort us to our room, since we've already had our room invaded two days ago. Second, you need to inform the park service that the pony-tailed man and his two other companions will need a helicopter just this side of the Mile-and-a-Half Resthouse. If you are going down the trail, they will be off the trail about a thousand feet to your left. Two of them may try to hike out, but the third will need help."

"You say they are injured?" the clerk asked.

"Yes, they're severely injured if we did our job right," I said with a smile. "These men kidnapped us. That's why we weren't here last night, and I bet they're wishing they never met our son." Looking down at Sean, then over to Suzy, I added the words that I knew would bring joy to them both. "And to reward this boy of mine, we're going to get him his dog."

33

OUR ROOM CHECK WAS NEGATIVE for any nefarious intruders, and we could relax, shower, and talk without the need to check our six. We went down to the El Tovar dining room to enjoy a late lunch.

Anything but gorp, peanuts, and warm water.

The Harvey House tradition of fine American cuisine did not disappoint us. While trying to think positive, we were joined by a gentleman from National Park Emergency Services. smartly dressed in the uniform of a high-ranking and physically fit medic. Close behind him came a Park Ranger supervisor, spit and polish all the way. No one could survive working in the canyon without being in excellent physical shape. This superintendent was no exception. Pulling up chairs to our four-top lunch table, they begged forgiveness for interrupting our lunch.

"Mister and Missus Amity, it is urgent that we talk to you so we can understand," the supervisor said. "Could you start at the top and explain to us what happened?"

Suzy and I alternately listed the things that had transpired overnight—my kidnapping by one or two men. I detailed the hood, the zip tie restraints, the locks, the location of our hidey-hole, and our escape. Suzy related her assault and kidnapping by a single man, who unknown to her was someone who knew and detested us. She related with a smile the reaction of our son, Sean, who kicked him in the shins so hard that his leg grew increasingly unusable.

For now, she left out the part of the story where Sean kicked his kidnapper while he was down—at my request.

Before the two men could ask, I volunteered that it seemed to be the strangest, most poorly planned kidnapping we'd ever heard of. I confessed that when two of the men bound and dumped my acquaintance at our feet during our ordeal, I did some persuasive things that caused him to talk.

"Phil Snart told us that his mission was to kill me. That is what makes this so bizarre. Why would he want me killed? I hardly know him. And his accomplices were dumber than rocks. So was Snart. None of it made any sense."

"Any motivation that this Snart character stated?" asked the supervisor.

"The first day I met him by accident several months ago, he described himself as an army medic who served in Vietnam. He told me that I deserved to die for being a pilot in the Air Force during the war. I never was anywhere near Vietnam. That didn't seem to matter. He told me yesterday that he lied to me. He's not a veteran but seems to hate them all. Then he mentioned that this was some sort of initiation to join a peacetime antiwar offshoot of the Weathermen organization. Remember them? The bombing of the Capitol?"

The supervisor sat silent for a moment, then turned deliberately to face the senior medic. To the surprise of everyone at the table, he stood up, pushed his chair away, and headed quickly to the exit of the dining room. We followed his fast pace out of sight, turned back to our medic, and blankly stared in confusion. I spoke first.

"Did we just uncover something big?"

"Looks like it. I don't understand what just happened myself, but I'd guess the Park Service is running to get help." The medic raised a clipboard with government forms attached and got ready to write. "Let's talk about these three men. We can't send out a helicopter without more information, and it sounds like we need more than evacuation services here."

I nodded. "I don't think they'll be eager to flag you down. In fact, there's a good chance that they'll kill this Snart guy, the one they dumped on us."

"Are they armed?"

"We never saw any weapons," I said. "I don't think they ever expected to be in the canyon more than a few hours. Then their buddy, Snart, started making mistakes. Really weird."

"Why would they kidnap you in the National Park? Seems like a dumb place to commit a crime. It's hot as blazes down there this time of year... or any time of year, actually."

"I could only speculate," I cautioned, "but, if their intent was to kill me, what better place to leave a body they don't want found?"

"Why did they want to kill all three of you?"

"I don't think they wanted to kill Sean or me," Suzy said. "I think that's why they dumped my kidnapper in our space. I remember something they said... asking him what Sean and I were doing there? They sounded hopping mad."

"Okay, then. Here's the bottom line. We need some backup to extract these three men. Can you describe their injuries?"

"Easily," I replied. Snart injured his leg. He complained of blood pooling in his feet. He wasn't eager to get on his feet or to even stand up. He may have a blood clot. That's my uneducated guess. The two big fellows are easier to diagnose. The one I'll call Mister Sumo has a crushed trachea and a gash on the side of his head near his ear. Mister Goliath has a couple of blows to his head along with several missing teeth. You'll recognize them by the blood."

"Did you do all that by yourself?"

"I put Mister Sumo down, but Sean polished off the other two."

The man from Emergency Services looked over at nine-year-old Sean in surprise. "You?"

"Yup," the boy replied. "Last night I kicked Mister Snart's leg over and over, and then this morning I beaned the other two with my throwing rocks."

I don't think the man truly believed us, until his park emergency radio began a frenzy of chatter.

34

A TEAM OF FBI AGENTS from the satellite office in Flagstaff was headed north, and the park staff was not happy. A lazy day at the park was turning into a nightmare. The park ranger supervisor came back to see me. Suzy and Sean were back in the room to rest. I was in the El Tovar Cocktail Lounge fending off malaria with a gin and tonic. I left word at the front desk where I could be found because I knew officials would be back in droves. An agent arrived sooner than I expected.

"You're on duty," I said. "Can I buy you a Coke?"

"No, thank you, but I'll take a glass of water," he said. "I'm heading down the trail in a few minutes. I never want caffeine or alcohol in this heat."

His manner was urgent. I extended my hand to a chair and offered him a seat. I asked the bar hostess for a glass of ice water. He continued.

"Do you suspect that there are others in the park in this Weatherman Wannabe group you mentioned?"

"Funny you ask that." I answered him after some hesitation. "We met four men who claimed to be former Marines. Their clothes were a bit out of the norm. They appeared nice enough, but they seemed to show up everywhere we were. Then when our room got broken into, they appeared out of nowhere soon after we discovered it. And when I was grabbed yesterday, I first assumed it was those men who did it. Of course, I was wrong."

"Can you describe them to me?"

"Sure, I can... even their first names as well. They said they take a yearly trip together."

He scribbled down my answers to his question. His face gave no tell of his reactions to my information. When I described the four of them wearing the same French Foreign Legion hats, he smiled briefly.

"They should be easy to spot with that on their heads," I said.

"Are they armed?"

"No, but then I wasn't looking for anything, either."

"Mister Amity, you may have made some federal agents very happy today," he said. "The FBI has been getting hints of this organization for the past couple of years. When some of those Weather Underground bombers got arrested, we knew we did not have them all. Then they began recruiting for a new organization with even more extreme methods. Instead of saying they wanted to end the war in Vietnam, these nut cases set a goal to punish those involved. Their goal was to strike terror among our veterans by randomly killing them. They were good at secrecy, until now. You might become a hero out of this."

Or be an even bigger target.

"You said they made mistakes?" the supervisor asked. "Could you explain?"

"If this was to be a hit job, why would they come here to do it?" I asked. "That idiot Snart lives in Oklahoma City. That's where I live."

"Sounds like he missed a deadline to take you out. Sound plausible?"

"I *did* get a call from a friend who warned me he was coming to find me. His name is Jay Goodwin. He was very worried for me. I may have blown off his warning too quickly. Jay implied that Snart was going to do me harm."

"Another mistake?"

"I've concluded the two big men grabbed me off the trail, but then Phil took my wife and son unnecessarily. When the other two found out about it, Phil's initiation into the Weather Hitman Club was over. If these guys are any measure of the organization, all those Looney Tunes are in trouble."

"Anything else?"

"Yes. The biggest mistake the two others made was tying up and throwing their partner into our area. It took only a couple of kicks to make him sing like a bird. That's one reason I concluded he had never been in the Army like he claimed. He told us everything."

I looked down, realizing I had neglected my highball, took a sip, and ordered a fresh one. The superintendent had been drinking his ice water with relish. When a refill came with my fresh gin and tonic, I sucked the remainder of the first warm one down like a pro.

"I may have more questions for you," the superintendent said, then stood up." Are you leaving tomorrow?"

"No." I was overwhelmed with fatigue. "We'll be here a couple more days at least."

"I'm heading down to meet my rangers. The helicopter is on the way already, but we may be a while finding them if they don't want to be saved. The FBI wants to talk to them, so we need to keep them alive. We will be looking for your other four friends, the Marines, too."

He turned with a salute of goodbye and left the lounge at a determined pace. The man of action was leaving the building. As for me, I had experienced all the action I cared to have in a single day. I leaned back in my lounge chair, took a slow sip of an ice cold second gin and tonic, and ordered a third when the waitress came by. "...and can you bring me a glass of water? I don't want to get too dehydrated."

35

SOON AFTERWARD I STUMBLED BACK to our room, still wired, but tired. I took the stairway, noting for the first time the soreness in my muscles. My back especially bothered me, a reminder that Mr. Sumo had rolled me into jagged rocks. Sore muscles recover. Rocks on my spinal column wouldn't heal as quickly. I entered our room, careful not to startle Suzy with the sound of my key in the door lock. Sean was on the rollaway bed, sound asleep. Suzy was sitting in one of our two upholstered chairs with their subtle Navaho-like fabric. She faced the window overlooking the North Rim, her view of our side on the South Rim blocked by trees. I turned the other seat around and pulled it up to hers. Sitting down without a word, we instinctively reached out our hands to each other. We paused for a moment just long enough to savor the warmth of our presence together.

"I bet Sean won't wake up for a while," I chuckled. Silence returned comfortably to us for a few more precious minutes.

"What just happened to us out there?" I asked quietly.

She was now ready to talk. "I've had time to ponder that question. I'm too stimulated to take a nap," she said. Her words then poured out in buckets. "At first, I couldn't understand the motivation to even think of killing another person. Then I got to thinking of our days in college. The Democratic Convention in 1968 was a real eye opener to John and you... and me. The antiwar crowd, those yippies, the assassins... they all reached a crescendo in

Chicago when protesters and police battled in the streets on live TV. It occurred to me that those same protestors are now sixteen years older. Normal people go on to live their lives, go to work, get married, have children. But some can't get past it."

She paused briefly. "Do you think they may be going through some midlife crisis, trying desperately to relive their glory days of protesting? Of free love? Even their worship back then of Chairman Mao or Che Guevara? Were these people simply missing their good old hippie glory days of protest and narcissism? Goodness, even Jerry Rubin turned capitalist to become a stockbroker. I hear he's now a millionaire. On the other hand, our acquaintances went from radical protesters to revolutionaries. They took their Che and their Mao admirations seriously. I just wonder. How many more like them are out there?"

She paused to look again at the view from our window. She turned to me, squeezed my hand, and put her head on my sore shoulder. Sean continued his deep slumber. I shared my own opinion.

"Vietnam caused so much bitterness, it has affected our lives ever since. I wanted to be a veterinarian when I grew up. I became a vet, all right. It was just the wrong one. Half the population wanted to end the war by giving up. The other half wanted to end the war by winning. Eventually, we failed at both ends. I remember several college students declared that they were getting married to avoid being drafted. Then the rules changed, and those same students had to be parents to avoid the draft. The rules changed again. If you wanted to remain in school out of the draft after getting your bachelor's degree, you could either go into medical school or divinity school. I have encountered some of these physicians and ministers. They are often bitter and unhappy. They are doing something in life that they hate—all to avoid the Vietnam War. Many students stayed in school, not because they wanted a college degree but to delay the draft. We've diluted the value of a college degree because there are more of them than the public wants. You've seen the ads. 'Become a plumber—bachelor's degree required.' Vietnam has had such a negative impact on society, and we no longer realize it. Sometimes I get bitter. I didn't achieve my childhood goals. I didn't win my war. It cost us both dearly. But, deep down in my being, I am happy. And since we cannot go back in time, what transpired before this moment, I am content to accept. Suzy, life is good for us. These men we met haven't accepted the life they were dealt. They needed to grow up about fifteen years ago."

We were quiet again, our venting over. My three highballs at the bar were taking their toll as I sat hand-in-hand with my beautiful wife. I promised myself I would not overdo the alcohol ever again. I drifted off in the chair, no longer looking out the window at the mightiest, most marvelous view in the world. At some point Suzy lifted her hand from mine and left me to my exhausted sleep.

WHEN I CAME TO FROM my nap, the soreness in every muscle of my body was making even the slightest movement to stand up from the chair a challenge. I forced myself amid involuntary groans to move. Suzy was still pondering the canyon from her chair.

"How long have I been here?"

My question made Sean stir into a sitting up position.

"Three hours," Suzy said.

"Let's go eat. We might even get to eat without people asking us questions."

"I could eat." She spoke devoid of enthusiasm.

She had not napped and still looked tired. When she stood up, she looked at me and groaned.

"Oh, my goodness," she said. Her chuckle spoke of muscle pain. "Now I know why you are hurting. I can hardly stand up and take a step."

"Welcome to hiking the Grand Canyon."

Sean, bleary-eyed with hair disheveled, brightened his expression at the word eat. His latest growth spurt meant his intake of food was a day behind his needs. We quickly checked ourselves in the mirror and attempted to comb Sean's hair. Realizing it was hopeless, we put a ball cap on his head and ordered him not to remove it. To our amazement, he had no complaints about soreness. As we painfully and slowly stepped into the hallway, Sean waited, smiling in amusement. Oh, to be young.

The Bright Angel Lodge, housing the last continuously operating Harvey House Cafe, was a real treat for dining. Because of the history of the railroads in the West, Fred Harvey revolutionized a traveler's dining experience. Where once the unsavory train station diner and an equally unscrupulous conductor collaborated to cheat the traveler out of a decent meal, the Harvey House turned railroad dining into a travel destination. The coffee was always fresh. The Harvey Girls, young and attractive hostesses, made a passenger's dining experience top notch. The food was fresh, the choices were many, and the experience was first class. And here we three were, needing to be pampered for at least one meal.

We hobbled outside with our tortured sore muscles and joints and headed west along the pathway of the South Rim. Entering the Harvey House Café, we were greeted by a considerate hostess. We had not made dinner reservations, but being briefly the El Tovar's most notable celebrities, she recognized who we were and found a table at the back for three without delay. We dined in quiet contentment. Suzy and I savored several cups of the famous Harvey House coffee, served out of large copper kettles, changed out for fresh brew every two hours without fail. Sean drank seemingly endless glasses of water and generic cola. We ordered our meals without concerns for calories or cost. We had been through enough stuff already to make this an evening of no diet guilt—no limits. We were glad to be together, safe, and undisturbed.

For the rest of the evening, we lucked out. No one disturbed us. We lingered to enjoy more coffee and to savor a rare treat of dessert, something we seldom ate at home. We returned after our dinner to our El Tovar lodgings, taking an opportunity to enjoy the ambiance of the lodge's great room. With walls of pine logs, a limestone fireplace, and mounted heads of wildlife, it was a boy's fantasy room. Sean was content to walk all around the room, studying the displays on each wall and in each corner. Plush furnishings supported by sturdy pine wood with slatted back and armrests invited us to sit down. Fred Harvey being one of the first major supporters of Southwest

Indian art, the floor and walls were lavishly adorned with rugs and art of the local Indian tribes.

We met several other families while sitting comfortably by the limestone fireplace. Fortunately, none of them knew of our recent encounter, so we could have simple chit chat. Suzy and I enjoyed asking the families where they were from, where they had been, and how many times they had been to the Grand Canyon. I met one older gentleman and his wife, both seasoned travelers, who also flew their own airplane into the Grand Canyon National Park Airport. My eyes lit up when the man told me he flew a Cessna 210, a heavy hauler with retractable gear.

"I used to fly a Cessna in the Air Force, except it was a jet."

"A Tweet?" he asked, making me cringe. I hated the name Tweet.

I learned he had first flown Corsairs with the Marines in the Pacific. He had never lost the bug for flying. I thanked him for his service, then joked that at least he won his war. He chuckled at that but said no more.

We met another family that was headed to Phantom Ranch, located near the Colorado River at the bottom of the canyon. This was their first hike into the canyon, and they were looking for people who had hiked it before. Since I previously had hiked it rim to rim, they had an enormous number of questions. I enjoyed sharing my experience.

The time soon turned to bedtime. Sean was looking tired once again, perhaps more from his sudden growth spurt than from his hiking fatigue. We bid our new acquaintances a goodnight, unaware that beginning in the morning all hell would break loose.

36

MORNING CAME WITH A MINOR disappointment. Overnight the wind shifted. Looking out our window, the view was obscured by a thick foggy haze. The El Tovar staff earlier warned us that the clear skies we enjoyed at the beginning of our visit were unusual. Coal-fired power plants in the Four Corners region were a primary cause of the severe haze evident most days of the year. With this stark change to the landscape, our trek back to the Bright Angel Lodge's Harvey House Café for breakfast lost much of its luster. Suzy and I were determined to enjoy our coffee this morning for at least the time that it took our son to become bored. Coffee together was a ritual that kept us talking in the morning about the news. We even read the paper together. I was a slower reader. She was the tolerant speed reader.

"Look at this," Suzy said. "We're famous."

Pointing to a headline in *The Arizona Republic* on page three, there was a brief article about a foiled kidnapping in Grand Canyon National Park. It mentioned our name and hometown but made no reference to the circumstances. It said the Amitys had escaped but that the perpetrators were still at large in the national park. It reported a search was underway for two or three men, with their descriptions taken from our interview with the National Park Ranger superintendent.

We were halfway expecting to be interrupted during our coffee therapy or our breakfast. Finally, I concluded that the personnel most wanting to talk to us were likely in the canyon as part of the search party. We continued to enjoy our coffee, order breakfast, then return to our room to do our regular morning routine. It was great to not have an agenda and wedded to the clock. We hiked to several places of interest at the rim and around the El Tovar. Another person had a cassette player playing Ferde Grofé's *Grand Canyon Suite.* He was a little late for the first movement, "Sunrise." Still, it was a nice touch. We stayed to talk to the man, who was from England and happy to talk about what brought him all the way here to meld the music with the view.

At some point in the morning, we hit the gift shop nearby. We watched Sean spend most of the allowance that he had saved up in the previous four weeks. He was thrilled. We soon found the need to try out lunch at the El Tovar, drink more coffee, eat a hamburger apiece, and leisurely sit at the dining table while Sean played absent-mindedly with his gift shop purchases.

The first hint that something was happening came from hikers arriving at the hotel from the Bright Angel Trailhead. Most were too tired to chat, but a few hikers came into the lounge excitedly telling tales of action on the trail near the Mile-and-a-Half Resthouse. The chatter went on for five more minutes before a half dozen male hikers emerged from the bar lounge, approached our table, and planted a gin and tonic by my plate.

"The bartender told me you drink gin and tonic," a grizzled and weathered hiker informed me, then turned to Suzy. "Ma'am, could I get something for you and your boy?"

Suzy uncharacteristically looked momentarily flustered. She pursed her lips, unable to know what to say. I had learned long ago that, when a man offers another man a drink, the right thing to do is to respectfully accept. When the chance offers itself, you can always reciprocate.

"My son would like a Coke, thank you," I said to the man. "Suzy, what do you want? This kind gentleman is offering. By the size of this crowd, I wouldn't turn it down."

The group of men collectively chuckled, and Suzy relented. "I'll have what he's having."

The laughter from the group further puzzled her, until the man beside the generous grizzled hiker spoke up.

"Would that be the boy's… or the man's? Which one are we talking about?"

Suzy laughed, seemed to relax, and pointed at Sean with her most charming smile. The second man turned and headed for the lounge for two additional drinks. He was sunburned on his face, had a three-day beard, and wore boots which looked too big for the rest of him. I looked at the dirty and sweaty crew with amusement. They were obviously excited to tell me something.

"You boys must know something we don't know," I said. "Did they finally catch somebody?

They all answered in unison, laughing as they spoke, and each vying for the first chance to share their news.

"You boys know each other?"

"Not until this morning," said a third man, wearing hiking attire that must have come directly from Land's End.

"Now we do," said a fourth who wore jeans, tennis shoes, a floppy hat, and an oversized shirt.

"Have you heard what happened?" asked the grizzled hiker as he plopped a Princeton ball cap on his head. "Oh! Here come your drinks."

"We *did* see a lot of animated hikers earlier," Suzy said, while the sunburned hiker set her generic cola in front of her, followed by Sean's. There was no pause in the dialog to break in with a proper "thank you." I raised my glass in a gesture of gratitude.

"They got three aggressive bad boys," the grizzled Princeton man continued, then turned to the others. "We had a good time, didn't we?"

They all cheered, laughed, and clapped like boys who had just gotten away with something. It was a good time to chime in because only now did I notice that they all had drinks in hand.

"Well, then I propose a toast to you boys," I said, painfully standing up and holding high my still un-sipped drink. "I hope you got a chance to knock the stuffing out of them."

"Here, here!" We cheered.

"And best of all," hiker number five informed us, holding up a large RCA camera. "We got it on video."

More laughs and delight poured out of the men. They had obviously had the time of their lives down there. Number Five, a big man dressed in cargo shorts, T-shirt, sandals, and sporting a Redskins ball cap, laid his video camera on our table. Next, he removed a satchel from his shoulder of a portable full-sized video cassette player with battery. It connected by heavy wires to his camera. For a couple of years, I had been interested in getting a video camera, and this one looked like the miracle of engineering I was waiting for.

"You wanna see it?" he asked, as if we could have said "no."

"You're gonna love it," another said.

He opened a side panel on his camera that revealed a small two-and-a-half-inch video screen. I marveled at what I could do with that camera. He turned it to face Suzy and me. Sean scooted over close to me to get a look. All the men rotated around the table to stand behind us. Our Redskin fan pushed the play button on the portable player. To my surprise there was sound.

Being small, the video was hard at first to see fine details, but the grizzled Princeton man narrated with his own color commentary. His helpful words painted a clear picture of what we were seeing. The camera's location was the Bright Angel Trail. In the distance were four park rangers coming toward the camera with two massive men in front and another smaller man carried on a stretcher. It was still too far away to identify them, but obviously, those were our three foolish antiwar would-be-assassins. As they got close, our color commentator warned us to pay attention.

"This is where the fun begins."

The tape continued to show them getting closer until all three were clearly identified. Bloodied and dirty, they looked tired and resigned to their capture. When the first one landed his foot on the trail, things took a turn. Goliath and Mr. Sumo each took an elbow to the park rangers escorting them. It was then that I realized they were handcuffed in the front, leaving their elbows free to swing a blow behind them. Both rangers fell backward, and the two men took off up the trail at a run. At the same instant, the stretcher bearers dropped their contents. Snart fell off the stretcher at an angle that tumbled him a few extra yards to the side of the trail.

The camera then panned left to pick up the fleeing men. They paused to confront a hiker. After Goliath put a grip on the man, Mr. Sumo reached in the man's pocket with his two bound hands and out came a knife, which they used expertly to cut each other loose from their zip ties. They were close to the camera when they renewed their run up the trail to the South Rim. I knew that they would have to run at least a mile before they reached the trailhead. A run like that could not be sustained, especially with their own hunger and exhaustion. The camera zoomed in closer. Momentarily, it went out of focus. Perhaps two seconds went by before the camera's focus returned. To our shock, while the tittering began from the men behind us, four young men in funny-looking French Foreign Legion caps appeared at the top of the screen approaching the two escapees. The two sides knew instantly that there would be a conflict. Mr. Sumo held the knife out to the one Marine I had days earlier concluded not to mess with. Randy, the intimidating one with the full beard down below his throat, deftly approached the giant, faked a move to one side, stepped to the knife side and locked an iron grip on his wrist. With his other hand he gripped the man's elbow and forcefully bent the joint backward. Mr. Sumo screamed in pain as he reluctantly went face first on the dirt path. Jack, the clean-cut redhead, planted a boot on the knife after it fell from the man's hand. Picking it up, Jack folded the blade and held it high so the real owner could see it. Mr. Sumo remained face down with his locked elbow and forearm bent behind his back, while the camera panned over to Goliath.

Again, the camera focus blurred briefly, but it soon clearly showed a man with missing teeth and dried, matted blood on his face and above his left ear. He was cursing all manner of descriptive and impossible scenarios. Blue-shirted Bob and Chet the tall and muscled Marine approached Goliath, who first looked at his companion lying face down in the dirt. He positioned himself in a boxing stance and waited. Our color commentator instructed us to listen carefully. The three faced off in silence. The cameraman stepped closer to the action.

Chet pointed at Goliath's bloody ear and lower jaw. "Do you *really* want me to hit you right there?"

The giant sighed, dropped to his knees, put his hands to his face, and surrendered.

The group of video viewers had a good laugh over such an utterly unconditional surrender of Goliath.

The video continued. Park rangers moved in again to take over the custody of the totally exhausted pair. Our commentator added that more personnel were now approaching from above and below the rim to assist. The camera, still on Goliath, Chet, and Bob, picked up more cursing and screaming. Temporarily searching for the source, the camera panned wildly, until zeroing in on a literally hopping mad Phil Snart. Trying to escape on one leg, while announcing his location with every curse, the man who hated anyone military now had the Marines after him. Suzy and I watched the scene with conflicted satisfaction. Sean was laughing at all the words he did not need to hear. At first Bob and Chet offered to help Snart up the side of the trail, but he struggled to get away. When they forcefully dragged him up the difficult few feet to the edge of the trail, he took it out on his helpers. An attempted right hook at Chet went awry. Chet simply caught the fist in his left hand and crushed it until there was a muted crack. The cries of pain continued for longer than anyone wished to hear. It gave Randy and Jack a chance to recover the stretcher and return it to the trail. They were standing next to the upright stretcher when Snart, in a last act of defiance, spit in the face of Bob. The response was instinctive and immediate. Bob's right fist was remarkably powerful. Without a second of warning, priggish and whiney Phillip hit the back of the stretcher like a fast ball in a catcher's mitt. Jack and Randy bagged the human missile and laid the hitless Snart flat on his back and ready for transport.

37

"THAT'S THE GREATEST MOVIE I'VE seen since *Ben Hur,"* I said enthusiastically after the last of the video played.

Sean was still taking in all the aspects of this bad behavior by adults. Everything he learned at school about behavior on the playground was on full hypocritical display by grown men on video.

"Sean, don't do this at school." He laughed with all the men at that comment. I raised my nearly empty glass. "I toast you, boys, for some great comic relief. We have gone through a lot the past day or two. Seeing your video is a gift to us. Here, here!"

The men toasted their empty glasses, which prompted me to declare.

"Since there are only a half a dozen of you, let me buy you all a drink. Tell the lounge to put it on my lunch tab."

Like any real man, there was no hesitation. In unison the six men cheered and headed to the bar. I turned to my amused wife and son.

"Suzy, I may have to join them for a few minutes. Do you mind? They won't let Sean in, I'm pretty sure."

"Let's see if they throw him out," Suzy said, then she paused for reflection. "We both know, don't we, that bending the rules is the only way to get anything done in life."

And so, we joined the men in the lounge for another hour of raucous laughter, which was well worth the cost of admission. It was gratifying to learn that my new friends were all veterans of the army or navy. It was special to be around them and to share a few stories of what men do when they're too young to have a lick of sense. Eventually, Suzy, Sean, and I were exhausted and begged our leave. Sean had successfully bent the rules of the bar, much to his delight.

Back in our room it was clear that the attention and good news had sapped our energy. The stress was more than we anticipated. Much to Sean's displeasure, we took a nap in the two chairs. But first, I gave him his first ticket of independence with our room key and released him to roam the inside and outside grounds of the El Tovar if he stayed in the area. On his first foray out of the control of his parents in an unfamiliar place, he lasted about twenty-five minutes before he returned to wake us up.

Sean discovered interesting things and wanted us to see them with him. It's hard to turn down a request like that. We knew that in three years when he was a teenager, he would not be so much into sharing. But we convinced him that people might again bother us if we went out of our room. He grudgingly agreed to wait and explore after we had dinner. Not to anyone's surprise, his own exhaustion finally caught up with him, and he shared another long nap with the two of us.

It was close to 5:00 p.m. when our room phone rang. Bleary-eyed and stumbling to get to the phone in time, we picked it up beyond the fifth or sixth ring. One more familiar voice spoke to me.

"Mister Amity, this is Bob, you may remember... one of the four vacationing Marines. We took the shuttle from the airport together."

"Hi, Bob." I woke up quickly. "I've already heard that you guys have been busy today."

"Well, that's why I called. We want to treat you all to dinner tonight. If you would allow us to pay, you would make us very happy."

"We hoped to run into you before you left, so this would be perfect. Where and when do we meet?"

"How about the El Tovar Restaurant at six o'clock sharp?" Bob said. *"Does that give you enough time?"*

"Let's make it 1830 hours, and we'll meet you on Marine Corps time."

"Okay, 1815 hours it is. We'll see you there."

I put the phone down and sighed. Being in demand was tiring. The old joke about wanting to end a vacation so we could get home and rest was certainly applicable. Suzy teased me about not giving her enough time to get ready. She put on her evening's finest. I pulled out my slacks and a button-down shirt with casual loafers. Sean was easy. We let him dress himself because we didn't care. We were on vacation.

I enjoyed dressing up with my trophy of a wife. Sure, I treasured her intellect, but being an honest husband, Suzy was a delight to be with when she got decked out. Putting on her finest seemed to alter the smile that we always shared. She looked happier and more excited when dressed to the nines. She had a way of walking that could melt hearts. Framing that image with the latest fashions was my daily delight. With each year we had been married, she seemed to gain beauty and sensuality. It wasn't until we married that I discovered the difference between sexy and sensual. One is transient. The other never goes away. It was natural for Suzy to never change.

She was sensual this night in her choice of wear—a long bias-cut V-neck dress with an empire-waist in a beautiful butternut yellow. It was a perfect style for her figure, emphasizing her female form with just a hint of her rounded hips and belly, plus a peek of cleavage to add intrigue.

With every year the presence of veterans in my life became more compelling and necessary. It was important for my own sense of worth to be with those who had served and to learn of the different sacrifices we made. Not every sacrifice was because of combat or serving in a combat zone. Most veterans of the Vietnam War did not serve in Vietnam. Unless you were in the brown water navy or flying combat missions, sailors were at sea or lending support elsewhere. If you were Army, serving in Germany where Russian tanks and nuclear annihilation were constant threats, you did not serve in Vietnam. The same issue confronted Marines and airmen. Only by talking to all veterans did I learn that we all sacrificed something. My sacrifice was that I gave up an education. I left behind my hopes of becoming a veterinarian. For others, it may have been a marriage that failed or a parent not cared for. The best news for ninety-nine percent of veterans is the pride we all share because of what we did. Looking back ten years later, the military made me a better person, and I'm glad I got to serve. Only because Ronald Reagan reintroduced the custom of honoring veterans did we crawl out of our cocoons and declare to the public that we served. I considered it an honor to share a meal with these four fine U.S. Marines.

38

OUR FAMILY ARRIVED FOR DINNER at 6:14 p.m. to find the four neatly dressed Marines seated at a table for eight. Already holding drinks, I figured they had arrived to make sure they beat us to the table—a typical enlisted trick with commanders. They spaced themselves out so that Suzy and Sean would be together, but I would be spaced among the four of them. They were demonstrably happy to see us and gave us that look that only comes from having sprung a surprise that morning. It was clear that they knew we were suspicious of them in the beginning. They all carried in their manner a pride for today's job well done. There was certainly vindication for them in our minds and hopefully in our expressions.

As we walked in, the four of them stood up and looked directly at Suzy. We shook hands all around the table. Suzy and I impressed them by remembering each of their first names. It wasn't until Suzy took her seat that they sat down again.

"Well, six thirty p.m. We're right on time," I said as a joke.

"Good job," Bob said. "We can get the boy out of the military, but you can't get the military out of the boy."

"How true," Suzy said. "I think we've had enough combat to go around this week, though."

Six males nodded in agreement as we laughed. Sean—chief of rock artillery—was now one with the big boys. The first order of business was my offer to buy a round or two of drinks in payment for dinner. With that simple business deal over, I could get to the meat of the matter.

"You Marines really beat the snot out of those big boys, didn't you?"

We couldn't help but laugh with them. Their enthusiastic guffaws moved to clever comments and laughter then dwindled to titters. They had clearly enjoyed the day.

That was the catalyst that got the party going. Those Marines were ordering the weirdest drinks, and I knew a lot of drinks. The waiter took their orders, but then they suggested that a flyboy like me needed to order an appropriate drink.

Randy the intimidator told the waiter, "Get the lady a gin and tonic. The boy over here needs a Coke, and the gentleman needs an Afterburner."

"Oh, no!" I replied. "No *way* will I have one of those."

Suzy told him that she would have what Sean was having.

"I thought all you jet jockeys liked Afterburners."

"No, only the crazy ones. How about Flamethrowers? You like those?" They all laughed at my question. "I take it that means no."

Their personal history lesson went on for half an hour before we decided to order our dinner. Sundown was an hour or more away, so we could enjoy our meal while watching one of the wonders of the world from the big bay window—the changing colors of a Grand Canyon sunset. The four men ordered another round for us. Later I found out they paid for these, in addition to our meals. After studying the menu, we ordered. These marines were all meat-and-potatoes men. I got razzed for ordering chicken.

"I don't picture you to be a chicken man," said Randy.

"I'm a pilot," I replied. "We like things that fly."

"Chickens fly?" The table laughed in unison.

"You're quick," I said.

It was time to tell them what happened to us and to confess we had a warning telephone call that made us suspicious of just about everyone.

"Well, eventually I want to hear from Sean," clean-cut Jack said, "but first, can I have my Kel-Lite back?"

"Oh, yes. Thank you for the loan. It came in handy. You don't mind wiping a little blood off, do you?" I replied in all seriousness. "I found out the hard way that it makes an effective club... and keeps lit the whole time."

"I think we still have it somewhere," Suzy added. "It went through a lot of hands."

"Until you find it," Jack said. "Sean! Tell me what you did. I heard you were quite a hero out there."

Sean looked up and smiled, obviously pleased to be the focus of attention. He grinned at me, then at Suzy as if to get approval to tell the tale. I nodded my approval. His face grew more animated, and he turned to the marines.

"Well, first I beaned them with my throw, then I kicked the snot out of Mister Snart."

"Sean!" Suzy scolded the boy. "That is no way to talk at dinner in front of your mother and father."

Sean looked surprised, then the first tear accompanied by a pout emerged.

"But Dad said *snot.*"

Suzy looked at me with rare but expressive displeasure, then turned to Sean. "Not at my table anymore."

"Suzy, we're all veterans at this table." I tried hard to be persuasive. "Talking formal-like would embarrass us."

"Rob," Chet said, while looking at each of his three friends. "It looks to me like we all better toe the line if you get my drift."

"Okay." Looking down at the table, I turned to Sean, "Son, it's my fault for leading you astray. Let's not say that anymore in front of your mom." Then I gave Sean a clandestine wink.

With perfectly poor timing, our dinner arrived with visions of improper words dancing in my head. Chet continued his questioning of Sean's role in the affair.

"Dad and I ran an obstacle course at a camp, then we did it for real on the rocks," Sean said. "Dad pushed me up to a ledge about a hundred feet high. I crouched down so the men wouldn't see me. Dad yelled *'NOW!'* And I threw a rock and missed, but I got better and beaned him on the head, and then Dad beat him up. Another man came up and I... oh, I got that wrong. I beaned the second man with a rock. Dad beat up the first man all by himself. So, I saved

Dad from the second man.... That's it. I threw a second beanball at the other man, and it knocked him down. I jumped down from the ledge, and Mom and I ran for cover."

"What about that other guy, you kicked the... whatever... out of him?"

"Oh, I can't talk about that anymore," Sean replied tentatively, looking over at his mother.

That was too bad for the Marines because Sean's monologue was allowing them to tear into their steaks at the rate of a quick step. I rested a fork by my chicken dinner to mention the bizarre nature of their motives.

"They were nuts—and stupid, to boot" I said. "The only problem was their stated intent to kill us... all three of us!"

"Why you?" Bob asked.

"I don't think they even knew why. At one time this Phil Snart fellow told me he got the wrong guy... something about a B-52 driver. Then old Phillip got tied up and thrown in with us because he kidnapped my wife and son... against orders."

"Then he sang like a bird," Suzy said. "Sean had already used his boot on Mister Snart... Phil... while he dragged us to their hideout. He only restrained me. I guess he figured Sean would follow wherever I was. Sean stayed with me and kept kicking him in the shins the whole way. At one point it must have really hurt because the man started limping. Then by the time the other two men threw him in with us, all we had to do was let Sean kick him again on his bad leg, and he started talking. Sean had to do it because we were supposedly still tied up to some sort of anchor and lock. If it weren't for Sean's secret pocketknife, they might have killed us. But we pretended to be restrained until we could figure how first to save Sean."

"Well, you turned out to be mighty tough," intimidating Randy said, pointing his hand in my direction. "Having escaped to tell a story like this is daunting enough. You must have a skill set that gave you an edge over them."

"I didn't know what I was doing," I said. "I have a friend who has taught me some martial arts defensive moves, and in college I knew several of the wrestlers. They taught me all the illegal moves that can wear an opponent down. That's all I knew to do. Then Sean, the bulls eye thrower, landed some of the best fast balls I could have hoped for. I tried to kill the guy because I feared if I let him up, he would kill me. That would put my family in danger. But I was exhausted and could hardly breathe. I let up on my choke hold only because I was out of the means to continue. Man, were we lucky. When the second guy pulled me up, my first man was out like a light."

"Speaking of luck," Chet said, "we managed to wrangle a reservation at the campout area on the Colorado River for last night. We were on our way down when we ran into your buddies. We earlier had talked about how cool it would be if that happened. I was surprised when our dreams came true so soon. We weren't even tired, yet."

"I think we had more fun than you three did," Bob said, intending to top our story with his own. "We all agree that we haven't had this much fun before… *ever*"

"Suzy and I have been wondering. Tell us how you guys got started adventuring together? Your foreign legion hats are a good place to start. What's with the matching outfits?"

They all chimed in at once. It became clear by the pointing that it was clean-cut Jack's doing.

"We've been friends since high school," Jack replied. "Joined the Marines together, got separated, but all ended up in Vietnam and managed to live through '68, the worst year in our lifetimes. That was the Tet Offensive, if you didn't know."

"I know," I said. "That was the year we won the war but didn't know it."

"Right on, brother," Jack said. "That was a scary time. By the way, were you in Vietnam?"

"I didn't get to go," I replied. "I stayed in South Texas. Instructor pilot in T-37 jet trainers. So, I can't say I did much."

"I would disagree," Randy said. "You flyboys saved our lives on several occasions. I can remember coming right up to the edge of engaging the enemy, when we would call in close air support and watch them come out of nowhere to place ordnance on the target with amazing precision. Those F-100s were beautiful."

"I still thank God for you guys every day," Chet said. "The FACs were always there for us. Those boys would plant their bombs so close to us, I don't know how they did it. You trained them. I thank you, too."

"Thank you, guys," I said awkwardly. This was one of the few times someone, veteran or not, said to me that the small job I did was vital to their returning home.

"Okay, then how did this yearly odyssey start?"

Randy continued. "We got out of active duty about the same time. We were all disappointed to discover how cynical the American public had become about Vietnam. We kicked the enemy's butt during Tet. Sure, it was tough going, but we eradicated the forces of communism. It was the press that waved the white flag. When we landed back home, lines of antiwar hecklers would call us all sorts of names. It was disconcerting, and we again bonded after that. We had each other to talk to. The best therapy known to man... someone else who has been there."

"Then this is your therapy?"

"I don't like the word *therapy,"* Randy said. "We just know that we share a lot of things, and life is good because of it. Ask Jack. He's the one who organized this year's adventure. Ask him how he got the job."

I turned to Jack with anticipation, cupping my hand to an ear in a let me hear it gesture. The others were relishing the story they shared if the goading comments were indicators.

"I won the most money at craps last year in Las Vegas at Caesar's Palace on the first night."

"The previous year's organizer gets to set the contest rules," Bob said.

"We don't know what the contest is until we get home," Jack said. "Who would guess that winning the most money would make me a loser?"

"You get them back by what? Making them wear dorky outfits and goofy hats?" I asked.

"That's one of my jobs... to pick the gear, the travel outfits, and, of course, the destination. I rather like what we wear on these adventures."

"Jack is our clothes horse," said Randy. "He made us wear Preppy uniforms when he drew the short straw about three years ago... in Nashville."

"So," I asked, "what's the contest this year?"

"Oh, I guess I can go ahead and tell you now," Jack said. "We *are* leaving tomorrow, after all"

The other three Marines agreed that this was the best moment because for the first time they had an audience. Jack pulled out his billfold and removed a small piece of paper. Inscribed in pencil, he'd scribbled the required guiding principles for their mystery contest.

Jack stood and called his mob of Marines to order. "This year's competition is for the dumbest and most life-threatening thing done in the Grand Canyon. It goes to the doofus who took on a knife-wielding gorilla and disarmed him with his bare hands."

Randy immediately stood up, threw his arms in the air, and danced around the table, doing everything but spiking a ball in the endzone. This attracted the attention of the El Tovar manager, who instead of talking to us directly, walked over to the head bartender. Randy calmed down at their suggestion.

"Hey, Randy," I said, hoping he would not resume his victory dance. "Where are you going to take them next year?"

"Back here to the Grand Canyon," he replied, "where we can kick some more ass!"

Suzy's stern look at me, with a sideward glance toward Sean, told me volumes. That's when I knew that dinner was over.

39

WE BANTERED WHILE THE WAITER arranged for another round of drinks, mine being amended to a shaken cold gin martini with an olive. I had my suspicions that the Marines were getting their drinks watered down. The small talk continued around the table. *Where are you from? When do you leave? Where do you work? Are you married? Who's the oldest?* Then it got good.

"You guys have any good basic training stories?"

The table was briefly silent. The four leathernecks looked at each other, then looked away. The explosion of laughter that followed was fun to watch as well as totally expected. Every veteran has his stories of basic training. There is an awareness of the absurdity of this training coupled with pride in getting through it. In retrospect, basic training is a culling out process, where only the physically and mentally fit survive. It is a well-earned badge of honor. Short of combat or confinement, it's the toughest obstacle a veteran will face. As many have said before, if it weren't for the laughter, we might not have made it.

Oddly, three of the Marines turned their heads to the intimidating one.

"Randy's the one who has all the stories of boot camp. No matter where he is, he'll be the one to step in a pile of…." Jack stopped himself, then turned with a red face to Suzy in embarrassment.

Sean, though, spoke up. "A pile of doo-doo?"

"Exactly," Jack replied.

The laughter came from everyone.

"Sir, your son sounds like a Marine in the making," said Bob.

Suzy asked. "Do you have any clean stories?"

The four Marines, in a precision response, spoke in unison. *"NO!"*

Again, the table exploded in laughter fueled by guilt, embarrassment, orneriness, and the joy of admitting the truth of a veteran's life. If you don't know how to curse before basic training, you are a pro by the end.

"I can tell one on a sergeant when we were in boot camp at Parris Island." Chet said. The muscular frame on the man tested the seams of his shirt. "That's in South Carolina. Hotter than blazes."

I could see the reaction of the other three out of the corner of my vision. They all knew the story. Chet continued.

"We had a parade for some reason. You know what summer's like in the South? The humidity was in a race with the temperature to see which one could go higher. A sergeant, part of the support staff, was rounded up to fill the ranks of us trainees. He must have done something really bad to get assigned that duty with all us recruits. When we assembled, there was an ambulance off to the side. That sergeant went over and asked the attendant if he had any ice water. The man said 'yes.' So, the parade began, and the sarge instantly passed out. Attendants carried him to the ambulance, and he drank ice water until the parade was over."

There were a few titters, but we were just beginning.

"How about that weird recruit that joined us midway through boot camp," Bob said, "what was his name...?"

"Anton."

"Yeah. Anton was the biggest doofus I ever saw. I think he got drafted and tried to get kicked out of the Marine Corps. He didn't know that if he succeeded, he'd get drafted again into the Army. I never met anyone like him. He did not obey a single order while in boot camp. He remained completely silent... never answered our drill sergeant. We had three of them screaming at him. Number Three had been the nice guy... sort of. He went up to Anton and screamed at him an inch from his face for so long a time that he lost his voice and had to back off. It was crazy."

"Did he get his wish?" I asked.

"No. They pushed him back to day one. They told us that it was his fourth time and let that be a lesson to us. Nobody had sympathy for the guy."

"How long was your boot camp?"

"Thirteen *very* long weeks," said Randy.

"That's a shame," I said. "Air Force basic training was only six weeks... and we had air conditioning."

Our Marines were not amused by my rubbing the easy life of an airman in their face. There was no laughter but some acceptance of a friendly inter-service dig.

"So, do airmen get any hassle from drill sergeants?" Randy asked. "Or do you spend all day thinking about what wine will be served at dinner?"

"Well, it's not very *good* wine," I replied. "I have a good story though. I was enlisted briefly before becoming an officer. I was one of the four appointed squad leaders in basic training. Two of us had undergone two years of ROTC and were college graduates with applications pending to enter pilot training, so Sergeant Garcia, my tactical instructor, expected more from us. We were always in his gun sights. One night near lights out, I had another basic trainee run up to me. He informed me that Sergeant Garcia wanted me in his office on the double. That was never a good sign. Who screwed up, and why didn't I know about it? I dropped everything and marched up to his door and knocked. I announced in a loud voice, 'Sir, Airman Amity reporting as ordered, sir!' The door opened. Sitting in a chair with a serious expression on his face was fellow favored squad leader, Airman Basic Masters. Garcia ordered me to 'Sit down!' I tell you I was scared... what shall I say...?"

"Doo-doo-less!" Sean said.

The table turned into pandemonium for a moment before Suzy chimed in. "Perhaps I should take Sean to our room."

Six males objected at once. I looked at Suzy and with a stern voice corrected her politely.

"Suzy. Our son was a hero a couple of days ago. I would say he's been in combat like these fine gentlemen here—in the field artillery. He was effective and indispensable to our escape and evasion. He deserves to be with these other veterans. He's earned it."

"From what I hear," Bob said, "so do you, Missus Amity."

"Oh, all right. Go on, then."

I turned back to my audience.

"So, where was I? Oh yes. There I was, scared... doo-doo-less. I had no idea why I would be in trouble, but why else would I be called in? Sergeant Garcia told me in a very gruff tone to 'close the door and sit down.' As per protocol I answered, 'Sir, yes, sir!' Airman Basic Masters blew his cover and smiled at me. 'Everything is okay,' he said. I looked over at Sergeant Garcia in confusion. Had our pilot training applications been accepted? Well, no such luck. Our tactical instructor leaned forward over his desk and said, 'I've got a great joke I've been dying to tell somebody.'"

My story was an instant winner. Even Suzy, hearing the story a hundred times, was laughing uncontrollably. Inevitably, the first question to follow was, "What was the joke?"

"I haven't a clue," I said. I paused to control myself. "I was so shocked and relieved, I probably never heard it... but I laughed anyway."

Sean was having fun with the big boys now. Suzy leaned back, becoming content with men being boys for a while.

"When I was in Vietnam," Randy said, "we adopted a pet monkey. We made him a little red vest and...."

His buddies quickly interrupted Randy and shut him down. "I don't think that story is going to be shared," Bob said to vigorous nods from the other two. "How much have you had to drink there, ol' Randy?"

"Too much, I guess."

"Hold 'er down," said Chet.

"I can only imagine what *that* story is about," Suzy said, teasing their consciences a little.

Suzy was not ignorant of the multiple stories the military told, usually attributed to some unnamed uncle's best friend's ex-wife, who passed on the story from her first husband. Randy's introduction sounded familiar to both of us. Jack availed himself of an opportunity to share his own tale.

"I had a gunnery sergeant who was a short-timer. He was getting a bit more belly on him than was good, and he had to buy new uniform pants that fit in the last few weeks of his enlistment. He was retiring and didn't"—he looked at Sean—"give a hoot. He started going to the Club on base with his belt secretly loose. He would belly up to the bar, then suck in his gut, and his pants would fall around his ankles."

Sean burst out with the loudest laugh of the night. It was the perfect story to tell a nine-year-old. He arched his back while he laughed, falling out of his chair and onto the floor. This made him laugh even more uncontrollably as he pictured in his head the gunnery sergeant standing at the bar, drinking beer, with his pants down—grade school humor at its finest.

"Did he survive his antics?" I asked.

"I don't know how, but he would remain like that, as if he didn't notice, continuing to drink beer after beer. Being close to retirement, everyone left him alone. Crazy things happen all the time, I guess."

We continued like this for several hours. Suzy left us at some point, taking sleepy Sean with her. The chance to share stories with these four marines was stimulus enough to keep me wired and awake until well past my reasonable bedtime hour. Eventually our stories turned more personal. They learned about John Alexander and his death in the desert of South Texas. Now they knew that Sean was his son, until I married his widow.

Their stories were a combination of intertwined diverting and reconnecting experiences in the Corps. All had their separate stories of being in Vietnam, using the GI Bill to enter college, falling in love, and getting married. Some had children. Some lost in love and marriage. Work varied from management roles to skilled labor. Their lives seemed to complement each other in their different directions. The three aspects that bound them together were high school, the Marine Corps, and a love of group adventure.

It was my best night out with the boys, since those younger days of dancing girls at the Laredo AFB Officer's Club, shared with my fellow flyboys a decade before.

40

THE NEXT MORNING WAS OUR last day at the Grand Canyon. From here it was back to the airport to fly home to Oklahoma City. I got up before sunrise, as was my frequent habit at home, put on some comfortable shorts and a shirt, and walked outside to find the rim of the canyon quiet but not deserted. Yet again, a tourist had a cassette player playing Ferde Grofé's "Sunrise" from the *Grand Canyon Suite.* I chose to leave her alone in this most private spiritual experience. I could look at the splendor of God's handiwork, marvel at its beauty, yet still conclude that there was no heaven on earth like Oklahoma. Returning to our own home. Sitting on our favorite love seat. Being surrounded by our own things. That was where life was good to me.

Suzy joined me, a cup of coffee in hand, simply to stand with me hand in hand. We marveled at a canyon so enormous that, each time we returned, we were surprised how much bigger it was than our brains could fathom. This was also a good day for flying. The skies were clear again with a million miles of visibility. The winds were blowing the power plant smog elsewhere. It was like my transformation over the past ten years to a better appreciation of what our servicemen sacrificed at the request of our government. It was clear to me now, that there would always be detractors, yet winds of change. What I now clearly knew was that I needed to meet this creeping antimilitary force with pushback. It was time now to express whatever it took to advertise my veteran status. Everyone would know that I served, and I would dare them to say something other than "thanks."

These thoughts reminded me of the one conflict that I had with another airman when I was in basic training. I turned to Suzy.

"Have I ever told you of the airmen in basic training who tried to intimidate me and got physical?"

She shook her head.

"In basic training, I had to get up in the middle of the night. As I left the bathroom, I noticed that the airman in charge of staying up to guard our barracks was not at his post. I investigated and found him around the corner asleep on the floor. If an instructor had checked on us, it wouldn't just be the sleeping guard in trouble. We would all be put on report.

"I crept over to our head squad leader, Airman Basic Masters, and woke him up, informed him of our sleeping guard, and together we rousted the derelict night guard out of his slumbers. Masters reported him the next morning to Sergeant Garcia. This airman was in deep trouble, but as lunchtime arrived, it got more serious. As I carried my lunch tray to a table, the same derelict body-slammed me behind my back against a table. I was in excellent shape, so I didn't fall over. I didn't spill anything out of my tray. I knew in that instant that it had to be our slumbering guard. He stepped right up to my face and threatened me with bodily harm. It wouldn't be a threat if he did more. It was a promise that more was coming. He was out for revenge. You realize, Suzy, that men always want you to know who's coming after you.

"All I said was, 'we'll see what happens.' He looked at me and laughed. I had had a similar experience in sixth grade with a bully. Back then, I told my teacher that if she didn't do something, I would slug the kid. I never had trouble with the bully again. This airman thought he could frighten me, but I had him booted out of our flight before dinner time. I knew the power I had, and I used it swiftly.

"I'm tired of people trying to intimidate us. They'll learn that I don't take crap off anybody. I go after them just as I've learned to do from experience. That approach has never failed us."

Suzy said nothing. She looked at me pensively and turned to the sunlight bouncing off the Canyon's myriad shapes and angles. She continued in silence for several minutes before turning back to me.

"We love our family. We love our fellow servicemen. We've paid our dues. It's time we defend our beliefs. I'm proud of our service and our sacrifice. I dare them to tell us otherwise."

These epiphanies come rarely in life. To say I'd come full circle would mean I hadn't changed at all. Perhaps it was true. I believed one thing in high school but went the opposite way during my enlightenment in college. My life was once again a one-eighty. Likely, other veterans who shared the same beliefs as I had for years—that we should sweep our pride under the rug—shared my change of heart. Even World War II veterans had advised me to keep quiet about being an Air Force pilot. Then Reagan won election as president, and veterans came out of the woodwork. What I didn't expect was the growth of groups that still loathed us. And now, we had encountered our first fanatics.

How many others will I have to fight in the future? The enemy isn't just the communism of the Chinese aor the Soviets, but Americans as well.

Even though our personal fanatics turned out to be stupid and ill-suited for doing much harm, I knew that the tide would not stop, and their new leaders would grow smarter. I could not simply confront them. I was geared up now to lead any charge to defeat them.

These were the thoughts I would share with Suzy over the following months. The only other epiphany I experienced for sure was that love can be so strong, that it finds loveliness even in the first signs of aging. There stood my wife, a few blemishes and a scratch or two from our ordeal marring her perfection, and nothing could be as beautiful. Real love will do that to a man.

We went inside to get a still sleeping Sean awake so we could have an early breakfast. Sean seemed to always be hungry and was growing like the proverbial weed. When he didn't get out of bed quickly enough, we allowed him to join us at breakfast when he got dressed. Entering the now familiar restaurant, we took a table near the window with a less obstructed view of sunrise in the canyon. We ordered our standard fare of coffee, eggs and bacon or sausage, and juice. Sean came down to join us within five minutes.

"I locked the door," he said to assure us.

We marveled at Sean's appetite. He wolfed down his breakfast, then waited patiently as we had more coffee, read the headlines of the Phoenix newspaper, and discussed our return flight in our Bonanza.

"I assume you still have the plane keys somewhere?" Suzy asked.

I put a hand in my pocket out of habit. Panic rushed through me as soon as she asked. "Is that what the intruder took? The keys to our airplane?"

We abruptly finished our breakfast, racing back to our room to call the airport. After a check with the FBO, the man on the telephone assured us that our Bonanza was still safely tied down. He then disappointed us by saying that there were no stray keys found by anyone. We called our hotel front desk about the keys and got the same disappointing answer. An extensive room search confirmed our gut feeling. The keys were gone. Probably stolen on purpose by someone who knew we flew in. The obvious culprit was our old buddy, Phil Snart, now in police or FBI custody. A call to several agencies soon located our airplane keys in the personal effects of the accused. With a little persuasion, they agreed to expedite delivery to the airport in time for our planned departure.

We went back to the restaurant to retrieve Sean, who had eaten each of our breakfasts in our absence. Despite ordering some additional a la carte breakfast items to fuel us before our flight, we were able to pack quickly, simply because we hadn't brought much. After paying our El Tovar Hotel bill, we boarded the shuttle to the airport.

41

WE RECOGNIZED A FEW OF the people on the airport shuttle, but the trip was mostly quiet and hot. Summer heat and altitude are a pilot's enemy when taking off. Both were going higher as we approached the airport. Adding our weight, we would be a full load of three persons with bags. The runway takeoff would be even longer. Our Bonanza would use up more runway than I liked. There was no way, after all the danger we were in, that I would do us harm on the runway. I would be calculating the takeoff roll with precision.

The first sighting of the control tower signaled the end of the eight and a half miles of a seemingly continuous traffic jam to the airport. The shuttle stopped in front of Grand Canyon Airlines, our FBO. After retrieving our bags and tipping the driver, I stopped at the front desk to inquire about the delivery of our airplane's keys. They informed me that they were still awaiting its arrival. This afforded me the leisure to file our VFR flight plan with Flight Service and check the weather. The weather looked good, but there was a chance of power plant haze to the east. At a planned flight at 11,500 feet altitude, the addition of haze in our route would be a disappointment. We would not be enjoying a clear view of the unique Arizona terrain below.

Until our keys arrived, we would wait. To fill the time, we elected to go outside and walk around our airplane. Our checklist was locked up inside, but by this time I had the outside check memorized. Simple things you forget can become fatal things. Checking for oil in the engine is a good one. It's surprising how many pilots shared stories of losing an engine after takeoff. Several involved low or no oil. Taking the cover off the pitot tube was another. It's hard to land safely if you have no indication of airspeed. Unlocking the flight controls would seem to be fundamental. It would be like driving around town with your steering wheel immovable. Suzy and I went through the airplane check together. It was now a welcome habit that even Sean was becoming proficient. I was under the wing looking at our landing gear strut, when Sean cried out for our attention.

"Mom. *Mom!*"

Suzy stood up first to take a hurried look at what caused Sean's continued screaming. To her astonishment, it was a woman running full speed toward our Bonanza. By the sound of her own screaming voice and the tool in her grip, she was not there to welcome us.

"Rob! *Quick!*" Suzy moved frantically to meet this unknown threat.

The not so lady-like woman let out another primal scream. I stood up to see Suzy stepping in front of Sean to block any attempt by this woman to do harm. She was almost to them. Being on the wrong side of the wing from Suzy, I was unable to assist her. The charging assailant raised an aircraft tow bar above her head as she aimed her glower directly at Sean. Suzy did not move. She planted her feet for impact. In one amazing feat of control, she extended her left hand, fingers up and palm out in a display of defiance, and yelled like the no-nonsense librarian she was.

"Stop!"

The attacker, counting on a cut and run reaction, came to a sudden stop. Her angered expression suddenly morphed into a look of fear. She screamed in rage as she turned to me.

"You're a baby killer! War monger! I hope you rot in hell!" She turned back to Suzy and Sean, standing defiantly still only ten feet away. I continued around the Bonanza's wingtip.

"What did you do to my husband, you little brat?"

The world suddenly morphed into slow motion. It was only a split second, but Sean stepped around his mother, an expression of shock on his face. He uttered the words that filled in the blanks.

"Missus *Snart?* What are you doing?"

"I'm going to kill you for what you did to Phil!" She glared at Sean, then turned to me. "Then I'm going to kill *that* murderer over there."

She again raised the tow bar high above her head. Blanketing the parking ramp with high volume colorful profanity, she rushed toward mother and son, just as I reached up from behind her and grabbed the heavy iron tow bar. She didn't let loose as I planned. Her forward momentum caused her to swing around to face me in a struggle to possess her makeshift bludgeon. Her rage seemed to have no limit. She tore into my face with her fingernails, then placed her mouth by my ear and exploded in primitive deafening screams. The pain in my ear overwhelmed the pain of her claws on my face. Jay Goodwin's defensive martial arts training kicked in. The many hours of practice made my moves almost automatic. While holding the tow bar at bay with my left hand, I tilted her off balance causing the woman to lose her grip on her weapon. I quickly tossed it aside before she went straight at me again with fingernails. She emitted guttural sounds that sent flecks of spittle on my face. I was used to throwing down a much bigger man, so when I flipped her over, her lighter weight allowed me to send her to a much harder landing on the cement tarmac. The impact was brutal, but her adrenalin was taking away her pain and maintaining her rage-filled strength. I moved to the side to get between this maniac and our son. She stepped to the side attempting to out flank me. As she charged toward Sean, she failed to see the heavy tie-down cables on the parking ramp. Hooking both feet on a five-inch-high cable, and at full charging speed, her whole body pivoted on the axis of her ankles, brutally slamming her head face-first onto the rock-solid tarmac. Lying next to her left hand, as she lay bleeding and unconscious on the hot pavement, were our Bonanza airplane keys.

42

WE AGAIN WENT THROUGH THE joy of more police interviews. They were now taking this affront to their usually routine workday more seriously.

"She seemed so nice," said the ranger supervisor. He could not stop his explanation, which made it sound more like an apology. "She was embarrassed for her husband's behavior. She offered to bring back your lost keys so she could apologize to you. Between our office and here at the airport, she changed into someone else."

"We had Medusa delivering our keys," I said sarcastically. A medic from the ambulance attended to the scratches on my face and hands. Suzy and Sean watched with concern and curiosity.

"I guess she's a part of this group with their harebrained scheme to kill veterans," the supervisor said. "They're going to be busy trying to kill tens of millions of us."

"It's probably ten million to one, veterans to vet haters," I replied. "There should be enough of us available to pound each one of those cretins into the ground... just like we did this week."

The medic swabbed blood from the top of my ear and behind my neck.

"They'll be back, I assure you," the supervisor said. "These things have a way of growing out of control. Nothing is inconceivable anymore. Just look at Charles Manson. He had a whole family of people blindly doing his bidding."

"Cultural tattoos," Suzy replied.

"What do you mean? Explain," the supervisor said.

"That's just a name I call it. You take a bunch of misfits and provide them a leader. Those people, as in the case of Charles Manson's family, get into the culture of murder so far that they can never shake the behavior from their sense of amorality. It's like when someone gets a tattoo. Once inked into you, it never goes away. The Manson family and this week's bag of nuts? They're all cultural tattoos. We'll never be able to get rid of them."

"And they're breeding like rabbits." I sighed and shook my head. "God help their children. Amen."

"That reminds me of something else," Suzy said. "Do you remember the lady we ran into and the screen door?"

Sean started to giggle. "I remember that. I like it. It was funny."

"Yeah, I remember," I said. "Talk about cultural tattoos? Perfect example."

Sean was looking at the supervisor, who in turn looked at me and at Suzy. Sean's grin of anticipation was contagious. Suzy turned to me.

"You better tell it. You're the man."

"Okay. We went to a barbeque restaurant for dinner not too long ago in Oklahoma City. It's the kind of place that has a small alcove in the entrance. The place is not too fancy. I think they made the thing out of Visqueen and two by fours. It has a regular door that opens out, plus a cheap screen door that opens in. You probably know the kind of screen door I'm talking about… spring loaded. The kind your parents had when they yelled at you for letting it slam shut. Well, as usually happens, there was a backup of customers waiting to get inside to reserve a table. It was a hot summer evening. The crowd was largely students from the nearby college, mostly twenty-somethings. Groups of students talked while waiting… a friendly crowd. The line inched along. We finally got inside the alcove and were on the threshold of the real entry door. Someone always gets that involuntary task of holding a door open until the next in line moves forward. The same principle applied to holding open the screen door. There were three college men…."

"They were college hunks," Suzy said. Sean laughed. She always added her comment whenever I retold the story.

"Polite hunks," I said. "Well, the line began moving forward. Two of the

so-called hunks went into the alcove, while a third held the screen door for them. Behind them were three coeds, two of whom accepted his courtesy with thank-yous and entered the alcove. The third coed was not so gracious. She yelled at the young man. 'I don't need some man to hold the damn door open for me, thank you!'

"Taking that declaration as a request, the polite young man said, 'okay' and let go of the screen door. *Wham!* Right in her kisser. It practically knocked her over."

I turned to Sean, who was laughing uncontrollably.

"I failed to mention that the screen was wound extremely tight. I'm sure it hurt. The three young men were quietly laughing and quickly pushed their way inside out of harm's way. To my surprise, the two other coeds joined in brief laughter at their friend's expense. The victim of all this... how can I say it... was mortified, angry, shamed... you name it. She stormed her way into the entryway, where she continued to wait behind the three men she had just insulted."

I glanced at Suzy, who was trying to calm Sean down. The supervisor found this highly entertaining.

"I was truly sorry for the young lady, but I bet she'll never change. It's those cultural tattoos again. Between the National Organization of Women, the Equal Rights Amendment, and even that stupid song...what is it...? *W—O—M—A—N!*"

"Careful," Suzy said. "I like Peggy Lee. I think you meant 'I am Woman.'"

"Okay, then. Helen Reddy made that young lady crazy, too. Cultural Tattoos... all of 'em."

AFTER THE MEDIC FINISHED UP with me and filled out his paperwork, I realized that my flight plan had expired. I had to refile with my friends at Flight Service. This meant it would be close to sundown before we arrived at Wiley Post airport in Oklahoma City if nothing else happened to us. I stepped to the FBO desk to pay my bill for aviation fuel and ramp fees. The cost of fuel was the one confusing flying expense that I never figured out. The oil bust in Oklahoma and Texas had made avgas cheaper for our Bonanza, which held eighty gallons. Avgas was significantly more expensive than car gasoline, but it never dropped by the same percentage as the gas I put in my car. It remained a frustratingly high price per gallon, especially at a national park.

"What next?" Suzy was always interrupting my profoundly deep thoughts.

"Flight check," I replied. "Grab your bags before it's too late."

The three of us conducted another preflight check. I grabbed the checklist out of the Bonanza and went through the list again on the outside, then put our miniscule baggage in the back. Once inside I went through all the items on the checklist, starting with disconnecting the control lock—highly important—to checking the vestigial Automatic Direction Finder—not important.

There was one other important item not on our checklist. In the chaos of the previous two hours, it had slipped my mind. I wanted to reward someone for his great efforts over the past few days. Suzy and I agreed that the recognition was worth special treatment.

"Sean, let Mom get in the back. I want you to be my copilot today."

Sean kept his cool. No grins. No giggles. No wide eyes. He tried his best to take the assignment like a man. Suzy chuckled at his reaction. Rather than tease him, we allowed him to take his job seriously. He stepped back and let his mother enter first through the single door into the cabin. Next, he waited until I climbed inside to occupy my seat as pilot in command before he climbed in and shut and locked the door. Although he had flown in the same seat when we flew to camp, now he had his mother to think of. He took his job seriously.

"Sean, open the door again, will you? It's the only cool air we'll have until we're ready for takeoff."

With everyone inside, we donned our headsets, adjusted the microphone boom to our lips, and checked that we could hear each other. With all seat belts fastened, we were set to start our engine. With a quick call of *"Clear!"* outside my window, I turned over the engine which started the three-blade prop spinning. The masculine growl of the Continental engine shook our seats as the first ignitions of avgas brought the whole airplane to life. We made a few more checks, then contacted Ground Control for clearance to taxi to the runway. Things still looked promising. No more people came out of holes or cracks in the brick from nearby buildings to assault us. I was getting excited. We taxied to Runway 21 and did our runup check. Tower cleared us for takeoff. As we taxied onto the runway, there was something satisfying in looking at our son and his renewed big fearless grin. He closed our cabin door with no problems. We were sharing something extraordinary that few kids could understand. Motorcycles? Skis? Sports cars? Speedboats? Not us. We shared airplanes.

"Sean, you're my copilot, which means you have a job to do. See that window you see out of? It's there so you can look for airplanes, birds, even balloons. Anything that we never want to crash into. That would only make us late getting home." Sean grinned at my sarcastic gallows humor. "We have to clear the skies of anything we see... you see? Tell me early, not later, okay?"

He nodded his head, speechless with excitement at the chance to help pilot the plane. He tried to look serious, but it wasn't working.

"All right then... are you ready? Let's launch!"

We went to full power on our takeoff roll. Sean began to giggle with excitement, feeling our Bonanza push us gently into the backs of our seats as we gained speed. Nose wheel liftoff was far down the runway because of the afternoon heat and our full load. We became airborne with a positive rate of climb. Gear and flaps came up. He was glancing out the window, alternately looking behind him and down at the runway rushing past. We shared airplanes, and I liked how it lifted my spirits as we climbed out together side by side. It was good to again be so happy. Ten years after Vietnam, I could finally say I'd experienced combat... albeit with civilians.

And this time, we won.

43

AFTER A FEW REQUIRED TURNS to avoid adding airplane noise pollution over the national park, we headed in an easterly direction into increasingly hazy skies. At least tailwinds would push us along enough at 11,500 feet to make it home without refueling. Perhaps only our bladders would be the deciding factor whether to land short of our destination.

I took out my small pocket calculator. Using a rough estimate of wind speed aloft for 12,000 feet, reported to us on our preflight weather report, I determined that we were flying at an astonishing ground speed of 240 miles per hour. At this speed and a sixteen gallon per hour fuel flow, we could fly the nine hundred miles in about four hours.

"Who's game for flying all the way?" I asked.

"We've sweat so much in the past few days," Suzy said. "I don't think it matters. We could be good for a whole day."

Sean was silent and not listening to us. Instead, he was clearing for airplanes in the sky. We didn't want to telegraph anything more about his having to hold it. We pressed on through the hazy eastern half of Arizona.

It was mid-afternoon when we entered New Mexico airspace. The sun shone over and behind our right shoulders. Again, the terrain changed to match the state boundaries. The haze of the Arizona coal-fired power plants drifted south of our flight path. Visibility improved, giving us a chance to joke about seeing our house in the distance as we passed over the city of Gallup.

The view of New Mexico seemed completely different going east, a testament to the value of seeing both sides of anything in life. Suzy wanted to talk.

"Is the world going nuts," she asked me over the intercom from the backseat, "or do you think it will get better?"

"You would think it will get better after what we saw," I replied, "but I fear this is just a sample of what's to come."

"It seems like our country's new pride in the military has had the opposite effect for some people."

"Some people don't like change from what it was for them years before. We were in an antiwar and hippie revolution in the sixties and seventies. I'm convinced that the leaders in those groups were in it only for the power to control people. The war in Vietnam ended, so they quickly migrated to other causes where their crowds could continue to follow."

"We need more people who will listen, not just follow. Have you noticed how some of these so-called leaders will declare something bad and overnight there is outrage? How come they weren't outraged the day before?"

"We need to be the ones who don't jump just because others have," I said. "We might be surprised by how many people we can influence more successfully by leading through example."

"Remember Phyllis Schlafly?" Suzy asked. "She led the opposition to the Equal Rights Amendment to our Constitution. Everybody said her warnings were kooky, but I've seen several things she predicted already come true that the opposition first laughed at. Nowadays, that same opposition tries to make happen the very same thing they once laughed at."

"It might be fun to go against the grain of conventional progressive thought. It has to be easier than fending off killer kidnappers."

Our radio came alive as Albuquerque Center shifted us to a new sector and new radio frequency. I checked in with the new sector for flight following.

"Albuquerque Center, Bonanza three-seven-two-one-Quebec, level at eleven five."

"Roger, Bonanza two-one-Quebec, radar contact. You have traffic at four o'clock, your altitude."

The three of us craned our necks over our right shoulders, gazing at a spot on the horizon where the aircraft would be at our altitude. Nothing caught our attention.

"Mister Co-pilot, do you see anything over there?"

"I don't see anything."

"No joy," I replied to the controller.

"Two-one-Quebec, turn left immediately to heading zero-six-zero for traffic. Call when you have aircraft in sight."

I was well into my turn before he had finished his transmission. "Look to your left... on the horizon," I said to Suzy and Sean. They both looked but said nothing.

"No joy," I replied.

"Two-one-Quebec, climb immediately to twelve thousand."

As I pulled into an abrupt climb, sure enough, at our altitude and on a near collision course came a much faster twin engine Beechcraft Baron, obviously not under radar flight following and oblivious to our proximity. The airplane passed below us but near enough that I could see two occupants in the cockpit. If they looked up, they couldn't have missed seeing us. They were likely unaware of our presence so near them.

"Tally-ho on traffic for Bonanza two-one-Quebec. Thanks a bunch. That was close."

"You're welcome, Two-one-Quebec. You may resume normal navigation."

I gave the controller two clicks on my radio for acknowledgement and turned back to my planned course.

"And *that's* why we use radar flight following," I said and returned our course to the correct heading.

We flew in silence, trying to calm our nerves. I wondered if Suzy and I were sharing the same knowledge of how close of a call we overcame because of outside help. I offered a silent prayer of thanks to God.

Suzy was first to talk. "They had no idea what was going on around them. The same thing might apply to our kidnappers. Are they simply not paying attention?"

I was surprised at such an abrupt segue. We had just experienced a near death collision. It was apparent to me that our previous canyon experience was still priority number one. We all have our moments of ignorance because of inexperience. A near collision apparently was one of them for Suzy. Best I not tell her exactly how close it was.

"Perhaps, if those pilots get the you-know-what scared out of them, they too will look around and become more responsible. Like just now, that airplane and the pilots' ignorance forced us to deviate our course. We'll always have to remain vigilant for the halfwits of the world."

"I don't expect that the Snarts will be seeing the light, do you?"

"They're fanatical revolutionaries. They've got their blinders on to block any other opinions. Their marriage is synced up quite nicely, don't you think? They're both nuts."

"Missus Snart certainly took an active role."

"You called it cultural tattoos."

"You like that?"

"It reminds me of a student I had in pilot training. He was from a wealthy family in Nigeria. There were actually two Nigerians in the class. The other had decorative scars on his face. My student did not. He spoke English as a first language and was culturally savvy and refined to American ways. Well-educated student pilots usually made our job easier.

"I took him out for his first ride only to learn that when he took control of the airplane, he could not keep the wings level. I told myself that it was just nerves. On our second ride, after some discussions about the horizon, he repeated his poor performance. We would fly along straight and level, I would give him the controls, and the airplane would very slowly start to lean to the left or right. It didn't matter. I would talk him through it. 'Keep your wings level. Look at the horizon. Line your wings up with the horizon.' He would move the control stick some but never in any way that made sense.

"So, I thought. Why don't I let him go until we are truly out of control? Then, surely, he will see what is wrong. He took the stick with our aircraft wings level. I watched as we went left wing low five degrees, then ten. At this point we began to descend slightly nose low. We reached fifteen degrees left bank. More descent. I mentioned our descent, and he pulled back on the stick. That stopped the descent, but he continued his left bank to twenty degrees. The nose dropped. He pulled it up. Twenty-five degrees. Our descent was unstoppable. I waited. Thirty degrees of left bank had us descending at an alarming speed, considering our engines were at normal cruise power of ninety-two percent. I took control of our aircraft, leveled our wings to align with the horizon, and pulled up to get us out of our dive.

"No one in my flight of instructors understood how this was possible. My commander told me to try and teach him for two more flights. After that, I insisted a senior instructor take him up. It was the only way I was going to prove to them that this foreign student had no clue what a horizon or the word level meant. After the instructor came back from the flight with the well-educated Nigerian student, he shared his astonishment.

"'This is by far the weirdest student I have ever flown with,' he said. His eyes were wide in frustration and disbelief. 'I have no clue what his problem is, but he is done with trying to be a pilot.'

"I told him that it was about time somebody listened to me. My best theory was that where he grew up, he may have never seen a horizon. If he lived in a forest, in a city with smog, or even in mountains... anywhere that was lacking a clear and level horizon, he would have grown up with no concept of straight and level."

"Then it was cultural. He will never get the concept," Suzy replied. "He's an adult. He can't undo what he has already engrained in his brain."

"There you go. Cultural tattoos again."

"You think that's the problem with our pals, the Snarts? Their brains are tattooed with hatred that makes no sense, but it can't be undone?"

"But you see what happens," I said, suddenly inspired. "You knew that Missus Snart would halt when she ran toward you. You simply held out your hand in a motion that said 'No,' and you yelled 'Stop' in a commanding voice. She blindly followed your orders because you were dominant. I think that is how these followers get hooked on this stupid stuff. Their leaders dominate them, and they blindly follow."

Suzy was silent, her lips pursed in pensive concentration. "I didn't think about that at the time. I just did it... I said *'stop,'* and she stopped."

"So, the solution would appear to be that you need to destroy the power of their leaders."

"But in the case of your Nigerian student, it is too late to undo the learning that he never had. Is that the same case with the Snarts?"

"Sadly, yes," I said. "I think it's too late."

"Eventually, some things can never be taught. How sad."

44

WE CONTINUED OUR EASTWARD FLIGHT with only routine events to handle. Albuquerque Center handed us over to Fort Worth Center. The flying continued straight and level, like a long drive on the highway. Looking for stimulus to keep me alert, I remembered the second letter Hal Freed wrote me. It was the fat letter I had put down for later the night before we hiked into the canyon and encountered our interesting adversaries. I turned my head to the backseat.

"Suzy, look in your bag where you put the mail. Do you see an unopened letter from Hal Freed? There were two of them. I never got to read the fat one."

Suzy, curious herself, quickly pulled it out and open. "You're flying. Do you want me to read it to you?"

"Would you, please? I'm sure it's rated G. Sean should get some entertainment out of this, too."

"Hold on while I open this. There are a lot of pages to it."

Inside was a two-page letter with additional newspaper clippings that she left in the envelope. The contents were plentiful enough to keep us busy for at least a hundred miles.

"Sean," I said. "Don't forget your job. Clear the sky for more airplanes."

"Okay, here it is. Oh, my goodness. He used a typewriter." Suzy began reading to us over our intercom.

"Dear Rob,

"I couldn't help writing again because I learned of a great story that may reassure you that things are not much different than they were sixty years ago. I know we have both encountered some bad people in the past ten years who have no respect for us military types.

"I ran into of all people Jimmy Doolittle, III, the grandson of the real Doolittle. He's a nice guy. You may have met him when he had a temporary T-37 instructor assignment with us at Laredo. He told me a funny story about his grandfather as a flight instructor a few months after World War One ended."

Suzy stopped reading to ask, "Did you call Hal and tell him what just happened to us in the canyon?"

"No. That letter came to the house before we left Oklahoma City. He has no idea what we've been through."

"Then, is he in for a surprise." She continued Hal's letter.

"West Point just awarded General James H. Doolittle the Sylvanus Thayer Award, which is like an honorary degree from the Military Academy. Jimmy III was there. Afterward, his grandfather opened up about what it was like to be an instructor pilot at the end of the war. Get this. In five months as an IP, he destroyed one trainer buzzing soldiers, intentionally prevented the base commander from landing on the runway as a prank, and, on a five-dollar bet, rode the landing gear on a military trainer while his copilot reluctantly landed the airplane. The net result was that our Medal of Honor hero spent three months confined to post and a month and a half grounded from flying. I looked it up—he would have been maybe 23 years old. Sound familiar?"

From the back of the plane, Suzy turned to the next page and smoothed flat the high-quality parchment. Another pause, then Suzy laughed aloud, startling Sean and me through our headsets.

"You'll love this."

"You and I must be well on our way to general rank any day now."

It did seem ironic and reassuring to know that even the greatest among us were human. While I still chuckled, Suzy continued.

"Don't expect too many letters to you back-to-back, but I had to share this with you, if for no other reason to remind both of us that, despite all our pranks, clashes, and obstacles, we're both doing okay. I'm glad we're growing up, but I still miss the orneriness—and I wouldn't change a thing. All my best to Suzy, Hal."

Suzy paused for a minute before she asked. "What was that all about?"

"I think I get it," I replied. "Hal and I have experienced a mess of people telling us that we should be ashamed of our choices in life. In our case we can add the phrase, 'or we'll kill you.'

"He's said before that it's not the first time in history that there were people obsessed with the idea of forcing everyone to agree with them."

Sean interrupted his aircraft clearing and general window gazing to ask, "Mom, why did that man do all those bad things. Isn't that against the law?"

"Yes, it most certainly is."

"Why did he still do it?"

"Because he hadn't grown up, yet," I said, "Sometimes, it's just innocent fun, but for others, it's to control people. My orneriness turned out to be good training to push back to stop a bully."

"Is that like Mister Snart?"

"Yeah. He turned out to be not so tough after we pushed back. He wimped out real fast, right? A little rule breaking as a kid might have helped him grow a spine."

"Rob, don't tell Sean that."

"Is that why I got to go with you into the bar at the canyon? I wasn't supposed to be there."

"Okay, dear... and yes, Sean."

"I feel bad for Tanner. He has Mister and Missus Snart for a mom and dad."

"We need to set an example then," I said. "Show Tanner how to act. You can get him to follow your lead. Every child wants to know how to behave. It's knowing the rules of good behavior that makes us able to relax and enjoy life."

"I sure hope things get better over the next few years," Suzy said.

"It's all up to us." I replied. "Our children have always been the hope of the world."

45

WE FLEW ON IN COMFORTABLE silence for another few minutes until our airplane entered the vast Great Plains of the Texas Panhandle with its green miles of irrigated circles. The ground was a checkerboard of section lines with hundreds of round checker pieces and little green Pac-Men looking to gobble up their neighbors.

Sean found the shapes and clearly defined square miles fascinating and peppered us with questions. "What are all those green circles? What are they growing down there?"

"Wheat, cotton, and sorghum." The funny thing was that it was actually true. I'd read an article about agriculture in the Panhandle not long before.

"What's sorghum?"

"I don't know, son. I'm a city boy. Ask Mom."

She looked at me with a shrug of her shoulders and a tilt of her head to the right. She replied after some thought.

"Sean, I think it's a grain that looks tall like corn. They feed their cattle with it."

"How did you know that?" I asked.

"I read," she replied smugly. "I *am* a librarian."

"Sean. If you have a question about flying airplanes, I'm your man. All other questions? Ask Mom."

We flew with idle chatter for another one hundred miles until we entered the airspace of our own State of Oklahoma. To our north were the rolling Antelope Hills. To the south lay the arid regions of our state, more dependent upon rain than on irrigation. Unlike the Texas Panhandle, rivers flowed here. Sometimes drying up. Sometimes overflowing their banks. The rivers would swell in many locations into abundant reservoirs, good for agriculture, ranching, and recreation.

Long shadows signaled late evening, the sun hinting at turning itself a red fireball on the western horizon. I directed my passengers to look out the left side windows to see more graphically the seemingly uncountable full farm ponds that reflected off the setting sun. No one could easily understand how water had changed the state since statehood, unless viewing it from the air.

Oklahoma was a state where nearly everyone was an Indian or wanted to be one. In school as a child of Sean's age, I recalled my teacher asking us how many Indians or part Indians were there in class? All of us raised our hands, except for one little girl. When she looked around to find that only she had not raised her hand, she cried. It's that kind of state.

Flying over the Oklahoma fields, we descended eight thousand feet, to pass low over the places we knew so well. We looked down at the baled hay, those money rolls to the farmer. Fields were bare and freshly plowed in preparation for the planting of winter wheat. The western half of the state was part of the Great Plains, the wheat belt of the state. This looked to be a high yield year which meant that prices would drop, but cattle would be well fed. As we looked ahead of us, a large herd of heifers and steers were running in line to receive their evening meal, courtesy of the hard work of a rancher.

Scattered throughout this bustling farm and ranch paradise were the rusting monuments to a once prospering oil industry now laid scattered about the land like vanquished foes. We knew that oil had risen and collapsed many times before. Both agriculture and oil were like our own beating hearts—beat—relax—boom—collapse—*BOOM!—COLLAPSE!* That cycle would go on forever in this state. As distressed economically as it was in Oklahoma, we knew the boom would come back. It always had before. History is a good predictor. Discontent among the down and out was also inevitable.

Our recent adventure in the canyon was only a microcosm of a national movement which set as its goal to terrorize those who served their country in war. It was fueled by unemployment, blind supporters, college indoctrination, and idle hands. Instead of covering that trend, the press hinted at the dangers of a cowboy president in charge of an expanding military. Nationwide people were beginning to panic about the nation's newly flexed military muscle. Suzy and I did not share their fears. We slept better because of it. But it was obvious that under the veil of increased security was a subculture of sinister forces, not yet able to stand on its own, but still growing at a steady pace imperceptible to the public. We had seen it up close. Being realistic to history, we feared no one would believe us when we related the insanity that was our personal experience in the Grand Canyon.

Oklahoma's oil economy was always in rapid change, like that beating heart which changed each time it contracted and relaxed. As we flew low over the landscape, the sun falling nearer to the horizon, signs of short-term declines were matched by other signs of hope. There were brave souls who saved their wealth, took a chance, and built or expanded while others retreated. They had the courage of their convictions that life, economy, security—all would be better soon. The people doing something were the hope of the state. Suzy and I had to take the same risk for the life, economy, and security of our nation and its warriors. Because even in a downturn, up above as we flew along, the world and our state looked beautiful.

I looked over at Suzy, who was smiling vigorously. It was unexpected and odd behavior for her.

"What's wrong with you?"

"Oh, I thought I better share something with you."

Suzy sat up a bit taller in her backseat. I was trying to imagine what she had up her sleeve as we neared home.

"Do you remember that second day you came home from flying with Brad? You were happy about your flying possibilities, after a day that discouraged you so much. I had a bottle of Champagne waiting for you?"

"Oh, I remember. Sean sprayed ginger ale on us. I polished off most of the bottle. I wish you'd taken your share. I might have had less of a headache the next day."

"Do you know why I only drank half a glass?"

"No, why?"

"Silly boy. I'm pregnant."

Coming into Oklahoma City airspace, things were getting busy as I pondered the joyous words of my angel. I checked my radio for the latest weather conditions, then I called Wiley Post Tower to give them our location and distance from the field. The voice that responded was friendly and familiar. The wind was shifting to the north. Lining up on Runway 35 Right, with gear down, flaps down, and power pulled back to near idle, we made a smooth touchdown. A surge of relief at being home overwhelmed me. Taxiing off the runway under what was left of sunny blue skies, we could still see way ahead, including a boy, his dog, and a baby. Our future looked clear and bright, and we still had a million miles to go.

KENT McINNIS an Oklahoma-born chronicler of people, places, and good times, lives with his wife, Cheryl, in Oklahoma City. He served as an Air Force primary jet instructor pilot during the last five years of the Vietnam War.

For the next 33 years he worked in the pharmaceutical industry while pursuing his hobbies of writing, American history, and flying. After retiring in 2008, Kent assumed the position of Chairman of Westerners International, an organization with chapters on three continents dedicated to making the study of Western American History fun—"no stuffed shirts allowed." He stepped down nine years later to return to writing full time.

Kent is past leader of Order of Daedalians (a military pilot fraternity), Chisholm Trail Corral (a Westerners chapter), and Rio River Rat Pilot Training Class 71-06. He also chaired three high school class reunions. He is active in the Indian Territory Posse (another Westerners chapter) and the Oklahoma City Men's Dinner Club. For nearly a decade Kent has also judged Wrangler Award entries for the National Cowboy & Western Heritage Museum in Oklahoma City.

In his spare time, Kent travels by car with Cheryl to see America at ground level, visit their three grown children, and savor the joys of freedom in this great country.

Find Kent at RioRiverRat@cox.net or on Facebook.

Printed in the USA
CPSIA information can be obtained
at www.ICGtesting.com
JSHW021618020724
65465JS00006B/52

9 781633 738881